Sometime

Katrina wok   bolted
upright in be   piration
dripping down her face. Before she could move
another muscle, Travis burst through the door and
rushed to her side.

"I heard you scream," he said. He sat on the edge of
the bed and gathered her into his arms. "You must
have had a nightmare. Everything's okay now.
You're safe."

Katrina could feel his body thrumming as he held
her, and knew how badly she'd startled him. "I'm
sorry. It was all so real!" She ran her hands over his
back and shoulders, assuring herself that he was
okay. As her fears eased and relief flooded through
her, she allowed herself to rest in his arms. His heart
drummed against hers fiercely and steadily.

"It was awful," she managed. "I dreamed you got
shot."

Dear Reader,

Romance and high adventure are the keys to every fantasy I've ever had. I like rugged men who face seemingly insurmountable odds with courage and who will brave all for the woman they love.

I've wanted to write THE BROTHERS OF ROCK RIDGE miniseries for a very long time, and I was thrilled when Harlequin gave me the chance to go forward with these stories. The Redhawk brothers are a special breed of men, and each one was dear to me in his own way. Their dedication to their jobs and their values as Navajo men earned them a special place in my heart.

I hope our readers will fall in love with the Redhawk brothers as I did—men who are willing to fight for what's right and meet every challenge with the same passion they show for life...and for love.

Warmest regards,

Aimée

Aimée Thurlo
REDHAWK'S RETURN

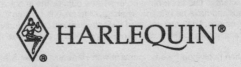

TORONTO • NEW YORK • LONDON
AMSTERDAM • PARIS • SYDNEY • HAMBURG
STOCKHOLM • ATHENS • TOKYO • MILAN • MADRID
PRAGUE • WARSAW • BUDAPEST • AUCKLAND

ISBN 0-373-22510-5

REDHAWK'S RETURN

Copyright © 1999 by Aimée & David Thurlo

This edition published by arrangement with Harlequin Books S.A.

® and TM are trademarks of the publisher. Trademarks indicated with ® are registered in the United States Patent and Trademark Office, the Canadian Trade Marks Office and in other countries.

Printed in U.S.A.

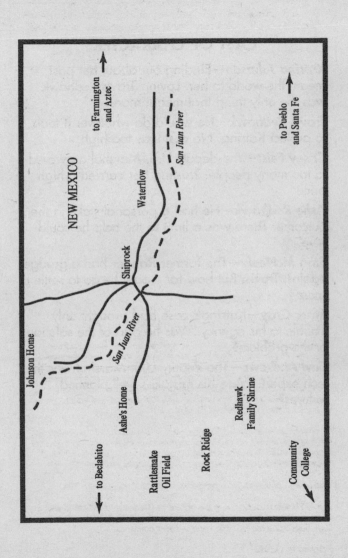

CAST OF CHARACTERS

Katrina Johnson—Finding out about her past meant the world to her. Loving Travis Redhawk was the only thing that meant more.

Travis Redhawk—He would do whatever it took to protect Katrina. No cost was too high.

Casey Feist—The deputy U.S. Marshal answered to too many people. Trusting her carried a high price.

Ashe Redhawk—He had a personal stake in the outcome. There was a limit to the help he could give.

Stan McNeely—The former Ranger had a grudge against Travis. But how far would he go to settle a score?

Marc Gray—Katrina's case had brought only trouble to his agency. Was he part of the solution, or the problem?

Carl Andrews—The deputy U.S. Marshal was the tech expert. Were his mistakes well-planned failures?

Prologue

Fall 1993

Travis Redhawk paced outside the Johnsons' home. He wasn't good at this. He should have kept his mouth shut, but, at the time, it had seemed like such a good idea. Fox's sixteenth birthday was tomorrow. He'd wanted to give her something really special that she'd always remember, not just a scarf or box of candy anyone could pick up at the trading post.

Katrina Johnson, the girl he'd nicknamed Fox, was very special to him. She was his foster parents' daughter, smart as a whip and beautiful too. But she was still just a kid, and needed someone like him around to keep her safe. At nineteen he was big enough and tough enough to see to it nobody gave her a hard time. Being an Anglo and living on the Rez wasn't easy for Fox.

Travis paced back and forth, waiting for her to finally come out. He thought of her golden hair and the way it caressed her shoulders. Heat surged through him as he gave his thoughts free rein for a few unguarded seconds.

"Hey," Fox's musical voice came softly from behind him.

He stepped dead in his tracks and turned to face her. Moonlight danced on Fox's hair, making it seem like spun silk. She'd fixed herself up, lipstick and everything, but had it been just for him? He wanted to think so. Seeing her sweet smile struck him dumb for a moment.

Travis looked away, determined to keep things from getting too hot and hard to handle.

"You said you had to talk to me tonight, alone, before my birthday," she prodded softly. "Is something wrong, Travis?"

His pulse hammered. Why couldn't he look at her lately without getting tongue tied? Frustration rippled through him. "I needed to tell you something and there's also something I wanted to give you for your birthday."

"You're broke." Fox smiled at him. "You shouldn't have bought anything for me."

"It isn't *that* kind of present," he said, then groaned. He was really messing things up. Now he sounded cheap, too.

She took a step closer to him, her eyes softening. "What kind of present is it?"

The evening breeze filled the air with the scent of roses and piñon pine and the warm, spicy scent that was Fox. He tried to break the spell, but he couldn't look away from her this time. Her mouth parted slightly and he held his breath. The invitation was unbearably potent.

When he didn't make a move, Fox stepped back, disappointment evident on her face. "We can't stay out here long. Dad's going to realize I'm gone, and then he'll want both of us inside."

Travis wanted to kiss her, but he couldn't. It was wrong. He felt it with everything in him. She was the only daughter of the Anglo teachers, who had been kind enough to take him and his brother in years ago when their parents had died in a car wreck. He owed the Johnsons and their daughter his respect. And he cared too much for Fox to steal a kiss. He thought it might be her first, and that pleasure should go to somebody who was really going to mean something to her, not a guy like him who was just passing through her life.

"You have something on your mind, Travis," she pressed gently. "What is it?"

"I haven't told anyone yet, not even Ashe, but I want you to know first. Pretty soon I'm going to be leaving the Rez. I'm going to join the army." The hurt he saw in her eyes nearly broke him. She'd never know it, but she was the main reason he was leaving. What he felt for her was too strong, and it could only lead to trouble.

"So you're leaving me, too," she said, sorrow laced through every syllable.

"Don't feel that way, Fox," he said, his heart heavy. "That's why I wanted to talk to you privately tonight. I want you to know that no matter how far I travel, I'll always come back if you need me. I give you my word."

"And I know you'll keep your word," she said, her voice trembling, "but that won't make me miss you less while you're away."

When she lifted her gaze to meet his, he saw himself reflected in her eyes. Fox had always made him feel all-powerful. Although it wouldn't be fair to her to say it out loud, he was going to miss her like crazy, too.

He struggled for the right words. "Fox, you and I have something special, something that neither time nor distance can change."

She smiled sadly. "I keep remembering what you told me not long after you came to live with us. It sounded so hard, but now I know it's true. Only the land lasts forever. Everything else slips away."

He stepped forward and cupped her face in his shaking hands. "Do you remember the rest of what I told you that day? I said that there were only two things that nothing could ever destroy—the land and blood ties, because it's blood that binds people's hearts and even death can't touch that.''

''We're not blood relatives.''

''Then we'll make a pact, an oath sworn in blood. You'll then be blood of my blood. That will bind us as sure as anything.''

''I'd like that. What do we need to do?''

He took out his pocket knife and made a small cut on the pad of his thumb. A drop of blood appeared. Before he could even ask, she held her small, delicate hand out to him.

He held her palm up to his lips and kissed it, then pricked her finger with the tip of his knife. He held her warm, soft hand secure inside his as a few drops of their blood fell together to the sand, staining it crimson.

''The desert will bear witness to what we've done here tonight. We are now joined in spirit and in blood, and nothing will ever break that bond.''

''In spirit and in blood,'' she repeated.

He held Fox's hand for a moment longer, aware of the heat rising again through him. Her pale-blue eyes drew him, and her soft curves were a dangerous temptation. His heart was beating so loud by now, he knew she could hear it too.

''Travis,'' her voice was a mere whisper, but it resonated with a longing neither of them could mistake.

He gazed into her eyes and was lost. Lowering his mouth, he kissed her tenderly. She shuddered and wrapped her arms around him, giving him more than he'd ever dreamed. Nothing he'd ever experienced could have prepared him for the shock of that contact. Her lips trembled beneath his. There was an innocence about her that made him feel powerfully masculine.

He held her tightly, knowing that he'd never forget this day. She was only a girl of sixteen, but, now, in his arms, she was a woman.

"Katrina!" A familiar voice boomed from inside the house. "Time to come inside now."

"Dad, I'm coming." She pulled away quickly. "I'd better go. What if he saw what we've been doing?"

Travis let her slip out of his arms, and before he could say a word she was gone, running toward the front porch.

He stayed outside for several more minutes. He couldn't face anyone right now. His body ached with needs he knew could never be satisfied, not with Katrina. Tonight he'd found something in himself and in Fox that had taken him completely by surprise, and it just plain scared him.

Life, so far, had taught him that caring deeply for anyone was a highway that led only to pain. People left—sometimes willingly, sometimes not, like when his parents died suddenly. The only way to stay safe was to keep feelings locked away, buried deep inside himself. Fox was becoming a woman but he wasn't the man for her. She'd do a lot better for herself once he was out of the way for good. She deserved someone who would take care of her for a lifetime, not him, who had nothing to offer. His love always seemed to hurt the people it touched. The best way he could protect her, and himself, was to go as far away as possible.

He rubbed away the trickle of blood that had spilled down his hand. He would leave right after her party tomorrow, but he would always honor their blood oath. That way, Fox would be a part of him for always.

Chapter One

Present day

Fox was up, packing her belongings by the time the sun appeared in the east. It was almost time to leave the safe house, and she wanted to get it over with. Today she'd testify in court, finally putting her past behind her.

In these last few weeks she'd learned more about herself than she'd ever dreamed possible. She'd discovered her real identity and learned that she'd been a protected witness since the age of six; that the only parents she remembered were unconnected to her by blood. Somehow the Federal Marshals had always kept her safe, though she'd been marked for death since the day she'd witnessed the murder of her birth parents. But then a few months ago, a leak at the Marshals Service had brought her quiet life tumbling down around her. She'd been forced to face the fact that her secure, sheltered life on the Rez had been nothing more than an illusion. Growing up always exacted a price, but, this time, it had destroyed the very basis of her world.

The teenage hood named Prescott who had taken the life of her biological parents had, over the years, become a powerful and influential man. He'd finally tracked her down and done his best to destroy her. He'd come terrifyingly close to succeeding. To her eternal regret, her adoptive parents had become his victims as well, prey to the murderer's need to neutralize the fragile connection she could make to his past crimes.

The one comforting link to her past, the one bond that fate hadn't been able to shatter, was her relationship with Travis Redhawk. Strong feelings neither of them wanted to acknowledge still existed, no matter how hard they'd tried to deny it. When she was in danger, he'd come to her...just as he'd promised so long ago.

Many times during the past few weeks she'd regretted the teenage pact they'd made. She was a woman now, not a child. The more she thought about it, the more wrong it seemed to allow Travis to risk his life for hers to honor a promise made by two idealistic kids. But nothing she could say had changed his mind and some romantic part of her was secretly glad. He insisted he'd stick with her as long as she was at risk. And like the boy he'd been, Travis was a man of his word.

"Are you almost ready?" she called out to Travis, opening the door.

"Yeah, but it's too early to start. If we leave now, we'll get there before they're ready for us," he answered from the kitchen. "Have some coffee first."

"No thanks. We can drive around for a while if you want, but I just want to get going."

When he stepped into her room a moment later, Travis stood tall, his lean, muscular body poised and ready for any challenge. His copper skin gleamed in the morning light. He was all power and masculine strength. Despite his close-cropped hair and his civilian clothes, there was a wildness in him that reminded Fox of the Navajo warriors of old. She had no doubt that anyone who tried to harm her would find him a formidable opponent.

"You're almost to the finish line, Fox," he said quietly.

"Calm down and let events unfold. After you testify, you'll be free to live your own life again, any way you see fit."

Alone with Travis, in the confines of her small bedroom, it was hard to keep her mind focused on anything except him. Every inch of her body felt flushed with a fiery awareness. She struggled to keep her mind on the desperate matters at hand.

"I know. This *is* the last stretch, but isn't that when things get really dangerous? Everyone lowers their guard, then the unexpected happens. I don't want to be a victim anymore. If we stay unpredictable, the odds will tip in our favor. That's why I want to leave now, and I'm not going to take no for an answer."

"Fox, I've known you almost all your life. I've seen you grow up, but one thing's remained the same. You're still the most stubborn, headstrong woman I know."

There was no censure in his words, just genuine admiration. The slow grin he gave her was so purely masculine, so sensually appealing, her heart quickened despite her best intentions. But she still held her ground. They *were* leaving.

"I'm not going to change your mind, am I?" he asked.

"Nope." His eyes swept over her, leaving her tingling in some very disturbing places. It was always a challenge to hold her own around him, but she was glad she had the strength to do so. With his devastating good looks, he'd certainly never had any problems getting his way with women but, as far as she knew, she was the only young, single woman who'd ever remained in his life for more than a few weeks. And their relationship had probably only survived because they'd stayed out of each other's reach in the ways that counted most.

"I've learned to think for myself and trust my instincts. We need to play things by ear. Forget the detailed instructions the Marshals Service gave us, Travis. Believe me, following orders is not the answer now."

"Unless you're the one issuing them?" he teased.

Fox glowered at him. "You should only do what I ask when I'm right. And I'm right now." She finished packing then closed her suitcase. "Remember one thing. We still don't have all the answers. The evidence tells us ex-D.A. Prescott killed my adoptive parents, and my real parents before that, but we had to fill in a lot of those gaps ourselves. He hasn't confessed, or even been convicted yet. There may be other people connected to him who want me dead, too, and if they can find a way to do it, they'll strike now when we least expect it. Prescott and his kind aren't the type to accept defeat quietly. He rose from poverty to become a very influential attorney. I think he's yet to make his final move, and that's why I want to get out of here now. A moving target is harder to hit."

Travis gazed at her, his expression somber. He was the one who'd taught her that. "All right, we'll leave. But don't get cocky. I'm still your bodyguard and I'll call the shots from this point on."

"Whatever you say." Fox gave him a quick smile. "See how easy I am to get along with?"

He groaned loudly as she walked past him out of the room.

TRAVIS STOOD to one side of the window, careful not to turn himself into an easy target. He peered deep into the shadows cast by their vehicle and the few small trees within his field of view, looking for movement or anything out of the ordinary.

It was early morning, not his time of day. He thought of Fox and how different they were, even in a matter as inconsequential as this. Fox had always been an early riser, as if she couldn't wait to see what the new day would bring. Yet at night, when he came alive and his energy was at its highest, she was ready for sleep, her energy expended. This morning had been no exception.

As she gathered up her things, he stood waiting, restless, and eager to see this thing through. Yet, as much as he wanted to see it finished, a part of him wished that it wasn't all coming to a close. Once Fox testified, it would be time for him to return to his Ranger unit, which was now on a training mission halfway around the world.

"Okay, I'm ready," she said.

Fox was dressed in a simple pantsuit but there was a quiet elegance about her that was hard to ignore. She was like a pale flower that continued to bloom in the desert despite the heat.

He felt the familiar tug on his senses as their eyes met. "Let's go."

Travis hurried out with her. He was glad that he'd be driving Fox to the courthouse today. He knew the Four Corners area well, and, in case of trouble, would be able to easily evade anyone pursuing them. Antiterrorist tactics, including those involving the operation of a vehicle, were part of the training he'd picked up as an Army Ranger.

Travis kept to the highway, moving along at a brisk pace. "I'm going to start heading in the general direction of the courthouse now. I'll take the long way, but that'll still put us there just about on time."

"Good. Anything's better than sitting around in some hallway, waiting."

The tension in the car was palpable. He was aware of everything about her, even the soft sound of her breathing. Yet neither of them broke the silence. They both knew only too well the dangers that lay just ahead for them.

Over an hour later, as they finally approached their destination, Travis felt his gut tighten. This was it. He wondered about the predicted media circus at the Aztec courthouse. His brother Ashe was a master of understatement, so Travis was fairly sure it would be far worse than Ashe had intimated.

Ashe and Casey Feist, the beautiful U.S. Deputy Marshal who'd been Fox's handler in the Witness Security Program, would meet them there. They'd be escorting their prisoner, ex-district attorney Prescott, into the courthouse.

"Why is it so important that I arrive at the same time as Mom and Dad's killer?" Fox asked. "Prescott still gives me the creeps."

"It's easier to coordinate security that way. But don't worry. We won't let him near you. Besides, he'll be shackled hand and foot," Travis said.

Still worried about Fox, he glanced over and saw her sitting quietly, staring at her own clasped hands. He felt a strange twist in his chest. They were as different as night and day, yet desire flashed through him every time he looked at her. He stopped the thought dead in its tracks. She needed him to stay focused now, to keep his attention on outside threats, and that was just what he intended to do.

As they entered the small city of Aztec and approached the courthouse, he saw the crowd of onlookers and reporters that had gathered there. "Keep your head down, Fox," he advised. "No sense in advertising you're here."

"No way. Not any longer. I'm holding my head high and sitting up straight. I've done nothing wrong and I'm not cowering."

"For Pete's sake, jettison that pride of yours and concentrate on staying alive, will you? They can't take aim if they can't see you. Now crouch down."

"No. And stop giving me orders. I'm not a private in your special army." Fox looked straight at him.

"It's a good thing you're not, woman. I'd have had you on report from day one." He took a deep breath, then softened his voice. "Work with me, okay? Won't you please scrunch down in the seat so nobody will see you until we get out?''

"It's pointless. They already know I'm here," she said.

Travis cursed softly as they drove quickly past the crowd of reporters, cops and curious citizens. Moving to the county courthouse's back parking lot, he pulled into the loading zone. By the time he came to a stop, three other cars, two of them marked police cruisers, were right behind him.

His brother Ashe was in the middle car with Casey seated beside him and Prescott in the back seat. As two armed marshals came out the courthouse door, Casey and Ashe got out of the car.

''That's our cue,'' Travis said, stepping out, keeping his body between Fox and the crowd, which was less than fifty feet away.

Fox climbed out quickly. Their timing was perfect. Prescott was being unloaded at the same time.

''Can you believe a teacher is actually bringing students to see something like this?''

Fox pointed to a school bus in a visitor parking space a dozen cars away. "It's like stories of the Old West, where people would come for miles just to see the murderer hang.''

''Wait a second. Where are the students? I didn't see any school-age kids in the crowd out front.'' Travis glanced toward the courthouse, then over at Prescott and Ashe. When he turned to take a closer look at the bus driver, his blood turned to ice.

''Gun. In the bus!'' Travis yelled, warning his brother while simultaneously shoving Fox back down into the car. He dived in next, covering her with his body as the sharp crack of a rifle pinged against the metal of the car.

''Get her out of here!'' Casey yelled as another shot was fired.

Travis scrambled over to the driver's side of the car. "Stay down, Fox." He started the engine, threw the car into reverse, and jammed his foot on the accelerator.

As he tried to maneuver the sedan between the building and a police vehicle just entering the lot, another shot rang out. The windshield of the approaching cruiser exploded into a cloud of shattered glass and the squad car veered out of control. It smashed into the rear end of their sedan on the passenger side, jolting them painfully against their seat belts.

Glass from the rear windshield flew everywhere. Although Travis held on tightly to the steering wheel, the laws of physics were in charge. Their sedan spun around, hurling them against a parked van, then slamming them into the metal rail of a stairway leading to the basement of the courthouse.

Travis's head struck the side window hard, but he didn't have time to think about the sudden pain. Switching off the ignition, he turned toward Fox, who lay scrunched up on the floor mat beneath the dash. Her head was tucked down, covered by her arms.

Travis's heart pumped like a steam engine as fear pried into him. He'd failed her. In the end, his training hadn't mattered. Had she been struck by a bullet or injured in the crash?

Then he saw her move and, finally, he breathed again. She was alive.

Fox rose up slowly and climbed back onto the seat. "That was some wild ride. Where did you get your driver's license—at the rodeo?"

"A thank-you would have been nice," he muttered. "Get out of the car fast and go down that stairwell. Stay out of sight."

"I can't get out," Fox replied, grunting as she pushed

the door. "It's jammed. I can't even roll down the window."

Travis tried his door. "It's no better here. The collision pushed in the sides of the car like a stomped-on soda can."

"I have an idea," she said.

"What's new?"

"Will you just listen?" She never stopped to wait for an answer. "I'll climb into the back seat and give you some legroom. Maybe you can get enough leverage to kick open one of these doors."

As Fox crawled into the rear, Travis put his back against the hump in the floorboard and kicked at the passenger door. It squealed loudly and sprang open about ten inches before striking the wall of the building.

"Good going!" Fox said.

Ashe jogged over to them just as Travis sat up.

"Paramedics are on the way," Ashe told them. "Are you two okay?"

"We don't need medical help, if that's what you mean," Fox said, sitting up.

Travis slid over to the passenger side. "Is it secure out there?" Although Travis suspected that Fox hadn't been the sniper's intended target—no one could have been that bad a shot—it was dangerous to keep her here one second longer than was necessary.

"Except for the general chaos, it's clear. The shooter took off. You two need help getting out?" Ashe glanced back at the totaled patrol car, where others were helping an injured officer out of his vehicle.

"We can squeeze out," Fox said. "Go. Others are in trouble, and you have a gunman to track down. Be careful."

As Ashe ran off, Travis squeezed through the narrow opening, then leaned in to help Fox out of the car.

She'd just started to climb back into the front seat when

the police cruiser alongside them exploded into flames. As the blast rocked their sedan, Travis was blown sideways down the stairwell. In a desperate maneuver, he grabbed the bottom rung of the rail, breaking his fall at the last second. When he pulled himself back up, he was greeted by a vision straight from hell.

Their sedan had been shoved against the building, and the door he'd kicked open was now shut again, jammed against the iron stair-rail. Fox had been thrown diagonally across the interior of the car, and now lay on the back seat on the driver's side. She was covered in glass from the shattered rear window. Oily flames from the cruiser were already blistering the paint on the trunk of their car, and black smoke billowed up in a swelling cloud. Unless he got Fox out fast, she wouldn't have a chance. Their car had nearly a full tank of gas; he'd pumped it himself last night. It wouldn't take much more heat to make it blow.

He looked down through the opening where the rear window had been. "Fox, I'll help you out. Hang on."

"How? There's no way out. The back end is burning already. The doors are jammed on both sides and I still can't roll down any of the windows. Find something to break the glass—or maybe a fire extinguisher will help. Otherwise there's nothing more you can do here."

"Hang tight." She was right. He had to smash through the glass on the driver's side and pull her out the window. Travis wrapped his jacket around his arm, then slammed his elbow into the back-seat window. It hurt like hell, but the window didn't even crack.

Hearing someone shout his name, Travis turned his head and saw Ashe running up. "Give this a try!" Ashe yelled, tossing him a police baton.

Travis caught it in one hand. "Fox, cover your face." With one vicious backhand, he smashed the nightstick against the glass, shattering it. Ignoring the flames less than four feet away, he cleared the loose fragments of glass with the police baton and reached through for Fox's hand.

Travis pulled her through the opening, gathered her in his arms and carried her over to Ashe's truck.

"You'd better get her inside the building where she'll be safe!" Ashe shouted, joining them.

Fox squirmed, forcing Travis to set her down. Standing straight between them, she gestured around her. Smoke covered the parking lot like black fog. "Are you kidding? There's no safe place around here."

"I have to agree with her on this one, brother," Travis said. "That's why I carried her over here. We need to borrow your truck for a while."

Ashe handed Travis the keys without hesitation. "Casey will want to know where you're going."

"I don't know yet. Somewhere safer, I hope." Travis unlocked the passenger door and Fox climbed inside quickly. "We'll let you know as soon as we get there."

Before Ashe could argue, Travis started up the engine and raced out of the parking lot.

"Slow down, Ranger," Fox said with a wry smile. "We made it through that," she said, gesturing back toward the courthouse. "I don't want to end up wrapped around a light pole now."

Travis gave her an exasperated look. "Quiet. No one appreciates a backseat driver." As he looked over at her, he saw that her hands were shaking. "Don't worry, Fox," he added, his tone gentling. "We're out of it now. Did you get cut anywhere?"

"I haven't checked yet." Fox carefully brushed chunks of glass from her sleeves, then closed her eyes and shook more grains out of her hair onto the floorboards. "Do you know if Prescott was hurt?"

"No. But my guess is that *he* was the intended target, not you."

She lapsed into a thoughtful silence, then finally continued. "Have you noticed that whenever there's trouble, I always seem to be right in the middle of it. And, what's worse, a lot of people connected to me are dying, and I can't seem to stop it." Her voice broke, but she swallowed back her tears.

"I'm still here, and so's my brother," he said, his voice even. "There's Casey now, too."

"Yes, but don't you see? The only people around me who've managed to stay alive are the ones trained to fight. If I don't find a way to turn the tables on whoever's after me, I'll be dead soon enough, too." She raised a hand, stemming his protests. "It's time I went after these people and found my own answers. It's my only chance. The U.S. Marshals' work on this case has been plagued with setbacks. I need to know, once and for all, how I fit into this mess I've inherited."

"If you take the offensive, the road ahead of you won't be easy. The Marshals Service will do their best to stop you."

"They can't. It's my fight now. But I don't want you to worry about me. I can take care of myself. What's needed now is brains, not brawn."

He glowered at her. "Meaning what?"

"Nothing," she said quickly, with an apologetic look. "Just that I know you have to report back to your unit soon, and I want you to know I can handle this on my own."

There was no way he could leave her now. There was no telling how much trouble she'd be in without him. "I have plenty of leave, so let me worry about that. There's work we both need to do here now."

Travis glanced over at Fox. He'd loved the girl she'd been, but the woman she'd become drew him even more. She stirred his blood until anger and desire warred inside him in equal parts. Her will was more than a match for his own.

Yet there was a gentle side to her that spoke to him, as well. Her courage took its strength from her loyalty to those she cared about. He didn't believe for one minute that she fully understood just how hard the fight ahead of her would be. But, no matter what happened, he'd be there to equalize the odds.

Chapter Two

Fox studied the people getting in and out of their vehicles at businesses and along the streets, and the drivers of the cars they passed. Any one of them could be her enemy. The facelessness of the killer, or killers, on her trail scared her more than anything else, but she was through hiding. From this point on, she would become a hunter, too.

She glanced over at Travis, glad he was here, yet wishing he hadn't become involved. She knew that he would do his best to protect her, but the fact remained that this was her battle. She alone held the key that would lead them all out of danger, though it was buried deep within her memory, in a place not even she could find.

The loneliness that engulfed her now as she faced her situation squarely was nearly overpowering. Yet, it shouldn't have had that effect on her. Being alone was nothing new to her. After all, despite the love her foster parents had given her, she'd grown up as a white child among the Navajos. Her blond hair and fair skin had always marked her as different—an Anglo, as most fair-skinned people were called in the area. Although she'd been accepted, and in her own way had carved out a place for herself here, it was not the same as that feeling of belonging that came easily to those who were part of the majority.

Standing out in a crowd could be flattering, but it could be frightening, too.

As Travis drove back toward the Rez, she felt none of the comfort that traveling over familiar ground usually brought her. With her mom and dad gone—at least, the only mom and dad she really remembered—she felt empty inside. The bridges to her past were slowly disintegrating, but to find herself, she'd have to work her way back across them. Only then would she be able to find peace.

"What's wrong? You're too quiet," Travis said softly as they reached Farmington.

She shook her head, not answering his question.

"You've never kept secrets from me before, Fox. Why start now?"

He gave her that heart-stopping half smile that always sent a special thrill right up her spine. "We all have secrets, Travis," she said sadly. Then, after a moment, she added, "But, you know, I really think the worst ones are the ones we try to keep from ourselves."

"You *will* remember all the details of your past some-day, Fox. Just keep believing in yourself."

"You don't understand what this is like. You *know* who you are, Travis. You always have. Even when you and your brother left Rock Ridge to live with Mom and Dad, you had your own identity. From that came your confidence, and your ability to do just about anything."

"You're no different. You've always achieved whatever you set out to do, too." He paused, then continued. "In the Rangers we're taught to set an objective and do what-ever it takes to achieve it. You can be your own best friend or your worst enemy. If you refuse to admit the possibility of failure, you will win."

Travis reached for her hand, cradling it inside his own. His palm felt rough and strong, and incredibly masculine.

"No matter what the battle, I give you my word that you won't face it alone. I'll be right by your side."

His touch enticed her to surrender to the glorious feelings that contact produced. Only with effort did Fox force herself to impose caution and control on her thoughts. "Trouble comes in many guises, Travis. Help me keep watch for all of them."

Their eyes met and, for one wild instant, she felt the power of that indefatigable force that drew them together despite their efforts to resist. She turned away, disciplining her emotions, and brushed a few stray shards of glass from her blouse. She had to stop looking at him through the eyes of the girl she'd once been. He wasn't an illusion based on girlish dreams. He was simply a man—one who was undeniably attractive. She looked back at him again and, this time, saw only shadows of a fire that never was—and never could be.

FORTY-FIVE MINUTES LATER, as they reached the outskirts of Shiprock, Fox spoke again. "You're not going back to the safe house, are you?"

"Sure. Nobody knew we were there before." Travis shrugged.

"I don't think that's a good idea. There's a good chance the safe house has been compromised. The guy in the bus was waiting for everyone in the back parking lot of the courthouse. He knew our plans, or else was incredibly lucky to be at just the right place at the right time."

"I don't believe in luck, so your point's well taken." He considered their options. "There's only one other place I can think of where no one will think of searching for us."

"Where's that?"

"Our old home, the Johnson house. It's been locked up, now that none of us are using it. Most Navajos will be avoiding it, too, since nobody wants to be near a place where people have died. You know about fear of the *chindi,* the evil part of a person that remains earthbound after death.''

Fox nodded. "We'll have privacy there, that's for sure. And it'll give me a chance to go back through all of Mom and Dad's stuff. I have to start digging hard into my past, and I might as well begin there. Too many secrets lie buried with Mom and Dad—and with my real parents.''

Fox ducked down as they entered the Reservation town of Shiprock. "Let me know when we get to the turnoff. I don't want anyone to see me this close to home. They may guess where we're going.''

"Now you're using your head,'' Travis said.

"Why don't you duck your head, too, smart aleck?'' Fox glared over at him.

"I could do it, and still stay on course, but it would look weird to any passing car. So I think I'll pass. Navajos aren't supposed to show off, you know,'' Travis said with a straight face.

Fifteen minutes later they reached the end of a gravel road and pulled up beside the Johnson home. Travis and Fox hurried up onto the porch, and while Travis took a quick glance around the yard, Fox produced a key and unlocked the door.

As soon as they stepped inside, Travis got on the phone, which had not yet been disconnected, and called Ashe to let him know where they were. Fox stood by, and hit the speaker button as soon as Travis greeted Ashe.

Travis filled his brother in quickly.

"Stay on your guard and consider any approaching vehicles potential enemies,'' Ashe said. "You shouldn't have anybody dropping by since everybody in the area sees that house as one contaminated by the *chindi.*''

"How's Prescott?'' Fox asked.

There was a long silence before he answered. "He was

hit by the first shot. The rifle bullet penetrated the vest Casey had him wear. The paramedics couldn't stabilize him and he died en route to the hospital.''

Fox felt the blood rush away from her head. She sat down and then, after a moment, spoke. ''They don't want me dead, you know,'' she managed in a thin voice. ''What they really want is to destroy me by killing everyone I'm associated with.''

''No, I disagree, Fox,'' Casey answered, apparently having picked up an extension. ''I don't think there's anything even remotely personal about this. They're after something else entirely. But the attack on Prescott clearly indicates that there are more people involved in this conspiracy than we originally thought. Someone else started shooting after Prescott went down and pinned us long enough to give the sniper a chance to get away. Prescott was the intended target. We have no doubt of that.''

''So what happened to the gunmen?'' Travis asked. ''Did you catch them?''

''No,'' Casey replied. ''They abandoned the bus for another vehicle a few blocks away, and escaped before any of us could catch up to them.''

''We did find the real bus driver, bound and gagged, but otherwise unhurt,'' Ashe added. ''He was on his way back from dropping the kids off at school when he was hijacked at gunpoint by two men wearing masks. He couldn't identify either of them. The men are still at large, but we've got roadblocks set up everywhere.''

''This shooting can't have anything to do with Mom and Dad's death. Prescott killed them over a month ago,'' Fox said, her voice shaky. ''That means it goes back to my natural parents and the reason my family was in the Witness Protection Program. They testified against a group of Russian criminals, I know that. But it's becoming clear that they must have had other secrets, as well.''

"Your father was their accountant," Casey said, "but we don't believe he skimmed any of their money. He wouldn't have been living under the protection of WITSEC with just enough funds to get by if he had."

"*If* this is tied to your parents and your past, you're still not safe, Fox. We need to keep you hidden for a while longer," Ashe said. "But there is a chance that this has nothing to do with you. It may simply be a matter of Prescott's enemies wanting to make sure he couldn't cut a deal and testify against them. The bottom line is that, at this moment, we really don't know anything for sure."

"Not even where to start looking," Fox finished for him. She looked down at her hands, lost in thought. When she finally looked up, she held Travis's gaze with a steady one of her own. "I don't want any more protection. If whoever it is wants to find me, here I am. I won't spend the rest of my life running away from something that will endanger everyone who comes into contact with me. From what we've seen, they're prepared to murder anyone who gets in their way, but they don't really want to kill me. If they did, they could have done it before now. That's our one ace in the hole, and we need to let it work for us."

"Just because they don't seem to be aiming at you, Fox, doesn't mean your life is safe," Travis said. "Take today, for instance. Getting hit by a stray bullet could have been just as deadly. The wreck and the fire could have been fatal, and were very nearly so. You may not be their intended target, but they're quite willing to gamble with your life."

"Travis is right. You can't leave yourself open to these people," Casey said. "If it's information they want from you, once they get it, you'll be expendable. They won't leave a potential witness alive to testify. We saw that evidenced today."

A marble coldness enveloped Fox. "I can't just sit here. I have to take some kind of action. Too many people have died on my account, and it won't stop unless I do something."

"Fox, you're thinking like a rookie cop," Ashe interrupted. "You're ready to take on the world with no backup. Give Casey and me a little time to scout around. In the meantime, we'll increase our patrols around the house. If anyone tries to get at you there, Travis can handle it until backup arrives."

"We'll be here only for a short time. I can't wait. And you can't expect Travis to be patient and rely on backup. He could get himself killed, following those orders."

"You don't have a choice," Ashe replied. "It would be extremely foolish to make a move before you know exactly what you're up against. All I'm asking for is a bit of time."

"He's right," Casey added. "If you are valuable to a criminal still at large, we need to find out why. I expect we'll have more information in a few hours. Give us a chance to do some work on this and we'll get back to you as soon as we can."

Fox watched Travis as he hung up the phone. "Casey and Ashe are well matched. They make great partners—in work and love."

"My brother is crazy about her. I'm really glad they found each other."

A twinge of envy filled her as she realized that Casey and Ashe would be husband and wife in just a few months. They would probably have been married already if not for her and the murder case. The pair had banded together to keep Fox safe and to find Prescott, the murderer of her adoptive parents—Ashe and Travis's foster parents. As they'd worked to find the truth, they'd discovered love.

Wishing she could foresee a happy ending like Ashe and Casey's for herself, Fox went to her room, leaving Travis in the kitchen making coffee.

She sat at her desk, wanting desperately to feel some

connection to her past. The emptiness inside her was like a chill that had settled permanently over her soul.

As her gaze fell on her high-school yearbook in the corner, she began leafing through its pages, allowing her thoughts to drift.

Soon she reached her favorite section—one filled with baby photos of her classmates side by side with their graduation portraits. Her stomach flip-flopped as she vividly remembered a scene from her past. At the time it had seemed inconsequential but now, under the circumstances, it took on a different meaning.

One day after school, in preparation for that special collage planned for the yearbook, she'd asked her mom for a baby photo. She'd never seen one of herself anywhere, but the question had never really come up before then.

As memories unfolded in her mind's eye, she recalled her mom's strange expression as she'd explained that the pictures had been lost in a fire.

Fox knew better than to believe that story now. For the first time, she understood the echoes of sadness that she'd always carried inside her, weighing her down even on the happiest of occasions. It had been her soul crying out for the past only her heart remembered.

She picked up Chance, the scruffy dark gray teddy bear that lay against her pillows, as it had all through her childhood, and held it close. When the past was nothing but shadows, it was nice to have something familiar to hold on to.

"Fox?" Travis stood at the door to her room. "Why don't you come into the kitchen and have a cup of coffee with me?"

She smiled. "Okay, but I'll have to dilute it. Yours tastes like sludge."

"No problem. I just heated water for instant. I can make

a decent cup for myself and you can have the wimpy stuff.''

''My coffee's not wimpy. You just haven't realized that the spoon isn't supposed to stand up straight in coffee like it does in ice cream.''

Several minutes later, Travis and Fox sat at the table together. Travis stared at the words painted on her coffee mug and smiled. '' 'To move mountains, carry away small stones,' '' he read. ''I like it.''

''It's an old proverb I've always liked. Harvey Billey painted it on the mug and gave it to me as a present.''

''So, you've been seeing Harvey?'' Travis asked.

''Now and then,'' she replied.

''Is it serious?''

''Don't make it sound like a disease. We went out a few times but we really didn't have enough in common.''

As she sipped her coffee, Travis saw the strain of the last few weeks mirrored on her face. The dark circles under her eyes looked even more pronounced against the pallor of her skin. He would have given anything to hold her until her tension gave way to that look of hazy passion he'd seen in her eyes when he'd kissed her a lifetime ago.

''I'm so frustrated!''

Travis stared at her in surprise, then realized she was talking about something else entirely.

''The answers I want are inside me, Travis. I was there when my natural parents were murdered, and I shared their life, if not their fate. Why can't I just reach back into my memory and get the answers I need? Then I'd know who these criminals are, why they're still out to get me, and what they want from me.''

''Remembering may not be the solution you think it is,'' he warned. ''It could just end up giving you a whole new set of problems.''

"Maybe, but it's easier to fight an enemy you know than an enemy you don't know."

"You're right about that." He'd always preferred open confrontations. The cat-and-mouse games they'd been forced to play with the killers were not his style at all.

"I'm going to search this house from top to bottom. Mom told me once that all my baby pictures were lost in a fire but, in view of what I know now, I realize that may not have been true. She never threw anything out, so my guess is that she's got all kinds of mementos hidden here."

"It's possible. But it may also be that she never had anything from your past."

"I must have brought something along with me. I was a six-year-old kid, not a newborn. At the very least, I'd be willing to bet that there are photos of me when she first brought me home."

"Alice was always tucking things away, that's for sure. She saved the first report cards Ashe and I brought home after we moved here from Rock Ridge. And I know she kept bits of the first bouquet of flowers a boy ever sent you."

"She put the petals in her Bible," Fox said, nodding. "I'm going to start by looking there. But let me do this alone. It's my memories we're trying to trigger, and that's something you can't help me with."

"It'll go faster if we both search," he argued. Not that he wanted to search through the Johnsons' belongings. It seemed wrong, somehow.

"You'll only interfere with what I'm trying to do. Besides—" She stopped speaking and shook her head. "Never mind."

The fact that she was so adamant about not letting him take part in the search puzzled him. Then, in a sudden flash of inspiration, he understood why. For some inexplicable reason, she was trying to protect him. The thought was galling. He was a soldier. He didn't need protection. But, though he wanted to be angry with her, he couldn't quite manage it. She was an incredible puzzle to him. All steel and fire one minute, then as gentle as only a woman could be the next. Somewhere along the way, she'd turned into the most captivating woman he'd ever met.

"Just remember, Fox, your job is not to play detective. Anything you find out goes to Casey and Ashe."

"I'll tell them what I can, but I'm not sitting on the sidelines. I've been the protected witness already and look where it got me." Fox went to the Johnsons' bedroom.

Travis followed her inside and, as he did, felt a cold chill envelop him. He wasn't like his brother, Ashe. Travis harbored no fear of the *chindi*, the evil in a man that remained on earth to corrupt the living. Yet, strangely enough, it was taking every bit of willpower he possessed to stay in that room with Fox.

"The pages of this Bible are so thin, I'm surprised Mom was able to keep it in such good condition," Fox commented, her attention focused on not damaging it in any way. "I know this Bible was in her family for years. She told me once that, someday, it would be her legacy to me," she said, her voice trembling.

"This is harder on you than it is on my brother or me. She was the only mother you've ever known. Would you like me to look through it?" Travis asked, forcing his voice to remain even and not betray his discomfort.

"No. I owe it to myself, and to her, to do this on my own."

Although she found a number of little reminders of her childhood on the Rez, by the time she reached the last page, she'd discovered nothing of particular significance. Disappointed, Fox placed the Bible back on the nightstand.

"I'm going to take this room apart. You don't have to stay for this. You can't help now."

He took a deep breath. He had no desire to stay here, but knowing that she thought he couldn't handle it, exasperated him. He remained where he was.

"Look, I don't want your help," she said brusquely.

Despite her harsh tone, he saw the truth in her eyes. She intended to do what she thought was best for him, whether he liked it or not.

"Have it your way."

He strode out of the room, wondering how he could be so attracted to a woman who could make him so crazy at times.

GOING FROM ROOM TO ROOM, Fox looked everywhere for items that might have some significance to her, and provide a clue to her past. Finally, while carrying a box of old papers, she collided with Travis in the hall. The papers flew everywhere, despite Travis's attempt to catch the box.

"Where were you going?" Fox muttered.

"I've been watching you run around this house, opening drawers and boxes and mumbling to yourself. You need a plan."

"I have a plan. It's just not one of yours."

"I was only going to suggest you narrow your search and look for specific items, like your old clothes, or maybe photos." Travis kept his voice deliberately low. She needed his help whether she realized it or not.

An exhaustive search of the closets revealed nothing. "What we have to figure out is where she would have kept the things she never wanted anyone else to find," Travis said.

Fox sat on the edge of the bed, lost in thought. As he studied her expression, he saw a glimpse of the little girl she'd once been—the kid who could ace any science test, no matter how difficult, but who still longed to believe that elves and fairies could be real. The dreamer in her had always been at war with the practical, intellectual side of her nature.

Yet, from that unlikely combination of traits, came her strength as well as her greatest weakness. She was apt to joust with windmills, convincing herself that even miracles were statistically possible if she remained persistent. And, lately, she was jousting with him, too, on just about every issue that presented itself. The little girl was gone, replaced by a very strong woman with a mind of her own. Keeping her safe wasn't going to be any picnic if she insisted on playing Sherlock Holmes.

"The key to my past is here in this house," she said. "It has to be. But where?"

"We could try the special photo albums, the ones that have those old black-and-white and sepia photos of her family," Travis suggested at length. "She always kept those out of reach, so she may have hidden something else there."

"Yes, of course!" Fox went to the bookcase in the living room and looked around. "They were here, weren't they?"

"On the top shelf," Travis answered, reaching up and bringing one album down for her. "But, on second thought, you probably won't find anything in these. I doubt she would have risked having something that could compromise your identity so easily accessible."

"Sometimes hiding an object in plain sight is the best strategy." Fox took the album from Travis, then went to the couch.

As she sat there, cross-legged, absorbed in the photos, twirling a lock of golden hair around her finger, she suddenly looked like a sixteen-year-old again, not a twenty-two year old. Travis smiled, but as his gaze drifted down and he took in her body's gentle curves, he realized there was no escaping it: Fox was a woman now. There was a natural sensuality about her, too, which he found nearly impossible to resist.

But her innocence made her far more vulnerable than she realized. He could keep her alive by becoming bad news to anyone who tried to hurt her; but keeping her heart safe was a different story. In that respect, he was her worst enemy. He had to master his feelings for her, or his desire to make her his would destroy them both.

As Fox leafed through the album, she slowly shook her head. "There doesn't seem to be anything useful to us here," she said. But, near the end, she stopped and stared at the faded snapshot in the middle of the page. "Wait, here's something. This must have been taken right after they adopted me," she said.

There was no adult standing with her. Her heart twisted as intuition told her what was behind the somber expression she'd worn so long ago. "I was so scared."

"That was natural, under the circumstances. You had plenty of reason to be wary of people," Travis said.

"That's Chance, my teddy bear," she said. "I look as if I'm holding on to him for dear life. I wonder if he was a gift from Mom and Dad, or something I brought from my old life."

Travis studied the photo. "That bear wasn't new when that photo was taken. See how the ear is unraveling?"

"You're right. Poor Chance looked tattered even then. Mom sewed him up for me many times over the years." As she held the photo album closer to the light, she suddenly spotted a slight rectangular bulge around the center of the photo. "Do you see that?"

"There's something hidden behind there," Travis acknowledged.

"I'm afraid to pry up this brittle sheet of plastic from the sticky corners. There's got to be another way to get at what's beneath this picture without damaging anything."

She held the album sideways and shook it gently. As she did, a small photo slipped out from beneath the larger one, dropping onto her lap.

Looking at it grimly, she said, "Now we're getting someplace."

Chapter Three

Fox placed the album on the coffee table, then picked the photo up very carefully. It wasn't quite in focus, and the edges were damaged, but there was no doubt as to the month and year printed on the bottom.

"This picture dates back to before I was adopted. But how did Mom get it? And, more importantly, where was it taken?" She studied the photo carefully. It showed her, at age five, holding a party for two teddy bears and three rag dolls.

"You were in the Southwest," Travis said. "The dry, rocky terrain, and particularly the cactus and creosote bush behind you, remind me of central or southern Arizona."

"This photo must have belonged to my biological parents. And that looks like Chance." She pointed to the gray bear with its back to the camera. "Or it might be just another gray teddy bear," she added reluctantly.

"Let's take a closer look at that bear of yours." He went to her room and returned with the stuffed toy.

Fox saw Travis pressing into the bear's body with his powerful hands, searching for something hidden inside. She smiled. "There's nothing in that bear except very old stuffing. It's been squeezed and loved to death for many years, believe me."

He handed it to her. "You're right. It's soft enough that I can tell there's nothing inside it."

"Chance was my best friend when I was a kid," she said. "Sometimes when I look at him, I start to see these strange images I don't recognize. But when I focus on them, my heart starts pounding and it all fades away again."

"That's okay. Don't force it."

Fox set the stuffed bear down. "You know, there's another angle we can pursue. But we'd need the addresses of every single place Mom and Dad ever lived after I came into their lives."

"We can get that," he said. "It would be listed in their federal income-tax records and I know where Nick kept those." He led Fox to the workshop outside, then to two tall gray metal file cabinets. "Now tell me. Why do you want to know where they lived?"

"I'd like to talk to the people Mom and Dad knew back when I was little, right after they moved here to the Rez. Sometimes it's just too hard to keep everything a secret. What I'm hoping is that they confided bits and pieces to different people they trusted, just in the course of regular conversation. And, with luck, we may be able to piece together a lead we can follow up on."

"I don't think that's a sound course of action," Travis said. "If you actively pursue an investigation of your own, you'll be right in the line of fire."

"I'm there anyway," she countered. "I'm going on the offensive on this, Travis. You can't stop me. What you can do, if you choose to, is help me."

He considered it before answering. If he didn't help her, she'd do it on her own and try to cut him out of the picture. She'd left him with no real choice. "All right. We'll play it your way for the time being, and see how it goes."

"Good. I'm not making an arbitrary decision, you know.

It's our only option. We know Dad worked as an investi-
gator for the U.S. Attorney's office in Phoenix before he
opened the school here. Those files are going to be closed
to us, so we'll have to leave that part of the case to Casey
and Ashe. What we can do is tackle things from right here.
Since everyone knows everyone else's business on the Rez,
we may find quite a gold mine.''

They carried boxes filled with file folders to the house,
then began sifting through the oldest records first. "I remember going with your father whenever he traveled
around the Rez recruiting students," Travis said, spreading
the papers in stacks on the kitchen table and counter. "He'd
always point out the mission or public schools they'd
worked at before their school opened, and tell me about
them. There were several."

"The time between their arrival on the Rez and the opening of their own school must have been longer than I
thought," Fox mused. "I was little then, and I just don't
remember details."

"It took them several years to get things started. Since
they were really low on funds, particularly during the time
the school was under construction, they'd work anywhere
and everywhere. Alice got a job as a full-time teacher, but
Nick only did substitute teaching so he could be free to
oversee construction as often as possible."

"You know, I never realized that they'd had a rough
time financially," Fox said. "Mom always gave me the
impression that their school was a dream come true. She
never spoke of the hardships."

"Like it is with most people, they got what they wanted
because they were willing to work hard for it."

Fox stopped searching and froze. "Did you hear that?"

Before she finished the sentence, Travis was peering out
the window. "We've got company, and I don't recognize
the vehicle."

"I'll go back to my room and stay out of sight. I have a feeling it'll be safer for both of us if people think you're here alone."

"Fox, if there's trouble," he said, stopping her before she could leave, "climb out the back window and run down into the bosque as fast as you can. Head for town. I'll look after myself."

Travis strode quickly into the front room, not giving her a chance to argue. Seething, Fox put her coffee cup away so there'd be only one on top of the table. Travis just didn't get it. She wasn't running away—not anymore. Picking up a rolling pin from the counter, she continued down the hall to her room. If someone came after her, they'd get a cracked skull for their trouble. Travis had underestimated her badly if he thought she'd leave him to face trouble alone.

TRAVIS STOOD TO ONE side of the window, keeping out of sight as he watched the truck that was pulling up out front. Tense, he waited for a clear view of the two people inside. When the driver stepped out seconds later, Travis immediately recognized him. Stan McNeely was a longtime county resident and a former Ranger who had served with Travis a few years ago. The man had been booted out of the service after slugging a noncommissioned officer.

Travis watched the man as he sauntered up with the "I'm Bad" swagger many of the elite units had adopted. The passenger remained in the truck. Deciding to meet trouble head-on, Travis opened the front door and stepped onto the porch.

"McNeely," he greeted. "It's been a while. What brings you here?"

"Hey, buddy. Thought I'd pay you a visit. What do you say we go inside and talk a little business?"

Travis met the Anglo man's steely gaze with one of his

own. McNeely had an agenda. He'd never come to visit Travis before, and there was nothing casual about his arrival now. Travis considered not inviting the man in, but then concluded it would be better to let McNeely think he had nothing to hide—that Fox was nowhere around.

McNeely went in first. He swept his gaze over the area, like he was taking point in hostile territory, then he turned around and faced Travis.

"Let me get right down to it," McNeely said. "I've been following the news, and I know you and Katrina Johnson—Fox—are in a bit of trouble. I figured you could use some manpower to cover your backs. You've seen me in a scuffle a time or two, and know I can handle myself. I can be an asset to both of you, providing security."

Travis remembered a brawl outside the noncommissioned officers' club a few years back. It had taken four MPs to finally bring McNeely down. He was a stubborn, vicious opponent, but McNeely thrived on danger and met any threat head-on. That was fine in certain fights, but Fox's best chance lay in avoiding a confrontation, and that was what *good* security did best. McNeely's brand of help was the last thing either of them needed.

"I appreciate the offer, but Fox has the Marshals Service to take care of her, and they make all the calls on protection. After the Prescott case is closed and they're out of her life, I think she plans to take off and travel."

McNeely gestured out the window to the passenger in the truck. "My cousin Billy and I are looking for security work, and traveling is no problem. We'd be great bodyguards."

Travis shook his head. "Once this is over, Fox wants to be on her own. She's had it with bodyguards."

"That's too bad," McNeely said, heading back toward the door. "I could have done a fine job of keeping her safe. You know that. Talk to her, and let me know if she changes her mind. I don't have a phone, but my cousin Lori works at the Last Stop Café. You can leave a message with her.''

McNeely's eyes were cold as he met Travis's level gaze and held it. Finally, he looked away. Travis's gut feeling told him he'd just been challenged—a subtle warning between potential opponents. McNeely was a man for hire, and probably didn't much care which side he was on.

"Good luck at finding work," Travis said slowly. "But I'd be careful, if I were you, who you sign on with. For your sake, I wouldn't want us to end up locking horns.''

McNeely laughed. "If we ever do meet on opposite sides, I'll have the edge. You play by too many rules.''

Travis's smile was lethal. "In a fight for survival, there's only one rule—win.''

McNeely nodded, then walked out the door.

Travis stood by the window until the truck disappeared from view. Hearing soft footsteps, he turned his head and saw Fox approach.

"He's gone, right?'' Fox was wearing the dark-haired wig Casey had given her when she'd been under the lady deputy marshal's protection.

Travis hated the wig, but considering that Fox's blond hair was a sure giveaway around here, he was glad she still had it. He glanced down at the rolling pin in her hand. "About to make tortillas, or did you plan on taking a swing at McNeely?''

"I may not have your training, but I can and will defend myself. The instinct to survive isn't limited to soldiers. And while I'm on this subject, maybe we should consider finding another place to stay. Our next visitor may not be as polite as McNeely was.''

They spent the next half hour gathering everything they could that was linked to the Johnsons past. Old photo albums, the Bible, files and even Chance were carefully placed inside boxes and loaded into the Johnsons' carryall truck.

As she packed, Fox prayed for the courage she'd need to face what was yet to come. Instinct told her that nothing would ever be the same for her again after she left here today. She looked around with a heavy heart. It was time to say goodbye to the life she'd known, and start searching through its ashes.

Glancing over at her, Travis saw the pain mirrored in her eyes. "This is still your home, Fox. You'll be back before you know it."

"Until I know who I am and what part my being here played in Mom and Dad's death, I don't have the right to call this place home."

"Cut yourself a little slack," he said gently. "Things that are beyond your control are not your fault."

"Now you sound like Dad," she answered, sadness tainting her words.

"No, I'm not like Nick. I learned from him, and I'm grateful for what he did for us, but he and I were completely different from each other."

"You were never really that close to Mom and Dad, were you?" she asked, her eyes filled with questions.

"I liked and respected the Johnsons, and I would have done anything for them. But they weren't my real parents. I remember my mother and father too well ever to have accepted anyone else as a substitute." He was relieved when he saw understanding instead of anger in her eyes.

Although he owed the Johnsons a great deal, he'd never opened his heart to them. The one hard-and-fast rule he'd followed in his life was, *Never surrender both your heart and your mind to anything at the same time.* It left nothing to hold on to when things went wrong—and things always went wrong, sooner or later.

"I'm ready. Let's go before someone else shows up."
Fox reached for her windbreaker.

"Let's wait a little longer until Casey and Ashe check in with us. Once we have more information to go on, we can discuss our options with them."

"No, I'm through waiting to see what will happen next. It's time to *make* things happen. I'm going now. I have my own set of keys to the carryall. You can either come with me, or stay and wait." Fox opened the door and stepped out onto the porch.

"Wait, at least give me a chance to call them first." Muttering an oath, Travis jogged to catch her before she reached the truck. "Don't be so stubborn."

"You mean, don't do anything you disagree with." Fox turned to face him and then froze, staring at something behind Travis.

"What is it?" Travis turned his head, trying to see what had caught her attention. As he spotted the figure up on the hill, Fox started to walk quickly in that direction.

"I'm going to find out who that is up there," she said.

"No, wait! They could be armed." Travis ran after Fox, who by now was jogging toward the hill. Lunging forward, he pulled her to the ground, pinning her there.

"Let go of me!" She tried to break free of his grasp but he wouldn't release her.

"Stop fighting me and *listen*. I caught a glimpse of a flash that might have come from a rifle scope. You're not going to find anything but a bullet unless you chill out." Travis felt her squirming beneath him and had to bite back a groan. As her legs parted slightly and he settled between them naturally, desire blasted through him.

He couldn't think straight. Hell, he couldn't even breathe. His body was on fire and growing hotter by the second. He stared down at her. Fox's eyes were flashing and her face was flushed. Her chest rose in deep breaths.

His body ached for hers, but he knew his duty and would honor it.

He rolled to one side and pulled her behind the cover of some tall grass. "Stay put, will you?" he asked, his voice hoarse.

"Okay," Fox whispered, her voice as uneven as her breathing. "But I still want to see who's up there. How can we do it without getting shot?"

"We'll stay low, work our way around the side of the hill, and come out behind whoever it is." Travis moved forward in a crouch and motioned for her to follow.

The climb was a familiar one to both of them and it didn't take them long to reach the summit. But, by then, no one was around. The curve in the gravel road was only fifty feet away, and a faint trail of dust showed where a vehicle had passed. It was nowhere to be seen now, however.

Travis studied the ground, searching for footprints but finding none. "It looks like our watcher went to a considerable amount of trouble to smooth out his tracks before leaving. It's skillfully done, too."

"For whatever reason, he didn't want a confrontation here," Fox added thoughtfully. "Even if he did have a rifle."

Travis stepped over to a glass bottle that lay on the ground nearby. "It still has a bit of soda in it, and there's no cap. In the warm air this time of year, the liquid would have evaporated pretty fast, so our watcher must have brought it here. Let's take this down with us. Ashe may be able to lift some fingerprints from it."

Once back down the hill and inside the house, Travis called Ashe and quickly filled his brother in on what they'd found, and their plans to leave.

"Ashe has dispatched a patrol car to search the area for our visitor or anyone lurking around," Travis said after hanging up. "He'll also be by as soon as he can to pick up the bottle and talk to us. He asked that we wait here for him."

"I'll compromise with you. I'll stay until dark, but he'd better show up or he'll have the place to himself."

Travis watched Fox as she walked across the room, confident, unaware of her own sexuality or the effect it had on him. Someday soon she'd welcome a man into her life and learn to embrace the passion that was so much a part of her. Heat flashed through him as he pictured himself as that man, her soft breasts against his own naked skin, their bodies locked together.

He tore his gaze away, his hands curling into fists as he clamped down on his thoughts. Fox wasn't the type of woman a man could take and then leave. It was up to him to see that nothing happened that they'd both regret.

As NIGHT SHROUDED the upland desert, Fox stood beside the curtain, staring into the gloom. "It's dark now, let's go. Ashe can pick up the bottle when he's ready, whether we're here or not."

"All right, we'll leave, but let's do it as quietly as we can. I'll drive the carryall to the door, and you can join me. Don't lock up, and don't turn out any lights."

"I'll turn on the radio, too, and leave it on. That'll mislead anyone who comes up."

Hearing a vehicle approach, Travis started across the room to check it out. He was halfway there when the living-room window shattered, and a large rock bounced off the far wall. A bottle with a fiery rag came flying in next and smashed against the edge of the coffee table. They could hear the sound of someone running away outside as the smell of kerosene filled the air. Flames erupted on the sofa and spread almost instantly to the curtains beside it.

Fox ran toward the back door, but Travis caught her in

the hall and pulled her down to the floor. "We can't go out that way. The fire is just a diversion to force us out the back door into an ambush. That's where he ran after throwing the fire bomb."

"We'll die if we stay in here! The house is filling up with smoke."

He urged her into the kitchen, picking up his pistol from the table and jamming it into his belt. "Stay down and out of sight and breathe through a wet towel. I'll bring the carryall right up to the side and you can slide out the kitchen window." He climbed onto the counter and cut the screen away with a quick slash of his pocketknife.

"I'll get the cell phone. It's still in the front room," Fox said.

"Leave it. Just be ready to climb out the second you hear me pull up." Travis looked around. "Now we need our own diversion. I'll be right back." He disappeared for less than fifteen seconds, then returned with a big plastic bag full of firecrackers. Fox already held a damp towel to her nose and mouth, fending off the smoke thickening the air.

"You got those from Dad's desk. He was always confiscating fireworks from his students," Fox remembered. "You want me to light them?"

"Exactly. Just as soon as I go out the window, throw them into the flames in the living room. It should pin them down for a minute or two, at least." Travis handed her the entire bag, containing at least two hundred of the noisemakers.

As Travis crawled out the window and dropped to the ground, fear choked the air from her lungs, but Fox managed to pull the firecrackers out of the bag and throw them in handfuls against the flaming living-room curtains. They started exploding immediately, like machine-gun fire.

Thirty seconds later a few were still popping randomly

when she heard the carryall pull up. Fox was on the counter and out the window in a second. She dropped to the ground in a crouch beside the vehicle. Travis had thrown the passenger door open and Fox dived into the front seat.

An instant later someone shouted, then bullets from somewhere behind them peppered the back of the carryall. As Travis floored the accelerator and shot down the gravel driveway, Fox slammed the door shut. The vehicle bounced hard on the uneven road, making it almost impossible for her to fasten the snap of the seat belt. Finally it clicked into place.

Just as she wondered if the shooting would ever stop, it did. A trickle of relief touched the edges of her mind when suddenly a bright, white flash lit up the inside of the carryall. The powerful explosion that followed rocked the earth beneath them.

With a startled cry, Fox looked back. The Johnson home, a quarter of a mile behind them, was now a wall of angry flames.

Chapter Four

Travis's gaze darted to the rearview mirror often as they drove down the two-lane country highway. The route he'd chosen was full of small side roads they could turn onto if necessary, and traffic was light. "We've lost them."

Fox shook her head. "I don't think they ever tried to catch us once we got to the highway. They'd already accomplished what they'd set out to do. Casey told me not to take this personally, but how can I not do that? They're deliberately cutting me off from my past and leaving me with no place to go."

Travis wanted to hold her and whisk her away to where nothing would ever hurt her again. But fairy tales were no part of the hard, cold world he knew.

"Life is filled with new opportunities," he said. "No one can steal your past. It's not only within you, it's all around you."

Fox said nothing for several minutes as they continued along the highway, heading east toward Farmington. The lights of scattered houses were visible from time to time along the river valley. The familiarity of the scenery comforted her. "Do you ever miss your life here?"

He considered his answer carefully. "Sometimes I do. But the job I've chosen gives me a sense of purpose I've never found anywhere else. I've learned a lot as a Ranger—

about myself, and about the world in general. Every day brings challenges that require all my training and skills. I like that.''

Fox said nothing. She understood Travis very well. For him, the greatest security would always be found in movement. To remain anyplace for too long meant roots, emotional commitment and eventually stagnation. To him, that was the same as a death of the soul. The Johnsons had taught her that the Navajos began as nomads, wandering all over the West. Travis was closer to the old ways than he suspected.

''I have to stop and make a phone call,'' he said, pointing to an all-night gasoline station ahead. ''I need to tell Ashe about the attack and assure him we're fine, but I won't tell him what our plans are. I trust my brother and Casey, but I can't say the same thing for everyone in their chain of command. I think the less they know, the better it'll be for all of us.''

''I agree. But we're still going to have to arrange to meet with Ashe somewhere. We need another cell phone, and some camping equipment would probably come in handy, too.''

Travis nodded. ''I'll have my brother meet us south of Shiprock and bring what we need. I'll also ask for a two-way radio. There are too many places around the Rez where a cell phone is virtually useless.''

Fox waited in the carryall while Travis made the call. She could feel danger closing in all around her. Yet, as her gaze came to rest on Travis, some of her fear eased. She studied his straight back and his broad, muscular shoulders. Everything about him radiated confidence and power. Slowly, a different kind of tension began to spread through her. His sexuality packed a wallop that was impossible to ignore.

As Travis strode back, she could sense his determination.

"We have to stay low and wait a few hours before going to meet Ashe. He needs time to gather up the things we need, and also has to stop by the house and talk to the arson team."

She said nothing. The acrid scent of smoke on her clothes was a constant reminder that the only home she'd ever known had been destroyed.

"It's okay, Fox," he said as if reading her thoughts. "We're tougher than they are." He gave her an encouraging grin.

As his eyes met hers, her breath caught in her throat. Light and shadow played on his face. He was like the desert that surrounded them, filled with mystery and a power that remained forever untamed. She wondered if any woman would ever claim his wild heart.

With a soft sigh, she looked away. There were other, more important matters to be faced now. "If what these people want is to bring me to my knees, they *will* fail," she said.

"I know," Travis replied.

After killing two hours driving around, they finally stopped near an old shack several miles off the main highway. Not long after that, they heard a vehicle approach.

Travis studied it closely. "It's Casey and my brother. But there are two men with them I don't recognize. Let me get out and meet them first. My brother wouldn't have brought them here if they weren't to be trusted, but I want to see what's going on for myself."

"Ashe is saving you the trouble," Fox pointed out. "He parked the car and is coming over here."

Ashe stood by Travis's door a few seconds later. Assuring them that everything was okay, he led them back to meet the others who were standing with Casey by the unmarked tribal-police vehicle.

The presence of two men wearing business suits during

summer put all of Travis's instincts on alert. They were either city cops or lawyers.

Casey gave Travis a quick nod, then smiled at Fox. "This is Marc Gray, my boss and the U.S. Marshal in charge of this district," she said, gesturing to the middle-aged, slightly overweight man beside her. "And this is Deputy Marshal Carl Andrews, our technical expert," she added. The short, youthful-looking deputy with close-cropped blond hair looked out of place in the suit. He had a bored expression, but his brown eyes were as sharp and alert as a falcon's.

Fox shook hands with both men.

"I've brought them here because we all need to talk," Casey continued. "I've spent the last few hours trying to gather more information about your biological parents and, in the process, I've uncovered some very disturbing facts."

Fox didn't flinch, she didn't even move. Once again, Travis couldn't help but be impressed by her courage.

"Go on," Fox said.

"Figuring that the Phoenix police might have something that wasn't included in our files, I accessed their data banks. But then I found there was no open case on record matching the details and the date of your parents' murder."

"I don't understand," Fox said. "Was the murder solved at some point, or did the Marshals Service confiscate the data file?"

"Neither, and that's what puzzled me. The initial crime report was taken by the local PD and should have been on record. At that point, I decided to backtrack, cross-referencing against the data we have in our WITSEC file. I was trying to find a link between our records and theirs."

Fox nodded. "You were thinking it was misfiled or mislabeled?"

"Exactly. That's why I did a more comprehensive search, looking for possible key words that would link our files to theirs. I learned that your real parents' names, prior to them being given a new identity, were Yuri and Raya Sorge. But then, when I tried to get further information about their case, the computer told me that no one by that name ever entered WITSEC."

"But that's got to be wrong," Fox said.

"It is. We know your parents were protected witnesses. So that leaves us with only one possible explanation. Someone tampered with our case files."

"What about talking to the marshal who originally handled the case? I certainly don't recognize the names you mentioned," Fox said.

"Unfortunately he passed away several years ago," Casey said.

"The hard copies we have on file reflect what's in the computer now," Gray added. "We've searched for the original documents, but my guess is that they're lost forever."

"How did someone break into your computer files? You must have your databases password protected and encrypted," Fox said.

"We do. My guess is that we're up against a very gifted hacker," Andrews replied.

"Or a traitor in your ranks," Fox said flatly.

Gray nodded, his face hard. "That's been a possibility all along, though we did hope that problem was solved after we arrested Prescott."

"If the information in my case file is not accurate, that means we know even less than we thought we did." Fox leaned back against the vehicle and regarded them thoughtfully. "But there are a few facts we can rely on. Prescott *was* someone connected to my past. I knew him from somewhere—though I don't know any more than that. Also, he obviously thought I was enough of a threat to come after me. And someone else considered him so dangerous that it cost Prescott his life, once he was taken into custody. Now it looks like they're after me."

"All true," Gray said.

"What I'm doing now is trying to find anyone who worked with your family's original case handler," Casey told her. "That person might be able to give us a few leads, like maybe your family's real name. And yours."

"Whether we like it or not, it looks like the details of my past are only known to my enemies now," Fox said.

"You can count on one thing," Travis said. "They won't get to you. The WITSEC Program may have a leak, but I'm a wild card they weren't expecting."

Ashe's eyebrows rose. "Ain't that the truth."

TEN MINUTES LATER, as the others drove off, Travis stood by the back doors of the carryall, stowing away the equipment and supplies Ashe had provided. The cell phone had already been placed on the front seat. Travis looked over the radio, checking it out, and making note of the frequency Andrews had assured him would always be monitored. Satisfied, he placed it inside the vehicle.

"You never told them about the photo," he commented.

"I can't bring myself to trust two men I've never met before, particularly when we know that there's a leak in their department. I'll tell Ashe and Casey later."

Travis nodded slowly. "Yeah, that's the way I felt about it, too, and why I didn't say anything, either."

"What now?" Fox asked as they climbed back into the vehicle. "Any suggestions?"

"We should go up to Ashe's and my mountain lodge for tonight," Travis said after a moment. "We need someplace indoors where we can unpack and sort through all of Nick's tax papers. I think we should follow through on your idea to make a list of all the places they lived or worked at in the Four Corners area. But then we should turn that information over to Ashe and Casey. We can help out more by steering the police and deputy marshals in the right direction than by becoming targets.''

Fox didn't argue, but she had no intention of going along with that part of his plan. She had her own agenda to follow and she intended to see it through. But she did need that list of addresses before she could take the next step. The cabin near Rock Ridge, admittedly, would be a great place to work without interruptions. Ashe and Travis's own parents had built the wooden one story lodge years ago, and the boys had decided to share it with their new family. It had become a special haven to all of them—one that few people outside the family knew about.

They arrived at the mountain lodge two hours later after a slow, bumpy ride through Rock Ridge into the mountains west of there. Every part of Fox's body ached with exhaustion. Though she hadn't been physically tasked, the emotions that were tearing her apart had drained her. She was angry, frustrated, and anxious to deal with her demons.

They carried the basics inside and, as Travis searched the contents of his athletic bag, she sat down on the sofa.

''What are you looking for?'' she asked wearily.

He pulled out a small roll of clear plastic fishing line. ''I'm going to set out some trip wires as an early warning system. With both of us tired, we need to hedge our bets.''

''Good idea. Let me help,'' she said.

''Okay. Bring the empty soup cans that are in the bag.''

Outside, on the small forest path that led to the lodge, Travis got down to work while Fox held a flashlight. He threaded clear fishing line through holes he punched through the tops of the cans, then put a few pebbles in each can. After fastening the line at both ends, he concealed the entire thing with brush.

''That's as good as I can make it. Though I suspect that the people after us may have some training, it's dark, and with luck, they won't spot this line until it's too late. And if they try to come up on us through the forest to avoid the path, there's enough brush around to make their passage extremely noisy. We'd still have plenty of warning."

Fox turned off the flashlight. As she looked at Travis and saw the glow of the moon reflected in his eyes, her pulse quickened. There was a wildness in him that fit perfectly with these surroundings. As Ashe had said many times, Travis was as gentle and as dangerous as Wind, the fourth guardian of Sun's house. Wind had supporting power, and could be beneficial or destructive. With Fox, Travis was like a soft summer breeze, soothing and caressing. To her enemies, he'd be like the gale-force winds of a storm, leveling whatever stood in its way, showing no mercy.

She was safe with Travis beside her. Or was she? Her eyes strayed to his mouth and, for the millionth time, she wondered what it would be like to kiss him now that they were both adults.

"You okay?" he asked, interrupting her thoughts.

She felt her cheeks grow hot, and was grateful that the dark would hide that from him. "I'm fine."

Daydreams had their place, but knowing when to indulge in them was the key. Sometimes it was just too dangerous. When you wanted something really badly, logic had a way of getting all scrambled. Obstacles that should be as plain as day would become harder to see clearly. If she allowed Travis and herself to grow close, saying goodbye to him when he inevitably left, would be as bitter as a winter storm. It was foolish to tease her heart with images of something that could never be.

They were halfway back to the lodge when she stopped in mid-stride. "If the people after me have some of your training, they might just be expecting a trip wire. We should use that knowledge to our advantage. Since we have three more soup cans we haven't used, why don't we set up a second trip wire here? Then we can go back and make the other one a little more visible. When they spot that one, they'll get complacent. Then, when they least expect it, they'll encounter the one here.''

"Every once in a while, you're positively brilliant," Travis said, giving her a crooked grin.

"I'm brilliant all the time. It's just your ego that keeps you from admitting it," Fox countered.

"My, you're modest."

"Don't forget truthful," she teased, undaunted.

They finished the second trip wire, taking special pains to conceal it, then went back and made the first one easier to spot. "This should do it for now," Travis said, placing his hands around her waist and lifting Fox carefully over the trap.

For a brief eternity they stood face-to-face. The warmth of his touch left her feeling weak at the knees. Her heart was racing. The way his breath caressed her face, his raw sensuality—all sparked sensations that made her want to sink against him.

He leaned down as if to kiss her but then, at the last moment, brushed his lips on her forehead instead. "Let's go," he said brusquely.

Forcing herself to hide her disappointment, she followed him back up the hill.

Once inside the log house, Fox moved about restlessly. Then, looking for something to do, she lit the kerosene lantern and handed Travis a sandwich from the pack that Ashe had given them. Taking one herself, she sat down on the couch. At one time this lodge had seemed like a summer home to her but, now, she felt disconnected from everything—like a stranger, no matter where she went.

Travis ate his sandwich as he went back to check the other two rooms one last time before settling in for the night. Alone, Fox took Chance out of her overnight bag.

The teddy bear was one of the few remaining connections she had to her past. She stared at the toy, willing images to come but, once again, she drew a blank.

"Too bad you're such a lousy conversationalist, bear," she whispered.

Holding the worn stuffed animal close, she leaned back and shut her eyes. So many changes...so many questions... And now she was so tired. Allowing the gray mists to enshroud her, she surrendered to the peace of a dreamless sleep.

WHEN TRAVIS CAME BACK into the room, he saw Fox on the couch, fast asleep, holding Chance. She looked so young. But that was only an illusion. The little girl who'd always looked up to him for answers was long gone.

He took a blanket from the chest by the couch and draped it over her. Fox had always held a special place in his heart. She'd been the one who'd fostered his unshakable confidence. As a boy, reflected in her eyes, he'd become an unbeatable opponent and a steadfast ally. Fox had made him feel like a hero at a time when few had seen anything more in him than a kid looking for trouble. Through her belief in him, he'd learned to believe in himself.

As he adjusted the blanket around her neck, his gaze fell on the tiny locket that lay against her pale skin. Travis couldn't remember ever seeing Fox without that locket. Was it another memento from her early childhood? He suddenly wondered whether it had a photo inside. He'd never asked, but he would tomorrow, first thing in the morning.

"Sleep tight, Fox," he whispered, blowing out the lantern. "I'll watch over you—like you have over me."

Protected by the darkness, Travis stood by the window and listened to the sounds of the night. Not many things had the power to scare him, but the thought of something happening to Fox made his gut turn to ice. One way or another, he'd make sure no harm came to her. Her enemies would have to go through him to get to her, and, if they tried, they'd find him a deadly, well-trained adversary.

As Fox shifted in her sleep, Travis glanced back at her. She didn't know it, but she was the only person who had ever made him break his one hard-and-fast rule of survival: *Never surrender your heart and your mind at the same time.* But his mind ruled his heart, and that was the way it had to stay.

"I won't bind you to me, my Fox. Settling down is not for this Redhawk brother. I need new places and new challenges. I don't want to get too attached to anyone. It just doesn't pay. But you're like the Earth people who need roots and stability to thrive. What I can do, and will do, is make sure that you have the chance to go after your own dreams. Your enemies won't take that away from you, I swear it. Until the day comes when you can make your own choices without fear, I'll be right here beside you."

He stretched out in the chair by the window, knowing he'd be uncomfortable enough there to sleep light. As he closed his eyes, and her perfume filled his lungs, he dreamed of the only woman who'd ever made his scarred heart sing.

TRAVIS WASN'T SURE WHAT woke him, but he was alert in a heartbeat. He sprang up, feeling danger all around him. As he glanced over at Fox, he saw her sit up, listening.

Travis heard the rattle of pebbles in a can, followed by a low curse. In a flash, Fox shoved Chance and the cell phone into her overnight bag and picked up the radio. Travis grabbed the food cooler, his athletic bag, and the flashlight, and together they slipped out the door.

When they reached the carryall, a bullet suddenly shattered the driver's-side window as gunfire erupted. One of their enemies had circled the lodge, anticipating their move this time.

Travis threw their equipment into the vehicle, pushed Fox inside, then turned and fired back twice.

Quickly, Fox crawled behind the wheel and started the engine.

As Travis scrambled in, Fox floored the gas pedal and they hurtled down the dirt track. One bullet struck the back of the carryall, but in a matter of seconds they were out of range, dropping over the steep slope of the hill.

Fox scrambled for her seat belt one-handed while Travis topped off his pistol's clip with ammo from his athletic bag. "How could they have found us?" she asked, never slowing down. "Nobody knew we were here."

"Someone did, unless we were followed all the way from the house by experts, and they just waited for a chance to strike."

Over an hour went by before Travis agreed that they could stop. This time they made camp in a shallow arroyo in the foothills, the carryall hidden from view from any road.

The September night was cool but still pleasant. "Are you okay?" he asked, helping her unroll their sleeping bags.

"I don't think I'm going to get much sleep. My heart's still drumming." Fox gripped the bedding tightly.

"We got away, focus on that. It was our win this time, too, not theirs."

"I just wish I could make some sense out of this. What do these people think I have on them? Even if I witnessed something as a child, those memories would be from the perspective of a frightened little girl. They must realize that I don't really know anything that could be used against them, or the police would have been on their trail all along. And now, for some crazy reason, they've decided it's okay to start shooting at me. Why are they changing their tactics? What are we missing, here?''

"They shot at me and the vehicle, not you. The rounds weren't close to you. Of course, you're right about one thing—they are obviously taking more chances around you."

"But why? What's changed?''

"I don't know. Maybe they're pressed for time or feeling the heat as more law-enforcement agencies get involved in the investigation.''

Fox considered his answer as she watched him pull what he needed for trip wires out of his athletic bag. "Where will you be setting those up this time?''

"One uphill and another downhill from here.''

"I'll go with you.''

Once finished, they headed back.

"I'm still too keyed up to sleep,'' Fox said, looking at the sleeping bags, then shaking her head in frustration.

"Then let's go through the papers we brought from the house. First thing tomorrow morning we can send Ashe and Casey the information we compile.'' He lifted the first box of tax papers out of the carryall and started unpacking the folders.

Time passed as they worked together searching the files slowly by flashlight. Fox was glad for the chance to be doing something other than waiting for someone else to find answers.

"Here's something,'' Travis said. "I remember Nick talking about this place. It was the first home they lived in.'' He pulled out the old tax return. "Nick rented a house near Beclabito from the tribe. That was when they lived next door to Philip and Lucinda Ben.''

"Mom spoke about them often.''

"The Bens are traditionalists, which means they normally would have avoided Anglos, but their friendship with Nick and Alice lasted through the years.''

''I understand they're very old now. I remember Mom mentioning that their family was worried because they'd abandoned the modern house the tribe had given them in favor of the hogan they had built closer to the river.''

Travis jotted a note beside the Bens' name on his list, then turned back to the papers. By the time they had finished the list and returned the boxes to the carryall, Travis looked beat.

''I have to get some sleep now,'' he said, crawling into his sleeping bag.

''Good night, Travis.''

After a short while, she heard his breathing even. As Fox watched him sleep, she fought the impulse to move closer to him. Everything he did, everything he was, drew her, despite her efforts to resist the attraction.

With a sigh, Fox closed her eyes. Not everything she wanted was meant for her. Hearing Travis shift in his sleep, she gazed back at him, making sure he was all right. His rest was not the peaceful one she would have wished for him, but that was understandable under the circumstances. He was out here to protect her.

No one could have asked for a truer friend. But she also knew that she couldn't allow him to continue fighting a battle that was clearly hers. Twice already, he'd shielded her body with his and she knew he'd willingly give up his life for hers. But no matter what happened, she couldn't let that happen. She had to strike out on her own before it was too late.

Fox waited for another hour until she knew from his breathing that Travis was fast asleep. Moving silently, she slipped out of the sleeping bag and gathered her things, leaving the cell phone for him.

Fox wrote a quick note asking him to forgive her, then

left it tucked beneath his boots. With one last glance at him she went to their carryall.

Knowing that the sound would wake Travis, she prayed that the vehicle would start on the first try. Fox turned the key and the engine roared to life.

Putting the vehicle in gear and pressing down on the accelerator, she sped away. Fox fought back the tears as she heard Travis yell out her name. It would be a long time before he'd understand that she'd only been protecting him. Her heart felt leaden as she raced out of the arroyo, leaving him far behind.

Chapter Five

The sound of Travis's voice calling out her name still echoed in her mind as Fox sped along the desert track. Fighting back tears, she assured herself she'd done the right thing. This battle was clearly hers to fight, and she'd spent far too much time relying on others. She was going to take full responsibility for things from now on.

Not that she wasn't scared; she was terrified. But she refused to sit still like a child while everyone around her took action, and risked their lives for her. It was time for her to meet the danger on her own terms. Life had forced this situation on her, but it was up to her to determine her response to it.

As she thought of Travis, Fox felt sadness and longing envelop her. He was muscular and strong, yet his touch was infinitely tender. That magical combination had woven a spell around her. There wasn't another man in the world like Travis. No one would ever stir her emotions as deeply as he could with just a smile or a glance.

Angry about her lack of focus on the real problem, she forced her thoughts back to the present. She couldn't worry about Travis now. He was like the wind, wild and forever untamed. He would find his way back to the highway and be fine. At the moment, that was more than she could say for herself.

Fox pressed down on the accelerator, but instead of picking up speed, the vehicle lurched and then slowed down. When she pumped the pedal, the engine stalled and the carryall coasted to a stop. Maybe she'd flooded the motor, or a wire had come loose from all the rough handling the vehicle had endured lately.

This was all she needed. She fought back her anger, grabbed the flashlight she'd dropped into her purse, then threw open the door and climbed out. She didn't know a thing about engines, but maybe there'd be something obvious she could fix if she checked carefully, like reconnecting a loose wire.

As she stood back, trying to remember if the hood unlatched from inside or outside the carryall, the acrid scent of gasoline rose up from the ground. She moved toward the smell, and aimed the beam of the flashlight down. The gleam of a liquid indicated that something was leaking from underneath the rear of the vehicle. Gasoline, or what remained of it, was dripping onto the dirt. A bullet must have hit the gas tank when they'd fled the lodge. When she left Travis behind, she'd only had whatever hadn't already leaked out, plus what was in the fuel line and carburetor.

Frustration tore at her. Now what? She could walk—she'd have to—but it would be a long way to the Bens' hogan from here. She'd left the cell phone with Travis, but there was still the radio. She nixed the idea almost as soon as she thought of it. If she used it now, it would only be to arrange for another vehicle. But to get that vehicle to her, she'd have to disclose her location and try to explain what had happened to Travis. Under the circumstances, that was the last thing she wanted to do.

Fox gathered up her things and tied them into a makeshift knapsack. She was only a few miles away from where Travis and she had made camp. The progress she'd hoped to make was now nothing more than just another wish that hadn't worked out.

Knowing she had to get moving quickly or Travis would catch up to her, she began her trek across the desert, her spirits as low as her energy level. She'd wanted to face things alone but, the truth was, she missed Travis's company, particularly now. He could be almost dictatorial, but that didn't seem quite so bad when she remembered that he always had her best interests at heart. Even when their wills clashed, which was often, she knew that she could count on him.

Fox forced herself to maintain a slow, steady pace, uncertain how long it would take her to reach the Bens'. From there, she'd have to find herself another vehicle, too. But one problem at a time. Fox took a deep breath and let it out again, concentrating on the ground in front of her. The first thing she had to do was find the hogan.

Taking a circuitous route she didn't think Travis would ever choose, she worked her way slowly across an exhausting, rugged stretch filled with deep arroyos and rocky, uneven ground. Finally, winded and tired after only a mile or two, she stopped and sat down, leaning back against a large outcropping of hard sandstone. It felt good to stay still and not move even one muscle.

Though her break would have to be short, she closed her eyes for a moment. A faint sound suddenly alerted her to danger. She sat up and listened carefully. Something, or someone, was running toward her, and drawing closer with each breath she took. She rose quickly, and was searching for a hiding place when Travis suddenly scrambled out of the arroyo, just a few feet ahead of her.

Anger sparked a pure fire in his eyes. "Do you have *any* idea how reckless you've been?"

"You're a great one to talk about being reckless," Fox

countered. "You're a Ranger. That's reckless in and of itself."

"Don't try to change the subject by putting me on the defensive. It won't work. I want an explanation, and I want it now."

"What's to explain? I left."

"Why?" Travis's voice was too controlled to be natural. She knew his patience had vanished as he'd crossed the miles at a jog, rushing after her.

There was no room for anything but the truth now. "I wanted to protect you. I'm willing to gamble with my life, but not yours. And I can't guarantee that you'll stay alive—no more than I can guarantee my own safety."

"Fox," he whispered, his voice reverberating with what seemed a lifetime of feelings. "I'm trained to survive. And the only risks I'm taking are ones I've chosen."

His eyes stripped her bare and for one endless moment, the desert itself seemed to tremble. "I don't regret what I did," she murmured, "even if you are angry with me. I'm trying to keep you alive and in one piece."

"By forcing me to run for miles across the desert? You can be the most infuriating female—" The stubborn tilt of her chin told him he was getting nowhere. With an exasperated groan, Travis took her hand and pulled her roughly into his arms. "Do you have any idea how worried I was about you?"

Before she could gather her wits, his mouth covered hers. His tongue plunged inside, sparring with hers, seemingly insistent on taming her, even if only in the most elemental way.

Sensing it, she was determined not to surrender to the sweet fires raging inside her. Yet, when she felt the shudders that ripped through him as he held her, her resolve vanished. Desire blossomed and she gave herself over to it.

Yearnings she'd never experienced before burned

through her. Her body became alive as she pressed herself against him, feeling his wildness.

When he eased his hold at last, she stepped back slowly, heart drumming. They stared at each other for one moment, their breathing harsh, their lips throbbing. She hadn't expected it to be like this. This went beyond physical need; it touched her very soul.

Travis tore his gaze from hers, and cursed under his breath. "I'm sorry, Fox. I shouldn't have done that."

She glared at him. "Of all the egotistical—" She paused, took a breath, then continued in a calmer voice. "What makes you think it was all your doing?" The grin he flashed her was even more irritating, but she refused to show him that he'd gotten to her. "Understand one thing, Travis. If we choose to stay together, then we *share* the responsibility for everything that happens. We're two adults. You can't pressure me into anything." She paused again, then added with a tiny smile, "Though I do seem to be able to pull a fast one on you from time to time."

He glowered at her. "Are you finished now?"

"That depends. Are you going to kiss me again?"

He smiled slowly, but there was a dangerous glimmer in his eyes. "Do you want me to?"

"It might be nice."

"I'll wait until you're sure." Travis started walking in the direction they'd just come from, obviously toward the abandoned carryall, without even looking back to make sure she was following.

Although she felt like throwing something at him, she decided to stay cool. The fact was, she was glad he'd found her. She'd missed him, though she would cheerfully have painted her tongue black before admitting that to him. "Why are we going back? The truck won't do us a bit of good now."

"I know. I smelled the gasoline that soaked the ground

back at the camp where it was parked. A bullet must have struck the tank or cut the fuel line.'' He turned around. ''That's why I knew I'd catch up with you sooner or later if I set out double time. After I found the carryall only a few miles down the track, I just headed in the least logical direction until I picked up your tracks.''

In less than ten minutes, they reached the truck via a route much less taxing than before. Travis jumped into the cab, released the hand brake, then climbed down again.

''Why did you say that the course I chose was illogical?''

''I didn't think you'd let that one get by. Just stop gabbing and give me a hand.'' He began to push the carryall.

''For your information, my choice wasn't illogical. I was trying to avoid you and figured you wouldn't pick that trail.''

''If I didn't know you, it might have worked. But I've learned how you think. You do exactly the opposite of what anyone of sound mind would expect.''

Realizing it was perhaps better not to pursue the argument right now, she helped him push the damaged truck into the dry wash.

''I want to hide this as best I can, so help me cover it with tumbleweeds and whatever bushes you can find.'' Travis stepped back and looked around for suitable brush.

After they'd done their best to disguise the vehicle's profile, he regarded the results of their work.

As he studied their efforts, she studied him. Travis looked singularly male in the short-sleeved, tan T-shirt that accentuated his muscular chest. Little sparks of fire danced along her spine as he walked around the carryall, all confidence and male power.

''We'll have to hike the rest of the way, and it's going to be a long, hot march once the sun comes up.''

As he stood ramrod straight, an air of defiance and arrogance defined him. Fox knew she challenged him in a way few men dared. Yet it made her feel powerfully feminine to know that her strength was a match for his. "Well, if you're through posturing, then maybe we should get going. It'll be dawn soon," she said.

Her words sparked something in him. Emotions she couldn't define flickered in his eyes for a heartbeat, then he gave her a crooked half-grin.

Fox would have given anything to know exactly what thoughts had prompted his enigmatic smile. It didn't seem fair that he could read her with such ease, yet half the time she had no idea what he was thinking.

As she thought about it, she suddenly wondered if he'd given her that peculiar smile just to annoy her. Taking the chance that her guess was right, she stepped around him and took the lead. "You can follow *me*," she said in a haughty voice. "I'll set the pace."

Travis followed her. "Good plan. I'll be able to watch your...back from here."

The thought sent a delicious liquid heat coursing through her, making her knees wobbly. She turned and looked at him, feeling terribly self-conscious all of a sudden. "On second thought, you lead. I'd rather watch your back." She matched his mysterious smile with one of her own.

Fox saw surprise flashing in his eyes. He hadn't expected that. Suppressing a smile, she waited for him to continue, glad to be "taking up the rear." That phrase suddenly seemed very appropriate to her, too. Her gaze settled on his strong back, then drifted lower. Travis had world-class buns. The road ahead promised to be far more entertaining than she'd ever expected.

Hours later, well after the sun came up, and after a grueling, seemingly endless hike, he finally stopped, giving them a chance to rest. Fox was exhausted, but she never complained.

Opening the water bottle she'd been carrying, Fox offered him a drink. He took a deep swallow, then handed it back to her.

As she pressed her mouth to where his lips had been, a thrill shot through her. Surrounded by danger, with no guarantees on their safety, she felt vulnerable, yet exhilarated.

"I know things look bad right now, Fox, but sooner or later, you will have the answers you want."

"And then I'll have to face whatever the truth holds. I have a feeling that may prove to be the biggest challenge yet," she said thoughtfully.

"It's very possible that what you learn may hurt you deeply," he said, regret heavy in his tone. "But, eventually, you'll go on."

"Like you? You never really got over your parents' deaths. I've always known that. And you're one of the strongest people I know."

"I'm not strong," Travis said, his voice a whisper in the wind. "I'm just a survivor, and that means learning to take life as it comes." He lapsed into a silence, then added, "The toughest part about my parents' deaths was that I never got the chance to say goodbye. There were so many things I would have liked to say to them, had I had the chance."

"It's been the same for me," Fox replied. "Both times."

"That may be the one thing that will haunt you as the years go by. But the pain you're feeling now will go away. Eventually, you'll stop looking back quite so often. Everything—good and bad—eventually fades away."

"You're wrong. Some good things last and last. Look at Mom and Dad. They loved each other and depended on one another to the very end."

"That's what you want for yourself, isn't it? A rock-solid relationship like theirs?"

"Well, of course! Doesn't everyone, sooner or later?"

"It doesn't work that way for some people, Fox. Love takes an awful lot of trust, and some say it's nothing more than a fantasy people try to make real. The Johnsons came from a different time, when life was simpler. Even a generation ago, the lines that defined expectations and responsibilities for a man and a woman were a lot clearer."

"And you like having those well-established boundaries," she finished for him. "That's why you joined the military."

"The military is the only thing I trust," he said with a shrug. "No matter where I live or what I'm doing, I know I'm a Ranger. I know what I should demand of myself and what I can expect from the other members of my unit."

As they continued their journey, his words stayed on her mind. They weren't as different as he had previously thought. They both wanted to find security and order in a chaotic world. The main difference between them lay in how they chose to pursue their goals.

As time went on, Fox's legs began to ache, but she did her best to keep her mind off it. The angle of the sun revealed it was almost midday, and the heat was therapeutic. "I still can't believe Mom and Dad are gone forever. I keep thinking that, any time now, I'll suddenly wake up and realize that their deaths were only a hideous dream."

Travis fell into step beside her. "You haven't accepted it all yet. But when it does hit you, you'll face it with the same courage you've always shown."

"I've never had to show much courage—until now."

"And look how you've held yourself together."

The admiration in his voice warmed her, but she fought the temptation to bask in that glow. She had to remain self-reliant. That was the only way she'd make it through this—and the aftermath, once Travis was gone. "I'll finish what I've started and find the answers, but after that—"

"You'll find a new direction. What do you want to do

with your life?" he asked. "Have you thought about it much?"

She pondered the question. "I've always wanted to be a teacher. I'm good at it. I tutored lots of kids when I was in school, and I was always able to explain things in a way others could understand."

"I remember." He nodded. "Maybe you'll reopen the Johnsons' school."

Fox said nothing. She'd be lying if she'd said she hadn't thought about it, but it just didn't feel right. The school had been her mom and dad's dream and she didn't have a right to it. Maybe, after the killers were caught... "I can't make plans for the future—not when my past keeps creeping up behind me, undermining everything I do."

"I can understand that. But you do have a future, Fox. And it's filled with endless possibilities. There's nothing holding you back. In a way, you're a freer spirit than I've ever been."

"Me? You've got to be kidding. I'm about as adventurous as a mouse. I don't take chances unless my survival depends on it."

"You do take chances," he said. "Look at what you did today, leaving me behind. You were determined to go it alone."

"If I took a chance, it was only because I was certain I was doing the right thing."

"You couple everything you do with instinct and a sense of loyalty. That's not a bad thing—though, at times, it's definitely misguided."

"I know what's right for me," she said, her chin tilting upward stubbornly.

"No, you don't. But you certainly think you do."

"You just don't like it when my ideas aren't precisely the same as yours," she countered smoothly.

"You're lucky that our ideas don't always coincide. You're safer that way." He captured her gaze and held it.

She suppressed the shiver that ran up her spine. "I'm not afraid." She didn't flinch or look away.

"You're playing with fire, Fox," he warned.

Her mouth went dry. "I'm not in the least afraid of you," she said, unable to back down, though instinct told her that if there ever had been a time to do just that, this was it.

Recklessly, she leaned against him and brought his mouth down to hers, kissing him like she'd dreamed, but never quite losing herself to the moment. She wanted to show him that she could yield if she chose to, but never without demanding some measure of surrender from him, as well.

Fox put herself and the multitude of feelings spiraling through her into her kiss. Her tongue danced around his. Then, finally, knowing they had to stop, she pushed him back and stepped out of his arms.

"Don't play with me, Fox," he told her, his voice husky. "You don't understand what you're doing. I'm a man, not a saint."

Somehow, as usual, he'd managed to miss what she'd been trying to show him. She was a woman now, with needs of her own, but one whose will could match his on almost every level. "There are times, Travis, when I think you'd be lost in your own bathtub without a map and a compass."

Fox stopped a few feet away from him. "You said you wanted to lead, so go on," she said in a haughty voice. "I can't follow, if you're just standing there."

"I wouldn't be if you hadn't sidetracked me," he muttered, going around her. "You have an incredible gift for muddling a man's thoughts, woman."

Chapter Six

They arrived at the Bens' solitary hogan in the middle of a wide canyon shortly after sundown. The six-sided log house had the traditional smoke hole in the center of the earthen roof, and a single blanket covered the entrance. Travis still couldn't get the feel and taste of Fox out of his mind. He wanted Fox more than he'd ever wanted anything in his life. He wanted her beneath him, needing him, crying out his name and helpless with desire. But if he allowed things to go that far, he'd end up hurting her and that was the last thing he wanted to do. No matter how tough she pretended to be, she believed in love and "forever after." Those were things he could not give her. He would never gamble with his heart. Nothing in life lasted forever, but love took too high of a toll when it finally faded away.

They stopped about fifty yards from the hogan and waited. "I wonder if they'll see us soon," Fox said, standing beside Travis.

"They will. Have patience."

A few minutes later, an elderly woman appeared at the blanket-covered door and waved at them to come inside. As they entered, Travis breathed in the delicious scent of fresh mutton stew. He hadn't realized how hungry he was until that moment.

Philip Ben, a slender gray-haired man with a blue headband, red flannel shirt, and worn jeans, hung up the bridle he'd been cleaning with an oily rag. Lucinda wore a simple cotton dress with a woven yarn belt. Her hair was pulled back in a bun. The couple invited them to sit on a sheepskin rug, then sat across from them.

"Are you in trouble?" Lucinda Ben asked, serving them large bowls of stew as if sensing they needed to eat. "It's not often we have visitors. And none of them *ever* walk all the way out here anymore."

Fox explained what had happened to them and why they'd come. "You were among the first friends Mom and Dad made when they arrived on the Reservation. Can you tell us how it was for them back then?"

Lucinda Ben nodded. "I remember those days a lot more clearly than I remember what happened a few days ago." She paused for a moment, then looked up and continued. "Blue Eyes and Smiles. That's what we called them."

Travis nodded, remembering the nicknames the traditionalists had given the Johnsons. Real names were never used because they were said to have power. To use them often would wear them out and deprive their owners of that source of aid in a time of crisis. Of course, to use the names of the dead was even more dangerous because it could summon the *chindii.*

"They were good neighbors. Blue Eyes would help all of us whenever our pickups broke down," Philip Ben said.

"They also helped at community events," Lucinda Ben added. "They even tried to learn our language. Navajo is a difficult language because a lot of the words sound similar. Blue Eyes would make us all laugh when he got words mixed up and ended up saying something a lot different than what he'd meant."

Philip Ben looked at the ground, lost in thought. "We make it sound happy but, in reality, there were a lot of hardships for all of us back then. There was never enough money. We all worked hard, but if it hadn't been for our gardens and our sheep, we would have gone hungry.''

"People like Blue Eyes tried to make things better," Lucinda said. "He wanted to teach and help our people get a real education. I didn't always agree with his ways, but he was a good man."

"Do you recall anyone in particular, from off the Reservation, who came to visit them?" Fox asked.

The Bens considered the question for what seemed an eternity before answering. As he waited, Travis ate the stew hungrily. His stomach had felt so empty it almost hurt. He looked at Fox, but she didn't seem to be anywhere near as hungry as he was. She was still working on her portion.

"Nothing sticks in my mind," Lucinda said, "except I do remember that, once or twice, some Anglo men in suits came to see them. Blue Eyes and Smiles never spoke about it, so none of us ever asked, but we were curious. I remember people saying that they may have been lawyers because they were dressed up all the time, not just on Sundays."

"Did Mom ever talk to you about my adoption?" Fox asked.

Lucinda shook her head. "At first I didn't even know you were adopted but, one day, I overheard her on the phone talking to someone about your adoption papers. I asked her about it, but she told me she didn't like to discuss it, and asked that I not repeat it to anyone. I did as she asked and I never brought up the subject again."

"Is there anything specific you remember about her conversation about the adoption papers?" Fox pressed.

"No," Lucinda replied after a thoughtful pause. "I just got the impression that they'd taken longer to process because there was something unusual about the adoption. But I knew your mother was an honorable woman and I felt she was entitled to her privacy. I figured that if she wanted me to know, she'd tell me."

As Fox rubbed her eyes, Travis realized how tired she was. She'd only had a few hours' sleep last night, and she'd been walking all day. "We've had a very long, tiring day. Would it be possible for us to borrow your truck to drive back to Shiprock? We'll have my brother return it to you tomorrow."

"You could, but I haven't been able to get it started in weeks. My old mare won't be much good to you, either. She can't go faster than a walk these days. But my son will be by tomorrow sometime, if you want a ride to town," Philip Ben offered.

"In the meantime, you can stay with us tonight," Lucinda Ben said, handing them blankets and two sheepskins. "You'll be safe here."

Travis glanced around, noting that the hogan had barely enough space for all of them. "We don't want to intrude. We can sleep outside. We've done that many times before."

"You'll be safer in here with us," Lucinda insisted.

Travis knew that to decline her invitation would be taken as an insult. Although he would have preferred to sleep outside, somewhere where he'd have a clear view of the area, he accepted their offer.

"Before I settle down for the night, I'm going to go out and look around. I want to make sure everything is all right," Travis said.

Philip Ben stood and reached for his rifle. "You're tired and you may miss something. Let me do this. If anyone has come after you, I'll know."

Travis knew the old man was right. This was his country. He knew every inch of the area like the palm of his hand. If something wasn't right, he'd spot it. "Okay, thanks."

Lucinda tended the fire, then lay down and soon fell asleep. As the even sound of her breathing filled the hogan,

Travis glanced at Fox. "You okay?" he whispered. "I saw the way you kept rubbing your eyes."

"I'm fine. I'm just tired and my body aches," she said, rubbing her shoulder with one hand.

He wanted to massage her all over, to touch her until what had started as comfort turned into pleasure. As vivid images filled his mind, blood thundered through his veins. He had to stop doing this to himself. He was going to make himself crazy if he didn't put a lid on his imagination.

He lay down just a few feet away from her, but despite the fact that he was dead on his feet, sleep eluded him. Having Fox so close made him remember how good it had felt to have her body pressed against his.

He turned his head and refused to even look at her now. Instead, he stared into the fire, wondering why the gods were testing him.

Knowing he had to sleep, Travis forced his mind to go blank and then closed his eyes. It was at that precise moment that she reached out for his hand. Biting back a groan, he held on to her and, after an eternity, finally fell asleep.

TRAVIS HEARD THE BENS rise shortly after dawn. Moving silently, they picked up their medicine bundles and went outside. It was time to offer prayers to the dawn. The ritual was an intrinsic part of the Navajo Way. Travis hadn't practiced it since he was a boy at Rock Ridge, but his brother had stayed with the custom. In that respect, Ashe had always been more connected to the Diné.

Travis rose slowly, releasing Fox's hand gently, pleased that she hadn't let go after she'd fallen asleep. He wondered if she'd even been aware of reaching out to him. She'd been near exhaustion last night.

Not wanting to wake her, Travis moved quietly, pushing aside the blanket and leaving the hogan. He stood in silence just outside the doorway and watched the Bens, pollen bags raised, offer the blessing.

A twinge of envy filled him. There was beauty and order in the Navajo Way. The ceremonies all celebrated life and the interconnectedness of man and nature. But those beliefs no longer had the power to support or sustain him. After the death of his parents and all the changes that came afterwards, he'd learned to believe only in himself. He'd walked away from the Navajo Way and embraced the Anglo culture instead. He'd found purpose there, though the outside world placed more importance on dominance rather than in finding one's place within creation.

As Travis watched the time-honored ritual, he remembered the life he'd lost sight of during his years on the outside. As his gaze took in the dark blue skies and red mesas that surrounded them, he felt a sense of homecoming. It was as if the land itself was welcoming him back. Terraced sandstone rock formations and the sweet scent of piñon and juniper all reminded him that this was home and, for a brief moment, he wondered how he'd been able to stay away for so long.

As his gaze swept over the adjacent hillside, he suddenly felt the familiar tug on his scalp that always warned him of danger. He narrowed his eyes and studied the mesa. He caught a glimpse of movement. Someone was just below the skyline, looking down on them from the shadows of a large overhang. Instinct warned him that it was the sniper again.

Standing in the shadow of the hogan so he wouldn't become a target, Travis asked the Bens to go inside. He explained why, quickly, though he was careful to keep his body language relaxed so he wouldn't tip off the sniper.

"Move slowly," he said, "and don't look around, especially toward the mesa where he's hiding. Don't let on that we're wise to him," he added.

Once they'd all stepped back into the hogan, Travis briefed Fox, who hadn't gone outside yet. As he was speaking, Philip reached into a wooden box on a shelf and handed Travis an old pair of binoculars. "Here. My sight's not very good anymore. You can use these more effectively than I can."

Travis took the binoculars from him. Standing to one side of the blanket-covered door and remaining in shadow, he zeroed in on the figure watching them. He couldn't make out the man's face, which was shaded by a cap, but he could see a long-range hunting rifle braced on a rock. "He's no amateur, or he would have fired already. He's waiting for a clear shot."

Fox gathered up their things in record time. "Or else his target hasn't come outside into the open yet. Either way, we have to leave and draw the sniper away from here."

"You can't go outside now," Lucinda protested. "You're safe in here. These thick logs will stop a rifle bullet, won't they?" she asked Travis.

"Yes. But we still have to leave in case someone decides to approach us from behind. Once we're gone, you'll be safe. We're the intended targets, not you two," Travis replied. "But before we do anything else, I'm going to call for help. It's pointless to maintain radio silence now, just so we won't be tracked. Our enemies already know where we are." He studied the cell phone as he switched it on. "I've got very little power left on this cell-phone battery, but it should be enough."

As Travis phoned in, Fox worked with Lucinda Ben, topping off their supply of water.

Travis broke the connection, then looked outside again. "If we just step out there, he'll pick us off. We need some kind of plan."

"It's foolish for you to go now. Stay here. The police

are coming," Philip urged. "We can guard the entrance until they arrive."

Fox shook her head. "We're exposing you to too much danger, and we have no way of knowing how many are out there. The hogan is safe for you, but not while we're here. This time, Travis is right."

"This time?" Travis repeated.

She shrugged. "I'm agreeing with you. Be happy." She looked back at Lucinda. "I'd like to ask a favor of you both."

"Name it," Philip Ben said.

"If you can stand it for a few minutes, I'd like to try and fill this area with thick smoke, the kind that comes from smoldering embers. I want the sniper to assume that we're having trouble with the cooking fire, and that we'll be easy targets if he just waits," Fox said. "Providing we work it just right, the smoke will become our cover. The air is very still and that means the smoke will settle over the area like fog. What do you think, Travis?" Fox looked over at him.

"A smoke screen will help us slip out safely. But the air inside the hogan will be unbreathable," Travis warned.

"For a bit, that's true," Fox conceded. "But, with that layer of smoke, the Bens won't be easy targets and neither will we."

"We'll start a fire right now," Lucinda said. "We can block the smoke hole with a wet blanket, and smother the flames a bit with some damp wood. Then we'll pull the blanket on the door back a ways so the smoke will float outside. We can even fan the smoke out faster by waving some towels, and that'll help make it more breathable inside, too," Lucinda added. "As soon as it gets real thick around the hogan, you two can make your escape into the brush. We'll lie on the ground next to the entrance with damp washcloths over our mouths as long as we can. Then, once you've had time to get away, we'll open the smoke hole, put the fire out, and stay inside until the police come.''

IT WASN'T LONG BEFORE a thick, gray cloud obscured the hogan. The Bens went outside, always careful to stay within the veil of smoke. They quickly pumped water from the well into two pails, then hurried inside as if a fire had erupted within the walls of the hogan.

They all held wet pieces of cloth over their mouths as they worked, fanning the smoke out the entrance. When the smoke grew so thick Fox could barely see two feet in front of her, she knew it was time to leave.

''Take care of yourself, child,'' Lucinda said.

The gentle words made a lump form in her throat. They'd brought danger to this couple, who certainly hadn't deserved it. Yet the woman felt nothing but compassion. Fox wanted to hug her, but refrained, uncertain how Lucinda Ben would take to it. She was a traditionalist, and touching strangers went against the teachings of the Navajo Way.

As if sensing her thoughts, Lucinda took Fox's hand and gave it a gentle squeeze. ''Your soldier will take care of you,'' she said, whispering in her ear. ''But you must take care of him, too. He's lost his way—more so than you.''

Fox wanted to ask Lucinda what she meant, but there was no more time. Travis took her arm, urging her out.

''Now's our chance,'' he said, stifling a cough. ''Let's go.''

He led the way, staying close to Fox as they hurried out in a crouch. Although the smoke was thick around the hogan, it didn't carry far. Twenty feet from the entrance it had already thinned out, but by then they were on their hands and knees in the underbrush, crawling away, hidden from the sniper's aim.

Thorns and tough brush penetrated her clothing, rubbing and poking her skin, and yet somehow, she managed to keep up. Soon they were able to move in a crouch, then, finally, stand upright. When they were a few hundred yards away from the dwelling, safe inside a deep arroyo, Fox knew she could finally speak in a whisper. "Will the Bens be okay? I hate to leave them on their own now."

"Philip Ben knows this area. He can elude anyone he chooses here. And the cops are on their way."

"Travis, are you certain of what you saw? If it was a sniper, it's strange he never fired even one shot."

"As I said, whoever's up there is a pro. That kind of patience is something you only acquire with training."

"Who did he want to shoot? Do you think he was hoping to injure me, or you, so they could slow us down and capture us?"

"I can't say for sure, but I suspect he wanted to take me out first so he could get to you. I'm his biggest problem right now."

"If they hurt you, they'll find I'm quite a problem, too," she said meanacingly.

He grinned. "I agree. You've been a problem for years now."

She made a face, then ignored his comment. "Maybe the police will catch him before he has a chance to escape."

"I wouldn't count on that. If it had been me up on that mesa, I would have realized almost immediately that the smoke was a diversion. I'd have left the area double time, trying to pick up the trail of my prey again."

"How's he finding us?" she asked.

"He must know something about both of us to be second guessing us like he has."

An undeniable heaviness descended over Fox. It just didn't seem right. Travis was in this mess because of her, but he was even more of a target than she was.

Chapter Seven

"You and Lucinda hit it off well," he whispered as they crossed a sandy arroyo, staying close to the sides. Hiding from the morning sun was difficult, so they had to pick their path carefully.

"I like her a lot," Fox said. Lucinda's words about Travis still echoed in her mind, but she said nothing to him about that. Now, with time to consider what Lucinda had said, Fox mulled it over. Slowly, it began to make sense.

Travis's reluctance to accept the intrinsic worth of his own culture blinded him, and caused him to lose his way. No matter which path he chose to pursue, Anglo or Navajo, he'd first have to come to terms with who and what he was, before he could ever find peace. Fox could understand that better than most, too. Her own situation demanded that she face her past and learn her identity before she could be free to move into the future.

"We're going to need a vehicle," Travis said as they headed in the direction of the highway, "or this investigation of ours will go on forever."

"I agree. Fun as it might seem to a soldier like you, these cross-country marches are costing us way too much time. But don't worry about anything. I've got a plan," she said and continued undaunted. "We'll call Ashe from the first pay phone or business we reach. We have the support of the Marshals Service to stay in hiding, but we do need to make contact now."

"If we continue heading northeast, we'll eventually arrive near the Quick and Go on the highway between Beclabito and Shiprock. Nobody will expect us to go in that direction because it would be so much closer to hike directly to Beclabito. It's also in a direction that will take us away from the closest settlement—the place our pursuers are most likely to check first."

"If you're hoping to find the Quick and Go, we're heading in the wrong direction. That's north of here," she said.

He glared at her. "We *are* going in the right direction, which is northeast. Your internal compass is turned around a bit."

"Well, don't blame me when we get to the highway and you find out you're wrong," she said with a shrug. "But it won't be a disaster. We'll just have to hitchhike from there."

"I know where I'm going."

"Let's say, for the sake of argument, that we luck out going in this direction and actually arrive at the Quick and Go. There's still a problem. What if our call to Ashe is traced or is monitored from the other end? For all intents and purposes, we would be broadcasting our whereabouts and destination."

"The only way I can think to circumvent that is for us not to stay at the Quick and Go for long, and for me to carefully arrange a rendezvous with my brother. I'll make a reference to a place he'll know, without mentioning it by name. I'm sure I can think of something between now and then."

"Of course you can. You'll have plenty of time to decide, because we're never going to find a phone heading in the direction we're going now."

"Then how come you're following me?" he growled.

"You're right. I'll go my own way. You go yours. Excellent idea."

He blocked her way. "You're going with me, even if I have to carry you."

"Will you make up your mind? Half a second ago, you suggested that we go separate ways."

"I was making a little joke."

"*Very* little." She knew that she was no match for him when it came to strength, and something told her that he *was* prepared to throw her over his shoulder. "Okay. I'll go with you. But once you find out you went in the wrong direction, I want an elaborate apology."

"What?"

"You heard me. I want you down on your hands and knees, telling me that you were wrong and begging my forgiveness."

"You've been out in the sun too long."

"And here I thought you were convinced you were right."

"I *am* right."

"Good. Then you'll do it?"

He nodded once. "And what if you're the one who's wrong?"

She considered asking him what he'd want, then nixed the idea. That left too much to chance. "I'll salute and call you 'sir' for a day."

"And refrain from arguing with me, or coming up with any more plans?" he added.

"Okay—that is, unless you change your mind and need my help. But trust me, you're wrong."

As they drew closer to the highway, Travis grew more cautious. Although she hadn't worn the black wig since they'd left home, now, as they approached civilization, she slipped it back in place.

"The Quick and Go is right over that hill," he said.

"You're dreaming. We're probably closer to the Rattle-snake turnoff. We'll undoubtedly have to go several miles before we get there, but we should eventually be able to find a phone."

As they reached the top of the hill, she stared down at what she'd thought would be just empty highway. But a large vehicle was there. It was the state library's bookmo-bile, pulled over to the shoulder across the highway, aimed west in the direction of Beclabito.

"Looks like we were both wrong," she said.

Travis pointed east down the road where the Quick and Go gas station stood. "I wasn't that far off the mark. But let's try the bookmobile before we do anything else. If Edna Yazzie is driving it, let me do the talking. I bet I can convince her to give us a ride to Beclabito, though she's not supposed to take passengers."

"Okay." Fox paused, then added clearly, "By the way, you *were* wrong about where we were," she repeated. "You missed it by at least a mile."

"More like half a mile. But you were off the mark al-together. You had no idea where we were. Rattlesnake is probably ten miles farther east," Travis said through clenched teeth.

"So I was wrong. At least I don't have as big a problem admitting it."

Travis said nothing, but she could have sworn he was grinding his teeth.

As they crossed the empty highway, Edna looked out through the driver's-side window. The middle-aged woman's expression brightened as she saw Travis. "What on earth are you doing out here? Don't you have a car?"

"We had some trouble with it," Travis said. "How about giving us a ride into Beclabito? It looks like you're headed that way."

Edna turned to look at Fox and then smiled. "Oh, it's you! I almost didn't recognize you in that silly wig."

"It's my new image," Fox muttered.

"I hear you're both in trouble," Edna said, her expression somber. "It was all over the newspapers. So don't give it another thought. I'll give you a ride. Come on around to the door."

Edna quickly finished rearranging some children's books in preparation for her next stop, then started the heavy vehicle west. As they approached the elementary school in Beclabito, Edna slowed down. "The kids waiting will see the bookmobile in another minute, and will come right up once I park," she warned.

"Then maybe you should let us out here," Fox said. "We don't want to attract any more attention than necessary."

Edna gave them a long glance. "I don't see how you can avoid it. Everyone knows you, Travis, and Fox's wig really doesn't pass muster close-up. You can tell it's not real hair—or at least, I can."

"Thanks for the tip," Travis said as Edna pulled over to the shoulder of the road. "Don't tell anyone you saw us, okay?"

"No problem. I don't want anyone asking me any questions. Giving you a ride could cost me my job."

Edna dropped them off by a gravel road that led to a tribal housing project, then continued toward the school. Fox looked around, finally realizing where they were.

"Edna's right, you know," Travis said after a moment. "We need to find a way to blend in. Maybe traditional clothes. Nobody gives a second glance to an old couple walking by the side of the road."

"You will never look like an old man, no matter what clothes you pick." As she glanced at his muscular body and broad shoulders, she felt her blood sizzle. Everything about him spoke of sheer masculine power.

Fire danced in his eyes and he smiled as if he'd read her thoughts. "We'll just have to try and act the part. Clothes will be a way to set the stage. Of course, once we get another vehicle it won't matter, but the rest of the walk into town might be dangerous unless we camouflage ourselves a bit."

Fox looked around, then pointed to a solitary house a hundred yards across the highway in the opposite direction. A full clothesline blew in the gentle breeze. "I can see a long skirt hanging there. Let's see what else we can find. We'll take what we need if no one is home to sell us anything. But we'll leave some money clipped in its place so it won't be so much like stealing. I have some cash with me."

"Let's do it."

No vehicle was around, and nobody came to the door when they stood in plain sight of the front window. Obviously there was no one at home, but Fox knocked anyway. Finally giving up, they walked around to the backyard and took a skirt, a shawl, and a scarf, and left some money clipped to the line. Travis noticed an old cowboy hat on the seat of a tractor, and grabbed it.

"Okay, let's get out of here," she said.

As they walked back to the highway, Fox ducked down beside a large culvert running beneath the highway and changed clothes. The slight dampness of the newly washed garments felt wonderfully cool against her heated skin. When she finally came out, Travis nodded in approval.

"Even I'd have a tough time telling it was you from a distance," Travis said, then added, "But you'd never fool me for long. In the clear light of day, or in the middle of the night, I'd know you, Fox."

The words made a wave of heat ripple down her spine.

Everything feminine in her responded to him. She searched his eyes, hoping to find confirmation that he, too, felt a similar stirring, but the only thing she saw for sure was the same concern that had compelled him to go with her on this quest.

A little part of her died of disappointment, but she hid it well. "But what about you? You still look the same."

"Jeans are common here. The old cowboy hat I found will do the rest," he said, pulling it low over his eyes.

She nodded. "That'll work, I suppose. It does cover your face." What it couldn't hide was that indomitable maleness that issued a silent challenge with each step he took. "Try stooping a bit."

He tried, she had to give him that much. But it was like asking a wild stallion to bray like a donkey. It wasn't convincing. "Never mind. Just avoid looking anyone in the eye."

He laughed. "Does that mean you don't think much of my acting ability?"

"Well, let's just say that I understand why this role is particularly tough for someone like you to play," she said, and shook her head when he started to ask more.

They stayed on the shoulder of the highway as many elderly couples did, and avoided walking side by side. He led the way, but never let her fall back too far.

Deciding that they should stay out of sight while taking a break, Travis found a spot behind a low, juniper-covered hill. They ate some of their remaining food, sipping lukewarm water from their canteens out of necessity rather than interest.

Soon they were on their way again. When they arrived at a small grocery store, several Navajo families were having lunch at a picnic table under the shade of a large tree. The pay phone was within sight of a dozen or more people. Knowing that word about a Navajo man and the Anglo woman with the wig would spread quickly, they decided to wait across the road, and stay low profile until the families left.

Two hours later, closer to dinner than lunch, the last of the picnic crowd left and they were finally able to get to the phone. Travis spoke to Ashe quickly in Navajo, never identifying himself by name, and then hung up. "He'll get us another vehicle, something that doesn't stand out. But we'll have to wait until tomorrow morning for it. He wants to make sure it doesn't come from the motor pool, because those are too easily tracked."

"Where are we supposed to meet him?"

"I suggested the place where Alice used to buy our jeans. Remember?"

She smiled. "The trading post near Rattlesnake, of course! You and Ashe both loved the brand they carried." Her expression grew somber as she realized that they were at least fifteen miles from there—more if they followed the highway. "That's a long hike, closer to Shiprock than here."

"I know, but we have until midmorning tomorrow."

She gasped. "Are you crazy? With night coming it'll be impossible to make it there in time."

"We'll make it. I know a shortcut." He gestured toward a mesa far to the southwest. "We'll go as the crow flies, veering just to the south of that mesa. It will cut two or three miles off our route, and we won't be seen by anyone."

"Just the buzzards," she muttered, wondering if she'd ever have a normal life again.

Chapter Eight

After they'd been on their way long enough to have left the highway far behind, Fox ducked behind an outcropping of rocks, slipped out of her wig and long skirt, and into her own comfortable jeans and T-shirt. Her large cloth shoulder bag was once again stuffed full.

She managed to keep up with Travis through the miles of rugged desert terrain. Two hours later they reached a crest that allowed them to see for miles to the east. A vast stretch of desert dropped off before them, interrupted by the San Juan River valley far in the distance. The lights of Shiprock ran along that valley, on either side. To the left, and thankfully closer, were the oil field and supply buildings of Rattlesnake. Only a few lights gave away its location.

Fox continued to match his pace, and realized her legs had finally stopped hurting. In fact, she couldn't really feel them anymore. But the good news was that it was largely downhill from this point on.

As the wind picked up and sand began to blast its way across the desert, she tucked her head down and forced herself to push forward. "This is going to get worse before it gets better," she warned. "We'd better find some shelter."

"If memory serves me right, there's an old, abandoned

hogan not too far from here, just this side of Shiprock Wash. It's a 'killed' hogan. You know what that is?''

She nodded slowly. ''It's one that has been abandoned because someone died there.''

''Exactly. My brother would never spend a night there, no matter what the circumstances. Fortunately, neither one of us shares his beliefs.''

Fox gave him a long, furtive look, but couldn't see any trace of reluctance in his eyes. Had Travis really left his roots so far behind? Accepting his word, she followed him toward the Navajo dwelling.

TRAVIS SLOWED DOWN as they approached the hogan. It stood in a small clearing on higher ground, just as he'd remembered. A hole had been punched in the north wall, and the dwelling abandoned to the ghost of the dead.

As they drew near, his gut tightened and the hair on the back of his neck stood on end. In defiance, he threw his shoulders back, clenched his jaw, and continued forward. He would not give in to superstition.

Travis stepped inside first and looked around. ''It's messy, but it's safe.''

She followed him in. ''It was harder for you than you'd anticipated, wasn't it?'' she asked gently. ''You looked as if you were in the middle of a battle—one you intended to win.''

Fox saw too much. Her perceptiveness unsettled him. He couldn't afford to be an open book to her. ''I was just preparing myself in case a wild animal had crawled in here.''

She studied the hogan. Once they dragged out a few tumbleweeds, it would be intact enough to give them adequate shelter. It had been a good choice.

As his gaze settled on Fox, Travis saw the weariness in her eyes. Her skin was no longer creamy white, but sun browned, and it seemed to deepen the lines of worry around her eyes. His gut clenched as he remembered the child who had laughed at every one of his jokes when he was a kid. She deserved far more from life than the fate she'd been handed.

Travis cleared off the ground inside, making sure no snakes or centipedes had made the place their residence. "We can't close up the hogan, so expect some dust to come in through the smoke hole and the two other openings. At least the entrance is opposite the direction the wind is blowing."

"The wind is mostly coming from the west right now, so not much will get through the north wall, either." She studied the circular, soot-darkened clay opening in the piñon-and-mud ceiling. "It doesn't look as if they ever had a woodstove. It's impractical to us now, but I suppose that before someone died in here, the fire pit and smoke hole were the heart of this hogan."

"According to the Navajo tradition, the evil spirits are blown out through the smoke hole and that brings peace to the family. One of the reasons the traditionalists who move to modern houses, with their tightly closed windows and doors, feel so trapped is because there is no place for evil to escape."

She gave him a surprised look. "I would have expected Ashe to know stories like that. But I never thought you paid much attention to that kind of thing, let alone remembered it."

"My brother and I share the same roots. We both grew up at Rock Ridge. We've chosen different paths, that's true, but the foundation of everything we've learned rests on the way of our tribe. That's not something anyone forgets. We *are* alike in more ways than anyone can imagine." He glanced at her and gave her a crooked half-smile. "Not that I'd *ever* say that in front of him."

She chuckled softly. "You two were always competing. I envied your relationship, though. You were there for each other. Always."

"And for you, too." As his gaze strayed over her, he saw the way her T-shirt clung to her body, accentuating her soft breasts. Her nipples tightened, as if sensing his hunger. He forced himself to look away, trying not to dwell on how responsive she was to him. She was a living, breathing temptation. Desire clawed at him, sudden and fierce.

She settled down on the ground, and as a blast of sand filtered down through the hole, she edged back against the south wall. "I'm going to try and get some sleep." Using her makeshift backpack for a pillow, she turned away from him and closed her eyes.

As the wind picked up and the entrance let in clouds of dust, he leaned back against the log-and-mud-chinked sides of the hogan and watched her. She wasn't asleep. Fox hated storms and the shrill cry of the wind whistling through cracks would keep her awake. She'd been restless and uneasy during storms for as far back as he could remember.

Despite that, he knew she wouldn't reach out for him now. Independence was important to her and although he admired her for it, it always challenged him. Even the thought of having a strong woman like her surrender to him made his body swell.

He closed his eyes for a moment. Although he was no longer looking at her, he was aware of her soft breathing and of her body near his. Fox was Earth and Fire rolled into one. The warmth of the sun lived in her smile.

He fought the urge to move closer to her and listened to the howl of the wind. It was said that Wind found purpose only in movement. His own nature was a match for that innate restlessness. But there was one major difference: he sought movement because he feared what would happen if he stayed still. He wanted no roots or ties that would hold him in place. Everything he'd ever loved had been torn out from under him. Home and family were for those who had not yet learned that love was simply the emotion that came before pain.

Although Fox had never even suspected it, she'd been one of the reasons he'd joined the military as soon as he could after high school. His feelings for her had been too strong even back then. Their first kiss had jolted him far more than he'd let on. Even as a boy, he'd understood the danger she'd posed to him. But fate had conspired against him, bringing him back to the Reservation—and to the girl he'd tried to forget.

As the sand and wind raged over the desert, he kept watch over her. He was a man now, not a boy. He knew what he needed to do. He was a loner who intended to remain that way. His heart would never be tamed or gentled by a woman's touch.

IT WAS MORNING WHEN Fox awoke. The sun was up, shining almost straight into the hogan from the east, where the entrance was, and the desert was still except for the chirping of birds. She stretched slowly, her body sore from the small rocks that protruded from the sandy floor. As she sat up, she saw Travis standing just inside the entrance, eating a candy bar. He'd been her sentinel, forever on guard.

"I hope you got some sleep," she said, suddenly feeling guilty that she hadn't spelled him.

"I slept," he answered, his voice taut.

"What's wrong?"

"I don't know. It's just a feeling I'm getting. But there's no one out here now. I'm sure of that."

Fox gathered up her things. "I'm ready to go whenever you are. But I have a favor to ask before we leave."

He turned around. "Tell me what you need."

Somehow those words made her breath catch in her throat. There was raw power in everything Travis did or said. "Please use the radio and find out if the Bens are okay."

"Ashe would have told me if they weren't," he assured her.

"But you didn't ask him specifically, and I need to hear it. It's important to me."

He hesitated for a moment, but then took the radio from the pack. Using the channel they'd been told would always be monitored, he called in.

Fox heard for herself when Carl Andrews assured them that the old couple had not been harmed.

"The sniper was gone when the police showed up," Andrews continued, "but the officers reported two sets of footprints and four-wheel-drive vehicle tracks."

"Ask him if he has any idea how they might have found us," Fox pressed, though she knew Travis wanted to cut the transmission short.

Travis relayed the message.

"I suppose it's possible they homed in on the radio beacon," Andrews said. "Though, frankly, I doubt it."

She saw Travis's eyes become the color of a stormy, nighttime sky. For the first time in her life, the emotions she read on his face frightened her.

"What the hell do you mean?" Travis's voice held a lethal edge. "What beacon?"

"It's a homing signal sent out continuously, but it's on a special long-wavelength frequency. It was meant as a safety precaution in case one of you got hurt or needed assistance and didn't know exactly where you were."

"We've been followed, and I'm willing to bet that it's due to that beacon. Someone obviously figured out a way to track the signal. Now tell me how to shut it off," he snapped.

Travis listened to the directions, then terminated the communication.

"Those bureaucratic idiots," he muttered. "It was bad enough when all we had to worry about was someone tracing any call we made using the cell phone. Now this. Maybe we should discard the radio altogether. There's no telling what other surprises have been fit into it."

"Do you really think there's something else they haven't told us?" she asked.

"Anything's possible," he answered. "But it couldn't be too fancy. They didn't have a lot of time to tamper with standard-issue equipment." He moved one of the setting screws on the bottom of the radio one half-turn with a pocketknife, according to Carl's directions, switching the beacon off.

"I vote that we hold on to the radio," she said. "We may need it if we get into trouble somewhere along the way."

"All right. But now we have to do some damage control. Just in case they've tracked us again, we have to leave this area fast," he said, tossing Fox the last of their breakfast candy bars. "Are you up for jogging after you've eaten?"

"I'll keep up. Whatever you can do, I'll match."

"Why did I know you'd say that?"

Shouldering his backpack, he stood by the door and looked out as she finished eating. "I have half a mind to wait right here for whoever's following us and finish this fight." He took the pistol out of his jacket pocket and checked the clip. "I'd get a lot of satisfaction out of pounding their faces into the ground."

"Maybe, but since you also like to win, a face-off right now is a bad idea. You'll probably be outnumbered and outgunned. Staying on top of things is going to take finesse and intelligence, not brawn."

He let his breath out in a hiss. "Yeah, you may be

right." He set out, leading the way. "Stay on the rocky spots whenever possible. Whoever's after us uses the land, working with it like an experienced tracker."

"Or a Navajo who has lived here all his life."

He gave her a curious glance. "Do you have someone in mind?"

"No. It's just a thought."

Travis kept the pace brisk but not punishing. "McNeely was looking for work. It's possible he joined forces with the people who are after you. Stan McNeely is one heckuva tracker. His cousin would have gone in with him, too, but the real threat would come from McNeely. I've met his cousin Billy once, and he's a follower, not a leader."

"Does McNeely know the area around here well?"

Travis nodded. "He was born and raised in Bloomfield. And, in the Rangers, he was the only man who could follow a trail as well as I could."

As they reached an area thick with boulders and underbrush, he stopped. "Hang on here a minute. I'm going back to leave a little surprise for anyone who tracks us to the hogan. I'll loosen a few ceiling beams and arrange for a log or two to collapse if someone steps inside. I doubt it'll kill anyone, but it should slow them down, and leave some nasty bruises."

Travis ran back, covering the distance they'd just traveled from the hogan in half the time, though it was uphill. He returned fifteen minutes later.

His pace was quick as they continued down a dry wash that wound in the direction they needed to travel, and gave them complete cover. After twenty minutes, he stopped. "Let's take a break. We can still see the hogan, and I want to have a look at our trackers." Looking over the west wall of the dwindling arroyo, he searched the area above them carefully.

"There they are, two of them. They're coming up on the hogan."

"Do you recognize either one?"

"I can't make out their faces from this distance, but they've stopped in front of the hogan." Travis muttered a curse. "One of them must have spotted my trap. They're not going inside."

"Then we'd better get going again, fast," Fox said, fear giving her added energy.

"We'll make it, Fox," he reassured quickly. "They'll never get near enough to touch you."

"All I want you to do is keep them at bay until I find the answers I need. After that, the rules are going to change. I know I have to confront my enemies sooner or later. But I want to pick the time and place."

"Do you intend on letting me in on this fight?" he asked sarcastically.

Fox said nothing and avoided his gaze. She still wanted to protect Travis if she could. Although she doubted that he'd ever agree to let her face her enemies on her own, she wouldn't pass up any chance to do just that, once she had some leverage against them.

She cast a furtive look at Travis and, seeing his expression, decided that some things were better left unsaid.

He glared at her as if reading her mind and muttered a vicious oath. "That settles it. I'm not letting you out of my sight from now on."

Chapter Nine

Travis knew she'd ditch him if she got the chance. Damnation, no other woman had ever seen *him* as someone who needed protection. That was what they looked to him for.

Still muttering to himself, Travis stopped and took one final look behind them. It had taken special training for the men tracking them to spot the wire that would have brought half the roof crashing down on them. His gut instinct now told him that McNeely was involved. They'd received identical training. McNeely would know most of the tricks Travis had up his sleeve.

Travis glanced over at Fox. He'd set a brisk pace and she'd stayed right with him. He couldn't help but admire that fighting spirit of hers, though, at times, he sure wished it didn't make her so hard to handle.

"You okay? You've been giving me the strangest looks," she said, interrupting his thoughts.

"I was thinking that for the girl who avoided high-school P.E. for three years, you've done really well for yourself out here."

"Don't kid yourself. I hate this. I thrive in houses with air-conditioning and big fireplaces—not the great outdoors."

"You know, it's time we started taking advantage of your skills. You've always been great in math and science, so next time we need to set a trap, I think you should design it.''

"You think he recognized your training and style?''

She'd read his mind again, he realized with irritation. "Yeah.''

"The tables will turn in our favor soon,'' she said with confidence. "I know it. Once we get transportation, it won't be a matter of tracking us anymore. They'll have to second-guess us to keep up.''

"True, but remember they already have at least some of the answers we're searching for. That'll give them a definite advantage because they know where we'll eventually have to go to look. And, if McNeely and his cousin joined up with them—as I suspect they have—they've added two more to their ranks. They can still pair up and look for us in two places at the same time.''

"Right now, all I'm worried about are the two after us,'' she noted softly.

They walked the next few miles in silence. Travis had chosen a route over rough terrain, leaving false trails and using every trick he knew to misdirect the men pursuing them.

Finally Travis stopped and surveyed the terrain behind them. "We can slow down our pace again,'' he said. "I think we've lost them for a while.''

Gray clouds had been building for some time, and suddenly a loud clap of thunder shook the ground. "Great. Just what we needed,'' she muttered. "It looks like we're in for a major downpour. The New Mexican monsoon season is finally here,'' she added, using the popular term for the late-summer desert rainy season. "I don't think we'll be safe in the arroyos for a while. We could get caught in a flash flood before we see it coming.''

Travis could see her cringe every time lightning flashed across the sky, but she continued to match his pace even after the wind arrived and rain started coming down in thick sheets. The big drops were amazingly cold against his skin. "I remember how you hated thunder when you were a kid," he said. "You'd hide in your room and turn up the radio as loud as you could."

"I'm not a kid anymore, but I still hate storms," she admitted.

Fox's honesty was typical of her. He wanted to say something to comfort her, but he'd never been very good with words. He took her hand instead and, to his surprise, she didn't pull away as they continued to struggle against the deluge.

As the air flashed with light, immediately followed by explosive thunder, he felt Fox shudder. He tightened his hold on her hand. She needed him now. Nothing was as important as that.

"You know the scientific explanation for lightning and thunder as well as you know the back of your hand. What about it scares you so much?"

She shook her head. "I don't know. It's not just the knowledge that New Mexico has the highest percentage of lightning strikes. Maybe it goes back to when I was very young. The noise just makes me feel like hiding. I can't explain it any better than that."

Her vulnerability touched him in a way nothing ever had. As she looked up at him, the need to protect her overruled everything else. He looked around for shelter, but there were no rainproof places within sight.

"There," she said, pointing ahead. "Look at the three boulders leaning against the side of the hill. They make a primitive lean-to of sorts. It's not much of a shelter, but it'll do."

The ground was getting so soft and muddy that their shoes were becoming packed with the sticky stuff. He could see that each step was becoming harder and harder for her, with the difficulty of traction and the extra weight building up on her feet. She was exhausted. "I've got to tell you, Fox, that's not a good tactical position," he said reluctantly. "If they pass by here, it's the first place they'll look. We really should keep going, if you can manage it."

"Travis, please. Just for a few minutes."

Her soft voice cut right through him. He could no more have denied her this than he could have quit breathing. "All right."

She crawled into the small crevice with an ease he couldn't match. As he sat next to her in the tight shelter the rocks provided, he could feel her with every raw nerve in his body. Obeying an instinct as powerful as the raging storm, he drew her against him.

"I don't know how you do it, but you make me feel things no one has ever made me feel before." He touched her hair, feeling its silky smoothness, then caressed her cheeks. As she leaned into him, he heard her breath catch with desire. Through the crimson haze of his own pounding blood, he took her mouth. Their tongues mated and the taste of her drove him to the edge, threatening his iron-willed control.

Fox melted against him, inviting more of the pleasures he could give her. Thunder boomed overhead and she trembled against him even as she deepened their kiss. She wanted him. Everything male in him knew it. Yet something was missing.

As he eased his grasp slightly, still holding her against him, he wondered if he'd gone completely insane. He could keep on kissing her and take pleasure in that. He was strong enough to refrain from taking that final step and making her his. So why was he drawing away?

As the thunder rolled and she shuddered, he had his answer. She was with him now out of fear. She'd surrendered to desire only because she'd needed him to push back the demons that haunted her. And that just wasn't enough for him.

"As soon as the rain eases up, we'll have to get moving," Travis said.

"I know."

Her quiet voice tore at him. She was a strong woman who was doing her best to face a fear she knew to be irrational. But holding her so close to his side was sheer torture. No matter how hard he tried to suppress it, the fire in him refused to die.

As the wind slowed and the thunder became nothing more than a distant rumbling sound, she pulled away from him. "I'm sorry, Travis. I've held us up. I'll pick up the pace," she said, avoiding his gaze.

He sensed her embarrassment. "You don't have to apologize. Not for anything—and never to me."

"You have fears, Travis, but you manage to control yours," she said. "We're in enough trouble. You don't need another complication right now."

"What's complicated about holding a beautiful woman?" Travis countered, unable to suppress a grin.

"You've had plenty of practice, I suppose?" she asked.

"I'm taking the fifth on that one," he said, then grew serious. "Fox, you have more guts than some of the soldiers I've fought alongside. You never lost your cool when the shooting started, and you've never backed away from any threat."

"And then something simple like thunder comes along and my spool unravels." She shook her head. "Some partner you've gotten saddled with."

"Everyone has fears. They're unavoidable. There are things that scare me right down to my boots."

"Well, now that you mention it, I've noticed that I intimidate you at times." She paused, then added, "But that's probably because you like to be in control and I don't like to relinquish it.''

"What?" He glowered at her. That was what he got for trying to give her some comfort. It was like trying to soothe a wildcat. "The day I can't handle myself around a woman like you, will be the day I resign from the army and start baking pies and cookies."

"I never knew you wanted to be a pastry chef," she quipped.

Fox quickened the pace to the level he'd set before, almost as if trying to prove to him that she wasn't weak. He just shook his head silently. Now, when they could finally afford to slow down some, she wanted to go double time.

"Thunderstorms fit you, Travis," she said, choosing to cross a large field covered with purple asters and sunflowers instead of paralleling the rainsoaked wash that ran down one side. "Wind and Thunder go together well. But as you said once, I'm more like the Earth people. I'm the kind who worries about Lightning."

The observation left him aching for what he knew could never be his. No matter what his feelings for her were, he'd never be the kind of man she needed. "It's all part of nature. Even things that can be destructive have another gentler side. Wind and Earth are partners, you know. Wind can take seeds, and Life, to places Earth never could without it. I guess what I'm trying to say is that some things are meant for a closer look."

Fox gave him a gentle smile. "So Wind and Earth can be temporary allies—just like we are now."

"I'm trained for battle. It's what I do and why I know we'll hold our own against them. But I prefer knowing my enemy," he admitted. "These men after us are like shadows with guns in a guerrilla war."

"Even as a kid, you were always one to confront your problems head-on," she said. "But you can't do that now.

And once we get something we can use against these people, the fight will be mine, not yours.''

"You're dreaming if you think you'll ever confront these people without me beside you. I'm going to stick to you like white on rice. You might as well accept that.''

"Not all fights are won through force.''

"But most are.'' He'd expected an argument. When he didn't get one, that was when he began to worry seriously. She was set on having her way on this, and that meant there would be major-league problems down the road—if they got that far.

HOURS LATER, THEY ARRIVED at the trading post. Every muscle in Fox's body ached. Wistfully she remembered her old home and the security she'd found there. But all those things were lost to her now.

She reached back, touching the surface of her purse. She hadn't told Travis because she hadn't wanted to appear like a child—but she'd brought Chance with her. The old stuffed bear was the only tangible link she had left to her past, that connection made the toy priceless to her.

Travis glanced around the parking lot, checking out the vehicles. There were two newer-model pickups, an old van, and a weather-beaten truck. He took a closer look at the latter to confirm his guess. "That's the truck Ashe left for us." He pointed to the oldest truck.

"How do you know it's that one? Any of these could be his choice.''

"There's a *jish*—a medicine bundle—on the dashboard. Ashe made it for me many, many years ago.''

"How come you don't carry it with you?'' she asked, following him to the truck.

"Medicine bundles and, more importantly, the beliefs associated with them, are more a part of my brother's world than mine. It didn't seem right to take it with me when I joined the Rangers. I would have had to leave it behind most of the time, anyway. That's why Ashe offered to keep it for me." He reached for the keys he knew Ashe would have hidden inside the bumper, below the license plate, in a magnetic holder. It had been their custom for years.

As he unlocked the doors and they climbed into the truck, Fox took the *jish* from the dashboard. "Will you wear it now? It doesn't seem right to just leave it sitting there."

He held it in his hand and stared at it, lost in thought. "Do you remember what the teachings say about medicine bundles?"

"I know they're meant for protection."

"It's more than that. A *jish* is said to be alive and, to remain strong, it must be exercised—used. Without that, it grows weak and, some say, it grows lonely. It's not something that stores power, but it's a source of power in and of itself. To some, like my brother, owning the *jish* becomes a sacred trust."

"I think Ashe is telling you that it'll help you now, if you'll let it."

Travis fastened the small leather pouch to his belt. "At one time I felt the need to walk away from those beliefs. But being back here on the Rez has put a different slant on everything for me. I'm a man now, not a kid who needs to prove his strength by standing alone and going his own way. For the first time in my life, I'm really prepared to carry this—if not strictly out of belief, out of respect for who and what I am."

His revelation filled her with a sense of wonder and a twinge of envy. Travis was reaching out to the teachings he'd grown up with, knowing they would sustain him now. She had no such comfort. The past held mostly sorrow and questions for her.

"You know, it's strange how things work," Travis said. "As a boy, I never thought I'd be saying what I just said."

A new strength seemed to burn within him. "I like the grown-up you," she said in a near whisper.

His sudden roguish grin took her breath away. His playfulness was back, sweeping away the seriousness of their conversation. "Are you flirting with me, Fox? If you are, I've got to tell you, I'm easy."

"So I've heard," she teased.

He was about to answer when a young couple came out of the trading post. Travis quickly started the engine and pulled onto the highway, heading north.

"Maybe you should have gone south, then backtracked. We don't want anyone to guess our next stop," she said.

He smiled. "Which is precisely why I went in this direction. I know how the Navajos who live out on the Rez think. They'll give any Anglo who comes looking for one of the Diné the wrong directions. If we'd headed south, they would have said we headed north. I just wanted to make sure they knew which wrong directions to give."

"Good strategy." Fox laughed.

Checking the glove compartment, she pulled out some topographical maps, a cigarette lighter, ammunition, and dried fruit. "Ashe is certainly trying to think of everything." Feeling something by her feet, she leaned down and picked up a can of lubricating spray for their vehicle, obviously something left by the owner. "Near as I can figure, he's covered all the bases," she added with a smile.

Travis chuckled. "Ashe always thinks things through," he said. "That's one of the reasons he makes a good cop— and why he was always a pain as a brother," he added with a wink.

Turning her thoughts back to their immediate problems, she added, "I know we have a list of places and people to see, but I have a better plan. Let's visit the community college north of Fort Defiance next."

"Why there? That place must have just been getting started when the Johnsons arrived on the Rez," Travis said.

"Jesse Bidtah works there. He's been Dad's friend for forever. I think we should talk to him."

"I know Jesse," Travis said. "He teaches Navajo language. He was a counselor when I was in high school. He didn't approve of my choices, but he was always there for me."

"In that case, you might have better luck than I would, talking to him. I've heard that he's gone on record siding with the traditionalists who believe that the Reservation should be exclusively for the Navajos and that no Anglos should live here."

Travis nodded pensively. "Ashe said as much in a letter he wrote me when I was overseas. Jesse has become more dogmatic and focused on the tribe and tribal rights ever since his son got killed."

"Poor Joey. He was such a great guy," Fox said. "He left the Reservation and became a state cop. Then one day he pulled a guy over. The man had an outstanding warrant and didn't want to be taken in. He shot Joey and left him to bleed to death by the side of the road."

"I understand Jesse doesn't leave the Reservation at all anymore. Part of Jesse must have died when his boy was killed." Travis paused. "That's why I know he'll help us. He knows what it's like to lose part of his family."

"While you talk to Jesse, I'll go to the library. I'm very good with computers. Let me see what I can turn up by doing a search through various databases."

"What exactly do you have in mind?"

"That'll depend on what I turn up," she said with a shrug.

He knew she was up to something, but she'd be safe in

front of a computer. That was one place where there was a limit to the trouble she could find.

They arrived three hours later, having taken the route south and then west through Window Rock before turning north again. Travis parked the old truck while Fox pulled out her wig and quickly slipped it on.

"I think I'd better wear this while I'm walking around here."

"Good idea. It'll help you blend in. Not that it would be hard for anyone to do that here. There are several non-Navajos on campus," he said.

"Good luck with Jesse," she said. "I have a feeling he could be a great help to us, if he chooses to be."

As she walked away from Travis, Fox could feel his gaze on her. Unable to resist knowing for sure, she turned her head. He smiled. She waved, feeling her entire body blushing. Why couldn't she ever leave well enough alone!

Fox headed for the library building, suddenly realizing that this was the first time she'd been alone in weeks. Normally, she would have been glad for the respite, but the danger that haunted her every waking hour kept her on her guard. She'd have to watch her own back now.

As she stepped inside the library, Fox saw that only a few terminals were available. She quickly got permission from a librarian to log on, and chose a terminal in the farthest corner. From there, she had a clear view of the entire room.

Hearing the hum of the machine, Fox finally relaxed. The sound comforted her. She'd always been as good with computers as she was in math and science. Numbers and machines weren't illogical like people could be. If you gave them the correct instructions and information, they could always be relied upon.

She thought of Travis, off interviewing Jesse. Travis was the perfect choice for that job. It wasn't just his past history with Jesse, either. It was the fact that, when he wanted to, Travis could bring out the best in people. He had an undeniable presence and charisma that people responded to instinctively.

Yet what continued to draw her to him went far beyond that. There was an elusive quality about him that was much harder to define. She considered it for several moments, then the answer finally came to her: Travis had heart.

Chapter Ten

Travis walked slowly down the sidewalk toward the Native American Studies building. This was the first time in weeks that he'd been away from Fox. That kind of closeness normally would have made him feel smothered, but this time, he couldn't honestly say that it had. Maybe it was because he knew that, right now, she needed him to be exactly who and what he was—a soldier who was as deadly as they came.

As a Ranger, he'd acquired a well-deserved reputation for never letting anything get to him. Yet, with a touch of her hand, or a look, or a smile, Fox could fill him with desire so intense, it totally scrambled his thinking.

He'd never felt this way about any woman before, and that scared him more than an artillery barrage or a minefield.

Travis forced his thoughts on the job at hand as he entered the building and went down the hall. He didn't have far to walk before he found Jesse. The man was sitting in an empty classroom, grading papers.

Hearing footsteps, Jesse looked up. As he recognized Travis, a slow smile spread across his weathered face. His eyes were bright and alert. "Ah, I thought I'd be seeing you before too long."

Travis smiled. "You never cease to amaze me, uncle,"

he said, using the title as a term of respect. "How on earth could you have known that I'd come here looking for you?"

"I can't predict what you'll do, but I know how Fox thinks. If the police were unable to find answers for her, she'd take matters into her own hands. She'd systematically backtrack through her parents' history on the Reservation, find her own leads and pursue them."

Travis nodded. "That pretty much sums up why I'm here. You know you can talk freely to me. I need to find out more about your friends, Blue Eyes and Smiles. There's got to be more to their murders than what has already come out."

"I agree," Jesse said.

"Can you tell me about them? I knew them mostly as a kid knows an adult. During those rare times when I returned to the Rez on leave, I always stayed with my brother, not with them. Your take on them would be completely different from mine."

Jesse paused, gathering his thoughts. "What I liked most about both of them was that they really cared about their neighbors. If anyone needed something, they were there, ready to help. Many times, when someone was out of work, they'd show up with a casserole or fruit from their garden. And they never made it look like charity. It was that kind of attitude that won people over."

"Did they ever have any unusual visitors from off the Rez, or was there ever any gossip about them that you remember?"

Jesse considered the question carefully. "Every once in a while, some suit-types came to their house. They weren't preachers or lawyers, either—not with two-way radios. I normally don't pry, but I remember asking them one time if they were in trouble with the law. They laughed and assured me that they weren't. But they never offered any explanation. Many speculated that the visitors had something to do with the school they were starting up, but I never believed that. To me, those people looked like government cops of some kind. Like FBI, maybe. I can tell you this—there was tension between Blue Eyes and Smiles every time the men came.''

"Do you think the visits had something to do with Fox?'' Travis pressed.

Jesse remained silent for a long time. "Maybe. I just don't know. But, if they did, that would explain why Smiles was so overprotective of her.'' He paused, then added, "They didn't call her Fox back then, by the way. They always used her given name.''

Travis smiled. "Yes, I know. I was the one who nicknamed her Fox.''

Jesse stared at an indeterminate point, a faraway look in his eye. "There's one incident that sticks in my mind. I remember that Smiles refused to allow Fox to go on a day trip to Albuquerque with the other students. There was a lot of ill will about that. Some thought that Smiles didn't trust the Navajo teachers.''

"Did she ever explain why she didn't let Fox go?''

"No, not even to offer an excuse. She refused to justify her decision to anyone.''

"That doesn't sound like her at all. She was always careful not to hurt anyone's feelings.''

"It was completely unlike her, but I know she was doing it to protect her daughter. Nothing came ahead of that, as far as she was concerned,'' Jesse said.

After thanking him, Travis walked to the library, lost in thought. Knowing what he did now, he could guess that the Johnsons had been visited by Federal Marshals. The thought of her adopted daughter being in constant danger must have eaten at Alice Johnson more than any of them had ever realized.

As his thoughts shifted to Fox, an uneasiness he couldn't explain began to course through him. Maybe he shouldn't have left Fox alone. He quickened his pace.

Travis entered the library and, a moment later, saw her sitting quietly at a terminal in one corner of the room. Relief swept over him.

As he approached her, Fox beamed him a bright smile. He pulled up a chair and straddled it. "What's up?"

"I decided to try and hack into the tribal police's databases. It took me a while, but I finally figured out Ashe's password and got in that way."

He laughed. "I'm impressed, but I doubt Ashe will be. What's his password?"

"Navajoway." She smiled. "See? It fits him perfectly."

"You're right." He grinned, picturing how his brother would take the news that she'd invaded his files so easily.

"I was hoping the police had made some progress with this case," she said, "but from what I've seen so far, they haven't."

Travis looked over her shoulder and read what was on the computer screen. "You're right. This is information we already know."

"There's something else I want to try now." She entered the time of death and the date of her natural parents' murder. The information from her WITSEC file was part of the data Ashe had included in his files. "Now let's do a microfiche search. I want to know what the Arizona state newspapers reported about the crime. Maybe we can find a clue that might be useful to us."

It took a while for them to track down newspapers matching the date of the murder. Their initial search through the major papers in Arizona revealed nothing.

"I can't understand this," Fox said. "How could they not report a murder?"

He could feel her frustration and the fear that lay just beyond that emotion. "It may have been suppressed."

She stood and paced in front of the microfiche projector. "No newspaper reporter would back off on police say-so. They would have mentioned it, at least."

"How about trying the New Mexico papers? Regional news makes our headlines."

"Great idea! And to think that women say you're just another pretty face," she teased.

"What? Who said that?" Seeing her laugh, he clamped his mouth shut. He'd been baited by an expert.

Sitting beside her on an adjoining reader unit, he studied several reels of microfiche. "I think you should look at this article," he said, calling her attention to a small column in the Santa Fe newspaper.

She leaned forward, twisting the focus knob.

"This couple was murdered in Santa Fe on the same date as your biological parents," he said.

She continued reading until she'd gone through the entire article. Fox finally sat back, her face pale, her hands shaking. "The police reports have misled us. I think the murders must have happened right here in New Mexico, not Arizona."

He nodded. "I agree. Every other detail matches. And did you see the last sentence?"

"Yes. The couple had a daughter my age," she said.

Travis scrolled down the viewing screen until he reached the last page of the newspaper. "Unfortunately, there are no photos attached to the article." His heart went out to her as he saw the anguish mirrored in her eyes.

"Let's have a look in the next day's paper," she said after a moment. "This story is so brief it's as if it broke just before deadline."

He knew they were on the trail that would lead to the answers. But there was something else going on. His skin was crawling and the hair on the back of his neck was standing on end. He wasn't sure how he knew, but he was certain danger was closing in on them.

Travis looked at the people working at the other tables, and at a man in a study carrel. Gut instinct was really nothing more than information processed by the subconscious. He had to find what had triggered his inner alarms. He scrutinized everything again, but nothing appeared to be out of the ordinary.

"Look," Fox said at length, bringing his attention back to the screen and to a photo she'd found of the murdered couple. "Those are my parents, Travis," she said, her voice unsteady.

He saw her trembling and every protective instinct in him responded. He put his arm around her shoulders, drawing her closer to him. "That's such a grainy photo, Fox. How can you be so sure? Have you remembered something? There's no name on the article, probably because you were a minor and state law protected you."

"Not with my mind, but with my heart. Those *are* my parents."

Chapter Eleven

Tears spilled down her cheeks as she stared at the black-and-white image on the screen.

Travis didn't hesitate, he simply acted. Pulling her out of the chair and into the space between two tall bookshelves, he gathered her into his arms.

"I'm sorry," Fox said. "I'm making a spectacle of myself, but I can't stop crying." She tried to pull away but his arms remained steady and strong.

"Just let it out. Don't worry about anything."

"Seeing their faces… It was a shock," Fox said, struggling to compose herself. "And as I looked at that photo, I suddenly understood how much has been taken away from me by the people who murdered them. I may not remember much more than their faces, but I feel the loss with every beat of my heart."

"They'll always be a part of you, Fox. Cling to that," he said, stroking her hair. He tilted her chin up and took her mouth in a gentle kiss that was meant only to comfort. But Fox seemed to melt into him, as if trying to push back the chill in her soul.

She needed him, and he couldn't back away. As her lips opened, he poured everything he was feeling into his kiss, warming her and giving as much of himself as he could.

Her arms wound around his neck and she clung to him

as their tongues mated and danced in the silent language of love.

Then, although it felt as if he were ripping away his heart, he gently pushed her away. "Your life has been filled with too many losses and betrayals. I don't want to add to that. I won't be around for long, and you deserve far more than anything I can give you."

Her eyes burned into him and she was about to say something sharp when one of the librarians came up to them.

"Are you finished with the microfiche? Someone else needs a viewer," the woman said.

Fox moved away from Travis. "We're done here, thank you." When she looked back at Travis, the only emotion etched on her face was determination. "Let's go. I have a plan."

His jaw clenched. "Remember when I told you that some things scare me right down to my boots? Well, those four words have suddenly gone to the top of the list."

"Relax. It's a great plan. I want to go to Santa Fe."

"You memorized your biological parents' address, didn't you?" he observed.

Fox nodded. "And that's where we're going next." She looked around nervously. "We'd better do it as quickly as possible, too."

He narrowed his eyes. "Is there something you haven't told me?" he asked as they left the library.

"Well, I didn't exactly get caught when I accessed Ashe's files, but—"

"But what?" he roared, hurrying with her across campus.

"Have you ever heard of 'cookies'?"

"As in with milk?"

"No. It's kind of an electronic footprint you leave behind when you access a site via computer. It basically identifies your computer's address, and leaves traceable code on your computer's software.''

He narrowed his eyes. "Are you telling me that the police can track our location now?"

"Yeah. It won't take long, either, once Ashe notices the log-access times and realizes there's been an unauthorized access. He won't know it was me, so he'll probably turn it over to their systems manager. After that, they'll be here on the double, I would imagine.''

"*Now* you tell me.''

"We've been taking chances all along. What's one more? And, you've got to admit, the results far outweigh the risk. Now we can set aside our other plans and go directly to Santa Fe to pursue this.''

"That's not such a good idea. I'm virtually certain that the criminals after you have your parents' old house staked out. Remember they know more about the crime than any of us do and would realize that your search for answers will take you there sooner or later. There's also something else to consider. Once we show up at that house, the danger to you will increase. They're undoubtedly going to assume that you've remembered more than you actually have.''

"I have to go anyway, Travis—with or without you. I have to follow the trail, regardless of the risks. Let's face it. They must be pretty sure I know, or have something that's a serious threat to them. I have to follow this through.''

"I'll take you, because nothing's going to stop you and I know it. But we can't just drive up there. We need a plan of action. Give me a chance to think about this.''

As they reached the pickup, Travis heard someone call out his name. He turned his head and saw a short Pueblo man of ample girth hurrying over to them.

"I thought that was you, Travis. I haven't seen you in a long time,'' the man said, struggling to catch his breath.

Travis smiled at his old friend, then introduced him to Fox. "This is Alfonso Suarez. He's from San Ildefonso Pueblo."

"There've been so many rumors about you two, lately," Suarez said. "And not just in the newspapers! What on earth are you doing here?"

"We needed to talk to some people, but we can't stay," Travis replied.

"You're still trying to keep your location a secret, then," he observed. "Okay, I can help. I'm finished giving a graduate level class lecture here, so why don't you both come to San Ildefonso? You'll be safe at our pueblo. Nobody will talk to outsiders about you being here."

"We appreciate it, sir," Fox answered, "but I'm not sure it's such a good idea. We could be endangering you and your neighbors. The people tailing us are very good at what they do and they're deadly. That's why the authorities have agreed to our plan to stay on the run. But we've already been at this public place too long." Fox looked around, half expecting to see a police car pull up, searching for whoever had broken into the police computer system. Since they still didn't know who the leak in the Marshal's Service was, the last thing they wanted was to give anyone a fix on their location.

Suarez chuckled softly. "Trust me. The pueblo is the safest place for you. My people are much more...shall we say, 'reserved,' than most Navajos like Travis, here. We like our privacy. Strangers aren't welcome unless they're invited. Any outsiders who wander onto our land are spotted and watched."

"And that includes Navajos," Travis added ruefully.

Suarez laughed. "Not you, old friend." Seeing the curiosity on Fox's face, he explained. "The Navajos were nomads and used to raid the Pueblos. There's still an old...good-natured rivalry between our peoples."

Travis saw the worry on Fox's face. "Alfonso and I go back a long way. He can be trusted."

"How did you meet?"

"Years ago Ashe and I heard about his talks on the history and customs of the pueblo peoples. We went to hear him speak whenever he came as a visiting professor to the Rez. It was his respect for all tribes that impressed us. Whenever we could, we'd stay and talk to him after he was finished. Eventually, we all became friends."

"So, will you come to my home?" Suarez asked.

"As long as you understand the danger, old friend," Travis said slowly, "we'll be glad to accept."

"But we have another place to visit first," Fox insisted, looking at Travis.

"We can make specific plans for that from the pueblo," Travis told her. "It'll be a lot closer from there, too." Travis noted the look on her face. It spoke volumes. He'd have to keep a close eye on Fox, or she'd sneak off and go to Santa Fe alone.

"You'll enjoy our pueblo," Suarez assured her, telling her a bit about it.

As Suarez spoke to Fox, Travis stood by the driver's side of the pickup, studying the campus grounds before them. Instinctively, he dropped his gaze to the rearview mirror and checked out the area behind them, as well. At first, he only saw kids getting in and out of vehicles and some walking around campus. But then, as he started to look away, a flash of movement caught his eye. Someone was coming toward them, weaving furtively between the thirty-or-so cars and pickups in the parking area.

The man's approach was methodical and careful. This was no innocent student just cutting through the parking lot.

"What's the matter?" Suarez asked, seeing that Travis's attention had shifted.

"Stay here and keep talking, and try to act casual," he told his friend. "Fox, I want you inside the truck, ready to roll." He handed her the keys.

Without explaining further, he crouched down as if to pick up an object, then moved away quickly, circling toward the back row of vehicles. He'd been waiting for a chance like this for a long time, and he intended to take full advantage of the opportunity.

He crept silently as a cougar, making no noise even as he moved across the gravel. Their stalker was someone dressed in a maintenance uniform. Travis came up from behind him and, in one deft move, slammed him against the car. Securing the man's arm at a painful angle, he immobilized his opponent by simply applying pressure to a key nerve on the back of his hand.

"Who are you and what do you want?" Travis growled.

The man groaned. "Ease up. You're paralyzing my arm."

The voice sounded familiar, but Travis was too angry to care. "You're lucky I don't tear your arm off and cram it down your throat. Now who the hell are you and what do you want?"

"It's me, Travis. Marc Gray. I'm the U.S. Marshal you met."

Anger and disappointment converged on Travis. "I could have killed you with one move," Travis retorted, and quickly released him. "This was *not* a good idea on your part."

Marshal Gray flexed his arm, then shook his hand, trying to get some feeling back into it. "I can see that now, but I really had no choice. Someone had to come and warn you, and I just happened to be closest. You two have to leave the area quickly. Your brother knows that a hacker at this college resource center used his password to get into the police database, and he called me first, suspecting it was either you or Fox.''

"If he didn't tell anyone else, then we're okay," Travis replied.

"You haven't heard the rest of it. Since he wasn't one hundred percent sure who the hacker was, he had to file a report and that's when the police chief got wind of it. Unfortunately, so did a reporter who happened to be at the station at the time. A few officers are on their way here from Window Rock and I expect the press will arrive shortly, too. This campus is going to be real crowded soon."

Travis nodded once. "We're outta here, then."

"I also wanted to tell you, face-to-face, to be very careful what you tell Carl Andrews, our tech expert."

Before Travis could ask him to explain, Fox came jogging up. "Are you okay, Marshal Gray? I saw who it was just as Travis corralled you."

"I'm fine, but we don't have much time. You have to go now." He glanced at Travis. "Remember. Double-check anything Carl Andrews tells you."

"Is he the leak?" Fox pressed.

"I don't know for sure. All we have at this point is just circumstantial evidence and speculation. Carl has a great record with the Marshals Service, but there's another side to the coin. I know he's been passed over for promotion twice. He's also heavily in debt, and is having marital problems. These things indicate he's vulnerable."

"How did you find us so quickly?" she asked. "Was it because I hacked into the police computers?"

"Exactly. Ashe suspected it was you because the user guessed his password. He called me and I had our people confirm your location through your radio's beacon signal."

Travis's expression darkened and Gray cautiously took a step back. "You knew the radio had a beacon, right?"

"I thought I'd turned it off," Travis said.

"No, it's still working," Gray said.

Fox pulled the two-way radio from her purse. "Do us a favor, then. Turn it off, please."

He took a screwdriver from his tool belt and turned the setting screw to the left of the one Andrews had told them about. "That's it. It's not exactly brain surgery. Now get going, you two. I'd offer to give you a ride, but I don't want to know exactly where you are, either, for security reasons. Good luck."

"We have a problem," Fox said slowly as Gray walked off. "Both these men can't have given us the right directions on how to disable the beacon. I don't know which one to trust. Do you?"

"It could be that Andrews simply made a mistake, or maybe Gray did. Neither of those men looks or acts like experienced field agents to me, even though Andrews is supposed to be a tech expert. They're more like bureaucrats."

"What we have to do is make sure that beacon really is disabled," she said.

Travis crouched between two cars and took the back off the unit, using his pocketknife. "This doesn't look so different from the ones that are military issue." He studied it for a moment, then disconnected the wire that supplied the transmitter beacon with power from the batteries. "This is the only way I know of to make sure it's not transmitting."

Suarez came up to them. "I stayed behind the truck while you were talking to that Anglo. I wasn't sure if you wanted him to see me or not, considering you'll be staying at my house."

"Good move," Travis said. "Let's go now. Time's crucial."

As he studied Fox's uncompromising expression, he found that he could read her mind as easily as she'd read his. She'd look for a way to duck out and follow her own course as soon as she could. She didn't want to stay safe nearly as much as she wanted answers.

Fox led the way back to the truck, and Suarez left them to find his own vehicle. Travis's gaze, and the thoughts that burned through him, stayed centered on her. She was an exasperating creature. She never backed down, even when she had every reason to do so. She'd frustrate him, and argue incessantly. Yet there was something about her that made her completely unforgettable.

Questioning his sanity, he bit back an oath and focused on what lay ahead.

SUAREZ'S HOME HAD AN undeniable atmosphere of comfort, especially compared to what they'd been used to lately. The leather easy chair by the window had the soft patina of frequent use, and the matching hassock showed the permanent impression of two feet. The walls were covered with massive, ceiling-high bookshelves filled with volumes on subjects ranging from anthropology to zoology. An Indian blanket woven in orange and black wool lay unfolded over the back of the sofa as if it had been recently used.

"You have a nice, cozy house. It has a lived-in look," Fox commented, wondering how long it would be before she had a place to call home again.

"Some say it begs for a woman's touch," Suarez said.

"Who doesn't?" Travis countered with a wry grin.

Suarez laughed. "Well, you haven't changed much. Come," he said, going down the narrow, whitewashed hallway to his study. "We'll be more comfortable in here."

The study appeared slightly larger than the living room, and had an atmosphere of purpose about it. Two computers, a desktop and a laptop, were placed beside each other on two connected desks. He gestured toward the easy chairs set by the windows. "Make yourselves at home," he said. "Now tell me. What's the best way I can help?"

"Don't let Fox go near those things," Travis said, pointing to the computers. "Hacking is her favorite pastime."

"Don't listen to him," Fox said, good-naturedly. "I've already gotten all the information I can about my past. There's no need for me to access other databases."

"If I may make a suggestion?" Suarez asked. Seeing her nod, he continued. "Perhaps you're going about this the wrong way. What you should concentrate on is learning more about your enemies. They seem to know a lot about you."

"That's true, but they're not exactly trying to help us," she said, her smile taking any sting out of her words.

Suarez glanced at one of his computers. "Maybe we can zero in on the one that's already been identified—Prescott."

"The police and the U.S. Marshals have an extensive file on him, but there's nothing there that's useful to us now," Travis said. "My brother and Deputy Marshal Feist have gone over that repeatedly."

Suarez considered the matter. "Let's look in a direction the police and the marshals haven't," he mused. "Do you know where he went to college? As a professor, I'm able to access many university databases."

Fox looked at Travis, but he only shrugged. Glancing back at Suarez, she shook her head. "I don't think that it ever came up in our conversations with the police."

"Well, let me do a search. If he practiced law in New Mexico, then there's a chance he went to a university here, and I know of only one, the University of New Mexico, that offers a law degree. If that's true, I'll be able to access his records and those may reveal something useful to you. One never knows."

As they waited, Travis turned toward Fox. She'd been

undeniably tense but in his steady gaze, Fox saw courage and inner strength. The caring and concern that had prompted him to reach out to her in this way was a balm over her troubled spirit. And in the gentle smile he suddenly gave her, she saw the reflection of love.

Chapter Twelve

Silence, marred only by the hum of the computer's cooling fan, hung heavily in the room as Suarez continued searching through the various databases.

"We're in luck," Suarez announced, interrupting the silence at last. "Prescott got his law degree at the University of New Mexico, just as I suspected."

Fox went over to where Suarez sat, and looked over his shoulder at the monitor. "That's a start. What now?"

Suarez continued to scan the pages scrolling down his screen. "His graduate-school adviser was Professor Samuels, and I know that man very well. He's been here as my guest frequently. I'll talk to him in confidence, and see what I can find out about Prescott and the person he was back then."

Suarez stood. "I'll call him up right now. You two make yourselves comfortable while I use the phone in the living room."

As he left, Fox noticed that Travis was pacing by the window. "You're just not comfortable here, are you?"

"It's the home of a friend, and you're safer here than any other place I can think of," he answered, avoiding her question.

"But you're still uncomfortable," Fox insisted. "Why?"

"The pueblo hems you in. It's like a closed society, Navajos are welcome but only to a point. It goes against the grain to let my guard down here.'' He stared at the floor, then back up at her. "Don't worry about it. I can handle it.''

Fox said nothing, determined to respect his privacy, though she would have given anything to have him reach out to her. Since he wasn't the type of man who ever opened himself up to anyone, it would have been a sure sign that he saw her as a trusted equal, not just someone he felt obligated to protect.

She waited, hoping he'd say something more. When he didn't, she sighed softly.

"You're taking this wrong," Travis said, sensing her thoughts. "If I were shutting you out, I would have denied that there was anything wrong. The fact that I'm admitting there is a problem, should tell you how much—"

Travis stopped and she held her breath.

"How much I...'' He shook his head as if he just couldn't make the rest of the words come out.

She knew that, deep down, he'd wanted to say more, and everything feminine in her had longed to hear it, but Travis was a man who had learned to use privacy as a shield. It went against all his survival instincts to completely drop his guard.

"It's okay, Travis," she said. "Some things just aren't easy to put into words.''

He nodded, visibly relieved. "I've never been good at that, you know.''

Suarez came into the room, smiling. His eagerness told her, even before he spoke, that he'd learned something that would be of value to them.

"I have good news. I was able to get more on Prescott's background, things you might find useful." He sat down. "Prescott's story is almost like the classic example of right instincts spoiled by too much ambition. When he was in college, his life seemed beyond reproach. He even turned down one of the highly competitive grad-assistant positions so that another student, with greater financial need, could get the post and stay in school. Prescott ended up working part-time at a car dealership in Albuquerque instead—Montoya's Imports. He remained there all through law school. On the surface, I have to admit, it really looked like Prescott worked hard to earn his degree."

"How can that help us?" Fox asked, disappointment in her voice.

"Remember that I said, 'On the surface,'" Suarez replied with a smile. "Prescott, apparently, always had money. Lots of it. His life-style was not ostentatious, but it was sufficiently above average that his adviser checked to make sure Prescott was entitled to the financial aid he was receiving from the government. That inquiry apparently put my professor friend in some hot water with the administration. That's why he still remembers the incident. It appears that Prescott had some powerful friends even back then."

"We should check out that car dealership," Travis said. "Do you know anyone who works there, by any chance?"

"No, I don't. But why don't you pay the place a visit? There may be somebody still working there who remembers Prescott. If you approach them just right, I'm sure you can get them to open up to you."

"We'll give it a shot," Travis said. "Thanks for the tip."

Fox stood and began to pace. "The answers are out there just waiting for us. But the longer we wait, the harder it'll be for us to pick up the trail leading to the killers." She met Suarez's gaze. "Your offer to have us stay here as your guests was very kind. And you've helped us a great deal. But I'm really afraid that if I sit still much longer, the answers I'm looking for will slip right through my fingers.

The people after me have already burned down the only home I've known. Given enough time, they'll destroy every single link I have to my past."

"You have to go, then," Suarez told them. "I understand. The rush-hour traffic to and from Santa Fe right now will help you stay low profile, too. But do come back when it's all over. It would be wonderful to see you both again."

He and Fox replenished their food and water supplies, and got new batteries for the cell phone. Once they'd gathered what they'd need, Suarez walked outside with them. As they stood by the door, he glanced down at Travis's *jish*. "Remember there's power and strength in your heritage. It sustained your tribe through years of hardships when the Anglo world tried its best to destroy them."

He paused, then continued. "When someone from our pueblo is faced with difficulties we say to them, 'Be as a woman, be as a man.' In other words, let the qualities of both guide you. In the Navajo Way, you say that only by joining can a male and a female be complete. There is a lesson woven into both our ways that you need to draw on now. If you work as one, blending your strengths, then you'll have everything you need to face your enemies. Nothing will be able to oppose you for long if you stand together."

A heaviness of spirit weighed Fox down as they left the pueblo far behind them, heading southeast. "I hope I get a chance to see him again," she said, turning around for one last look. "I like that man."

"So do I." Travis stopped the car by the side of the road and shifted to face her. "What you have to remember is that, no matter how trusted or well intentioned a friend, we can't really count on anyone now, except each other."

"It's enough," she said softly, reaching for his hand. She saw the softening in his gaze, then the surrender, as his iron will broke and more primitive emotions took control of him.

With a groan, he drew her against him and held her tightly, as if desperate to burn away her fears with his caresses. When he took her mouth, his kiss was harsh and hot.

She felt a blinding rush of feelings, a sweet burn that left her aching for more.

A moment later he drew away reluctantly. "I wish I could erase all the bad things that have happened to you. You deserve much more than what life has handed you."

"But, sometimes, what life gives me is enough, at least for the moment," she brushed his face lightly, then drew back.

He placed the vehicle in gear and got underway. Silence lay heavy between them.

As they went down the solitary road that would eventually join the main highway, Fox shifted in her seat. "I know you'd rather go to the car dealership in Albuquerque first, but we have to pass through Santa Fe anyway en route. I want to take advantage of that and go to my biological parents' home while we're there. Maybe something I see will trigger my memory."

Travis took a deep breath, then expelled it in a rush. "All right, but we won't stick around unless I'm absolutely certain it's safe. Agreed?"

She hesitated.

"I'm not going to take that exit until I have your word," he said flatly. "Your emotions are influencing your outlook and that's dangerous—for both of us. Like Suarez said, we have to rely on each other. You have the answers inside you and we must bring them to the surface, but you'll need a more logical approach to succeed. That's what I can provide for you now."

"Balance," she observed and saw him nod. "All right, we'll do it your way."

"There's a gas station with a pay phone a few miles from here. I'm going to call Ashe and tell him what we've discovered about Prescott. I won't go into specifics about staying at the pueblo or what Suarez found out for us, but I will tell him about the beacon. I think he has to know about that."

"That's a good idea. By calling we'll ease his mind, too. He may not show it, but I bet he's worried about us."

"Ashe guards his thoughts well," Travis said.

"So do you."

He gave her a slow, sad smile. "Men are trained to cry alone and only in the dark," he murmured.

His admission, so full of candor and vulnerability, moved Fox deeply. She reached for his hand, but as a powerful yearning rippled through her, she drew it away. Even the slightest touch was dangerous between them now. Too many raw emotions lay just beneath the surface.

They stopped a moment later and Travis made the call. Fox kept a sharp lookout over the back road, searching for signs of anyone following them.

Five minutes later, halfway to the main highway, their truck's front tire suddenly blew out. "Hang on!" Travis yelled, taking his foot off the gas and trying to resist hitting the brake, which could flip them end-over-end.

Fox grabbed the seat tightly as the vehicle slid nearly sideways in the gravel. "We're going to tip over!" she yelled, feeling the truck begin to tilt.

"I can hold it!" As Travis turned the wheel to the right, the vehicle straightened. Then, in the time it took to draw in a breath, the truck bounced and flew into the ditch that ran alongside the road. Brush on the outside whacked the vehicle like cannon blasts, forcing it to lose speed quickly.

By the time they came to a stop, the truck was wedged in the narrow channel.

"Did you hear it?"

"What, the tire blowing out? Of course I did!"

"No, just a split second before that, another pop. It was gunfire. This was no accident. Someone shot out the tire. Stay low and inside the truck. I'm going to take a look and see if I can confirm what happened. If I'm right, we've got to find a way out of here before we're the next targets."

He slipped out of the driver's side, and then edged around to the right front tire. It was as he'd guessed. The bullet hole was unmistakable, clearly visible on the sidewall of the steel-belted radial.

"They probably don't know if we're hurt or not, so they'll be approaching cautiously." Travis checked the pistol tucked into his belt. "I'm guessing that they'll try to put me out of action and kidnap you. If they'd wanted us eliminated, I'd have taken the bullet."

Fox fought the stab of fear that sliced through her, forcing herself to turn that emotion into anger. Getting ready to go, she reached down to the floorboard, and picked up the can of lubricating spray, which she'd seen rolling around under the seat. She had no idea how to use Travis's gun, nor did she want to learn, but she knew her chemistry. This aerosol can, along with a spark from the cigarette lighter she'd seen in the glove compartment, would make a very effective weapon at point-blank range. She slipped both into her jacket pocket, then grabbed her purse.

"Climb out my side, and let's go," Travis said. "We'll stay down in the ditch. There's no water running in it now."

"Shouldn't we try to get back to the pueblo and find help?"

"No, they chose the point of attack very carefully. The shot angle tells me they positioned themselves on an intercept course, hoping we'd run back in that direction. We'll go the other way. Our best bet is to make it to the highway where we can hopefully flag down a car. I don't think they'll be expecting us to do that.''

Their hike to the highway didn't take long, but the moment they emerged from the ditch and out from behind cover, a bullet ricocheted off the asphalt ten feet away, and a rifle shot rang out.

Travis pushed Fox to the ground; then, grasping her around the waist, rolled with her out of the line of fire and back down into the ditch. ''That was a high-powered rifle at long range,'' he said. ''The bullet arrived before the sound. They've anticipated us and, more importantly, they have a vehicle and we don't.''

''How did they find us this time? We can't seem to get away from them!''

''I don't know but, right now, we have to concentrate n keeping some distance between us and them.''

''We can't hike all the way to Santa Fe—not with someone who can drive right up to us at any time, chasing us.''

''We'll take a diagonal path toward the river, staying out of sight. That's our only hope. They have an advantage because they have wheels, but they can't track from their vehicle. They also won't be able to follow us easily if we vary the terrain, or end up swimming for it.''

Swallowing back the taste of fear in her mouth, Fox kept up with him as they jogged through the rocky, piñon- and juniper-covered area. Though she couldn't see anyone behind them, she could feel their presence; that gave her all the energy she needed.

As they reached the summit of a low hill, Travis stopped to survey the ground they'd covered. ''They're about ten minutes behind us. I think they're looking for a road they can take to cut us off before we reach the river. We're going to have to go north around Black Mesa. Vehicle or not, they'll have a tough time following us there except by cross-country, and they'll have to avoid being spotted by Pueblo authorities. The best part is that they won't be expecting us to circle around like that. That journey's a rough one by anyone's standards. They'll believe you can't make it.'' He gave her a slow, heart-stopping grin. ''But they don't know you like I do.''

''I won't even slow you down,'' she answered, holding his gaze.

''The way things are working out between us,'' he said in a husky voice, ''you may want to do just that, someday.'' His eyes shimmered with a fire that made her breath catch.

As they faced each other, desire sang in her and a storm raged in her heart. She wasn't sure how she found the courage, but Fox tore her gaze away from his.

''We'd better get going,'' she managed after a moment.

Their pace was grueling. When they reached the talus slope of the rocky fortress, where massive boulders had toppled down from the summit, Travis led them into the shadows. From there, he surveyed the area they'd just crossed.

''They're not as far back as I'd hoped. They've found a route, apparently, that others have taken before.'' He pointed to a slow-moving sports vehicle coming in their general direction, its windshield gleaming in the setting sun. ''But they still don't know exactly where we are.''

Sunset soon gave way to twilight. Travis and Fox looked around for a good hiding place as they made their way quickly up the side of the mesa. About twenty feet from the top, Travis found a shallow cave carved out by water and wind.

''It's dark enough now, they won't be able to see us unless we're out in the open. Let's hide here,'' he said, peering inside. ''We can't outrun them on foot, so we'll have to trick them. It's our only option now.''

He moved aside the tumbleweeds that covered the opening, pulled her in with him, then restacked the brush so they would be hidden from view. As they stood side by side, backs pressed to the sandstone wall, they heard the vehicle approaching from down below. Her heart was hammering so loudly in her ears, she found it impossible to believe that they wouldn't hear it.

As she edged closer to Travis, she brought the aerosol can and lighter out of her pocket.

Suddenly the vehicle stopped. There was the sound of one door, then another, opening, then whispers. The scuff of boots on rock told Fox they were climbing around the side of the mesa.

Fox could feel Travis's body as he kept perfectly still, his gun out and ready. Hearing the ominous click of a pistol being cocked just a few feet away, she held her breath. The advancing footsteps suddenly stopped, and she heard a low, throaty chuckle.

Fox felt her blood turn to ice. The men had approached from her side of the shallow cave. Travis was armed, but she stood between him and their pursuers.

One of the tumbleweeds hiding Fox's head was suddenly pulled away. Before Travis could reach around her with his pistol, Fox held up the aerosol can and lighter. There was no time for aiming, just action. Pressing down on the spray nozzle and flicking the lighter, she sent a column of flames and burning oil onto the man's shirt. He yelled and jumped back, knocking over his partner while he flailed wildly.

The sudden burst of light all but blinded her, but Travis grabbed her arm, pulling her out in his direction as bullets struck the rocks at the back of the cave where they'd been just moments before.

WHAT CAME NEXT WAS A dark, adrenaline-based blur. Gasping for air, Fox and Travis found themselves at the river's edge.

"They won't follow us now," he said. "They lost the initiative and one of them is injured, possibly seriously."

"Did you get a look at them?" she asked.

He shook his head. "All I saw was the fire that came shooting out of your makeshift flame thrower. We were lucky to get away without running in a circle or being shot."

"Aw, come on. I saved the day. Admit it. Besides, you recouped quickly enough. You led me here at a dead run as if you could see in the dark."

He shook his head. "It wasn't my vision that got us here. It was my memory of the area."

"Would it kill you to say 'Thanks, you were brilliant'?"

"It would, unless you meant it sarcastically."

Fox stayed by him as they got under way again, electing to walk downstream along the bank rather than risk an evening swim.

"By the way, that *was* quick thinking," he said at long last.

She smiled. "I bet that hurt to admit."

"You'll never know."

The minutes turned into an hour, then two. "Sometimes I wonder if we'll ever make progress on this case," she said. "All we ever seem to do is run. I'd sure like to see them on the run for a change. I'm tired of all this."

"Their turn will come soon enough. One thing I've learned is that life continually changes. The real problems come in when you're happy with the way life is going for you. No matter how badly you may want it to, nothing ever stays the same. And when good things get pulled out from under you, a piece of your heart gets torn off in the process."

"But what's the alternative? To force yourself never to

care? That's such a high price to pay! How can anyone be happy that way?'' Fox asked.

''I was…at one time,'' he said after a moment.

'''Was'?''

''Let's just say that life threw another curveball at me— one I wasn't expecting—and once again, things changed.'' He stopped and crouched on the ground. ''I'm going to use the radio. Would you get it out of your purse? We need some backup fast, and another vehicle and there's no way we can use a cell phone from this location. The mountains will block the transmissions.''

''At the rate we keep damaging trucks, they're going to give us an armored car.''

''I wouldn't mind.'' He chuckled, then shifted his attention to the radio.

Travis contacted Andrews, who was monitoring their channel. After a quick situation report, he added, ''There's one more thing. I have a feeling Stan McNeely, an ex-Army Ranger from Bloomfield, is one of the men on our trail. If he is, tell your people to proceed with extreme caution. He's one of the most dangerous men around, especially when cornered.''

Once Travis had switched off the radio, Fox spoke. ''How can either of us expect to outrun a man like McNeely?''

''There's only one way to defeat McNeely. Play by his rules, only dirtier.''

''You can't become what you're not,'' she protested.

''He and I are very much alike.'' He held up one hand, stemming her protests. ''I'll do whatever it takes to accomplish my goal—keeping you safe.'' He stood, then reached for her hand, holding it in both of his. ''You're the only thing that matters to me in this fight. We'll win, even if I have to sink to his level.''

There was deadly intent and an acceptance of what he

couldn't change mirrored on his face. But what touched her most was the realization that he cared what she thought. A rush of tenderness swept over her as he moved away. She knew with certainty now that his heart, though scarred, still had the capacity to feel deeply.

"No matter what happens, I'll always see you for the man you truly are—one who isn't afraid to fight for what he believes in and always follows his highest sense of right."

"Are you so sure that's the real me?" Travis took a step closer to her. There was a dangerous challenge in his gaze.

She knew what he was doing. He was trying to prove to her that his dark side merited her fear. She could not back away now.

Fox held her ground and then took his hand. His fingers curled around hers tightly enough for her to take notice, but not so hard as to hurt. Instinctively Fox pressed his hand against her cheek, then brushed a kiss over his knuckles.

His grip eased and his gaze softened. "I'll stand between you and harm. That's my promise to you." He released her hand. "It's time to go."

Silencing the yearnings in her heart, she followed him along the damp sand of the riverbank. Something special had just happened between them. Their hearts had spoken to each other, and that magical moment would be a part of her forever.

TRAVIS DID NOT SLOW DOWN until they were almost at the highway. It had been a long trek in nearly total darkness, and they were far south of the pueblo now. Ahead they could finally see the flashing lights of the police cars approaching from farther east, then turning on toward the pueblo.

"We know I injured one of the men and that'll slow

them down," Fox said. "With luck the cops will find McNeely and place him in custody."

"Unless the injured man *is* McNeely, and he's in very bad shape, the cops are outmatched. I know that in this terrain, I could evade the police for as long as I was able to keep moving. I expect McNeely could do the same."

"We're going to have to avoid the police ourselves now, too," Fox said thoughtfully. "If they take us in we'll spend hours being questioned when we have no answers, and wasting even more time."

"Better that than spending the night out here in the open. That's going to be too risky."

"I have an idea."

He groaned. "No, this time we're playing it *my* way."

"What do you have in mind?"

"For once, will you go along with me without giving me a hard time about it?"

"Only if you can convince me you're on the right track."

Her defiance sparked new fire in him. "We'll go down the dirt road just ahead that parallels the highway," he said. "There's an old flatbed truck coming up, and it's going really slow right now. If we're quick enough, we can hop a ride on the flatbed without giving ourselves away."

"I'm younger than you are, so I'm sure I'll make it. Think you can keep up?" Fox sprinted forward.

Travis caught up to her quickly, and jogged beside her. "Don't *ever* do that again," he growled.

"Or what?" she asked, laughing.

He gave her a slow smile. "Try it and find out."

Before she could gather her wits, Travis got busy rolling a large tumbleweed out into the center of the narrow road. Then, taking her hand, he hid with her in the thick brush several feet from the obstacle he'd placed in the truck's path.

"Stay out of sight until the driver either stops to move the tumbleweed, or slows to run over it. It's an open-bed truck, so it'll just be a matter of coordination to hop onto the back."

A few minutes later they were on the flatbed, lying low to escape detection. "Great job," he whispered.

"He almost came to a full stop before deciding to flatten the bush," she said. "It wasn't a real test of agility." She rose up slightly, taking a peek at the elderly driver. "Do you think he lives at the pueblo?" she whispered.

"No, he's going the wrong way. He looks more like one of the old Hispanic farmers who live along this stretch of the river."

Travis kept his arm around her waist as he lay behind her on the rough oaken floor of the flatbed. His grip was firm, and she felt the hardness and heat of his body as he pressed her against him. Sparks of awareness shot through her.

Deciding that she had to put some distance between them, she tried to wriggle out of his grasp.

He groaned softly as his body hardened in response. "Stop fidgeting," he said, his voice unsteady.

A new realization made her pulse race: she had the power to make Travis crazy with desire. And what was worse, everything feminine in her wanted to give him that pleasure and take all he could give her in return.

The knowledge both stunned and frightened her. She put a foot of distance between them. As if he understood, he didn't try to stop her.

When the driver finally parked his truck, she felt as if an eternity had passed. The elderly man walked away with a bag of groceries toward a low adobe house that looked almost as old as the earth itself.

As soon as he was inside the house and an interior light had come on, Travis helped her down from the truck bed.

"He's got a barn. That's where we'll stay." He gestured toward an equally ancient-looking earthen structure with two faded wooden doors.

Moving quietly, they made their way across an open area, then ducked inside. The barn's dirt floor was covered with several inches of straw. There were no animals penned inside, but two sheep were munching alfalfa from a wooden trough, and an opening in the back led to a fenced-in corral.

"We'll be safe here for tonight," Travis said. "I just hope he doesn't own a dog that might sound an alarm."

Fox gathered up some of the hay, trying to fashion a makeshift bed for herself. "Once this is all over, I'm going to buy a cozy little house. I'll never go anywhere that doesn't come equipped with soft beds and fresh linen."

Travis lay down a few feet away from her. "Setting down roots isn't the way to feel safe, you know."

"I can't go through life without forming attachments."

"It's not as hard as you think." Travis turned over onto his side, propping his head on one elbow. "After a while it becomes second nature. I'm so used to guarding my emotions now, I'm not sure I could stop doing that, even if I wanted to."

"You'll never find love that way," she said in a barely audible whisper.

"Love?" Travis shook his head. "That's not for me. I don't want it in my life. And, to be perfectly honest, it's beyond what I'm capable of giving. I can honor my word, and I can be loyal. But giving my heart away... That's an entirely different matter."

"Love isn't something you plan—it just happens."

"Not as far as I'm concerned," Travis answered quietly. "I'm too practiced at avoiding it."

The words wrenched her heart. "Are you so sure? Refusing to acknowledge feelings doesn't mean you don't have them. You have ties to other people, though you may not admit it.''

"There are only two people who are close to me. My brother, for one.''

"And the other?''

"You,'' he replied in a husky murmur.

"I know.''

Kneeling on the soft bed of straw, she took his hand and pulled him toward her. Travis rose to his knees and gathered her into his arms. Pressed against him, she could feel the hardness of his body and the proof of his desire.

"I should push you away,'' he said, as a shudder racked his body. Travis kissed her hard and felt her lips part beneath his. "But it's too late for that now,'' he said, drawing in a ragged breath. "Forgive me.''

Chapter Thirteen

Travis held her, feeling her body tremble against his. Fox wanted him, and the knowledge made his body grow as hot as a furnace.

As her hands slipped inside his shirt, kneading his muscles, he shuddered. The darkness became alive, keeping them hidden in a world where nothing existed except the fires their touch created.

She tugged at his shirt, pulling it away from his shoulders, then pressed a kiss to his chest, over his heart.

"Make me forget everything except you tonight," Fox whispered.

He kissed her then, his tongue thrusting past her lips and moving in a sensual rhythm that made her melt against him. Her gentleness cast a spell over him. He needed more of her softness. He undressed her slowly, kissing every inch of the flesh he bared, and leaving a hot, moist trail down the length of her body.

A storm raged inside him. Passion swirled around them like a hot desert wind. Desperate to hear her cries as she surrendered to the pleasures he could give her, he gently guided her down onto the bed of straw.

"It's so dark," she said, her voice trembling. "I can't see you." She reached out for him.

"Then feel me," he said, guiding her hand over his naked chest, then lower, to where his manhood pulsed, constrained against his jeans. "I want you. Never doubt that."

"Show me."

"I am," he managed. "And I will." No one had ever touched him so lovingly and no caress had ever burned him so deeply. He brought her hand up to his cheek and pressed a kiss into her palm. "Tonight is for you, Fox."

Travis then lay beside her, caressing her and wanting her, but knowing he cared too much about her to possess her fully without surrendering his heart.

Struggling against the fires that raged inside him, he drew her nipple into his mouth, sucking and teasing it with his teeth and tongue. She cried out his name, arching into him, eager for more. She was wildfire in his arms, and so compliant it took everything in him to hold back.

Travis raised his head, cradling her even more tightly against him as he murmured dark things in her ear. Then he kissed her again, letting her taste him as he moved his hand slowly down the length of her.

She writhed under his caress, helpless and needing him. Her entire being was focused on him as his palm smoothed over her skin.

Travis smothered her little cries with his mouth as his fingers breached her, pushing into her silken folds. She was so soft and so hot, he thought he would die.

As Travis stroked her, each strangled cry that came from her ripped through him like a bolt of lightning striking dry tinder. He was burning with the need to possess her, but the instinct to protect her overpowered everything else.

"Please," she begged, her body aching for release.

Shaking, he brought her to the edge. Then, as she arched upward with a gasp, he felt her shatter around him.

"I need you so much, my sweet love," he whispered, holding her close and absorbing the shudders that traveled over her.

Fox buried her face against his neck.

He cupped the back of her head as he continued to hold her. "You are incredible, my heart," he whispered in her ear.

"But you…"

"You gave me everything I wanted. Now, sleep while I hold you."

Travis felt her heart beating against his. He wanted her so badly it was a physical pain. He'd forgotten how consuming, how hot, it could be for a man with the right woman.

Feeling the moisture in his eyes, Travis held her tighter as the darkness continued to shield them. Until tonight, he hadn't understood that in an attempt to keep the world at bay, he'd condemned his own heart to a world of isolation.

TRAVIS WOKE UP JUST before dawn. Edging away from Fox, he stood up and washed his face using a nearby garden hose. The water was cold, but helped him wake up. A moment later, he picked up his shirt from the ground, slipped it on, and tucked it into his jeans.

He gazed down at her, watching the morning light dancing over her naked body, then crouched beside her and brushed the hair away from her face. "Wake up. It's time for us to go."

Her eyes opened slowly and she smiled. "So much for my beauty rest."

He turned his back as Fox cleaned up and dressed. The temptation to possess her was still too strong and he didn't trust himself.

Travis went to the barn doors. He could see movement inside the house through the open curtains. The rancher would be coming out to feed the livestock soon.

By the time he turned around, Fox was fully dressed. Almost as if she understood his need to focus on the pres-

ent, she refrained from talking about what they'd shared.
Instead, she joined him by the door, ready to go. "We
should head to the closest gas station and call Ashe while
he's still at home," she said. "But one thing worries me.
Do you think Marc Gray has had Ashe's phone tapped
without his knowledge?"

"You're trying to figure out how anyone could have
tracked us after we left the pueblo, aren't you?" He saw
her nod, and continued. "That's going to be a tough call.
But I can tell you this. If my brother even thought there
was a chance his phone was tapped, he would have warned
me."

"There are other possibilities. Both Andrews and Gray
found us at the college," she whispered. "Either of them
could have passed the word on to McNeely—if that's who
has been following us."

Moving quickly, they left the old man's property.

"Considering how little we know, I think it's best if I
don't call either my brother or Casey," Travis said at long
last.

"We still need another vehicle."

"I'll call a rental agency in Albuquerque where a friend
of mine works. John Francis will handle this for me so I
won't have to use a credit card and leave an electronic
trail."

Two hours later they met John near the turnoff to a
church near El Rancho, a small, old settlement farther east.

"I appreciate you meeting us here," Travis said, noting
that John's wife was in a second vehicle, probably the busi-
nessman's own station wagon. She waved when Travis
glanced over.

"It's not a problem, and nobody but my wife, Virginia,
knows I'm here." Sensing the urgency of their situation,
John kept things brief. "Once things settle down for you
two, stop by the agency and we can settle the account then.

I've filled out the paperwork in my own name, so you won't have any problems." He pointed out the various accessories of the sport utility vehicle he'd brought, as well as the camping gear inside. "I call this my Weekend Getaway Special and promote it for people who want to camp out once in a while without investing in all the camping equipment. The SUV is brand-new, with nearly a full tank of gas, so it'll take you anywhere you have to go. All you'll need is food and water."

"I won't forget this," Travis said.

As soon as John and his wife had driven away, Travis switched on the engine of the sports truck and they headed down the main highway in the same direction. "Santa Fe is our next stop."

"Good." Fox exhaled softly. "I was afraid that I'd have to talk you out of going on through to Albuquerque."

"No. This time we agree. The stakes are rising, so it's more important you take a look at your old house. With any luck, it'll trigger your memory."

For once, they seemed focused on the same goal. Fox studied his expression, wondering if what they'd shared had moved him as deeply as it had her. There'd been no promises made, and he hadn't taken her in the way she would have welcomed.

Yet there was a new fire in her soul now. In the midst of violence, a gentleness she hadn't expected had touched her.

TRAVIS GAVE FOX A LONG, furtive glance. He could see a change in her this morning. She seemed to have new confidence. The urge to talk to her about what had happened between them last night was nearly overwhelming. He had so many questions he wanted to ask her. Was she okay today? Would she remember what they'd shared and treasure it, or would she force it from her mind, and look at it as nothing more than a mistake? The answers were as important to him as the very air he breathed, but he remained silent.

Travis stared at the road, determined to stay focused on what they were about to do.

"Remember our agreement, Fox," he said. "I'll determine whether or not it's safe to approach the house. It's daylight now, and that makes it safer for us in one respect, but even more dangerous in another."

"I already accepted your terms. They made sense to me, and that's why I agreed to them in the first place."

Although her statement had been simply put, he sensed a challenge in her words. Fox was reminding him that she belonged only to herself. She'd shown him passion last night, but she remained her own person, relying on herself first, then him.

He was glad, for her sake. But the problem now was that he'd been so focused on protecting her, he'd forgotten to look after himself. What he felt for Fox went past the physical. Somewhere along the way, he'd surrendered a piece of his heart to her. His denying himself and putting her needs and feelings first had proved it.

But what the hell was he supposed to do about it now? He still had nothing to offer her. When this was over, he had to rejoin his unit.

From now on, he'd concentrate on the job. He needed to be ruthless—not vulnerable—in order to keep her safe.

FOX COULD FEEL TRAVIS'S tension. Last night they'd crossed a line that perhaps neither should even have ventured near. And now it was too late to turn back. She knew that her feelings for Travis had deepened.

Since the day he'd first kissed her years ago, she'd made love with him a million times in her mind. She'd envisioned every minute detail. He would enter her body and, before it was over, lay claim to her heart.

The reality she'd experienced last night, though less complete, had been far more intense, more passionate, and better than anything she'd ever imagined. He was a man who did everything with a power and gentleness that could shatter the dreams of a girl and reshape them into ones worthy of a woman.

She forced herself not to even glance at him now. She wouldn't burden him by asking for more than he could give. She'd known the score, and had chosen to gamble with her heart. Yet, no matter what lay ahead, she'd never regret last night.

"You're too quiet," he said. "We're going where you wanted to go. So what's up? Have you changed your mind?"

"No. I'm just trying to prepare myself. I keep thinking of something you said a long while back. Finding answers may unlock the door to a whole new set of problems."

"Are you afraid of what you'll learn, Fox?" he pressed.

She considered it carefully. "I'm afraid of how the knowledge will change me. By the time this is over, I'll have paid for everything I've learned. The person I'll be when we reach the finish line may be completely different from the person I am now."

"It's life that calls out to you. The People, the Navajo, define death as the inability to grow. When something ceases to evolve and mature—that is death."

"There's another death, Travis. A death of the soul. It happens when hope is shattered," she said, her voice barely audible.

He didn't answer right away. "Hope has a way of being reborn. It lifts itself out of the ashes like the phoenix," he said as they entered the rolling piñon- and juniper-covered foothills that signaled that Santa Fe was near.

A half hour later, the skies were dark and thunder rolled overhead as they finally entered a residential district east of the Plaza. Pueblo-style adobe houses were the standard in Santa Fe, a city with strict building codes that helped fend off urban sprawl and cookie-cutter homes. The established areas of the city never changed much at all. "Do you recognize anything around here?"

She remained silent, looking at each house, searching for something that would trigger a spark of memory. Then, as they reached the end of the next block, she saw the house that had always danced at the very edges of her mind.

"That's the address," Travis said, almost simultaneously.

"Yes," she said, in a mere whisper, as if afraid that it would vanish before her eyes. "I remember the long veranda and the way that old cottonwood shades the corner. I want to take a closer look. It doesn't look like anyone lives there now. See the For Rent sign?"

"We can't just walk up. For all we know, McNeely is inside, waiting."

"Okay, then drive on by and park down the street. We'll go up on foot," she insisted. "If we sense trouble, we'll cut and run."

"All right, but once we reach the house, let's duck behind the piñons beside the windows. Since it looks like the windows are open, we'll need to be quiet, but we can take a closer look inside from there."

"At least the neighborhood seems deserted. It looks like a middle-class section, so most of the people around here probably work. That's a good thing for us, too. The last thing we need are nosy neighbors calling the police."

"Some of these houses have garages, so don't count on the houses being empty," he warned. "There may even be a Neighborhood Watch program."

As they got out of the truck, half-formed images from

her past teased her, hovering just out of her reach. The threat of the upcoming storm tainted her efforts, continually distracting her. Then, a peal of thunder shattered the silence around them and a familiar terror gripped her.

Fox stared at the house down the street, her eyes on the veranda, and slowly a red haze, like a vision from hell, covered everything before her. Through it, she saw herself as a child huddled in the corner, her back pressed to the wall, the curtain of red shimmering around her. Shuddering violently, she stopped in her tracks.

"What's wrong?"

Travis's question, and the way he was gripping her hand, forced her back to the present. "I'm remembering something, but's it's mostly a jumbled image that makes no sense at all," she explained.

"We should come back in an hour or two," he said. "Maybe after the weather clears up."

"No. I have to see this through. That panic I feel whenever I hear thunder relates back to something that happened here, Travis. I know it." Fox stared ahead, willing herself to remember. "Something happened to me on a day like today, when the thunder was as deafening as it is now."

Travis gave her hand a reassuring squeeze, his gaze gentle as it rested on her. "All right. We'll see this through together."

They made their way slowly down the narrow street. When they got close to the house, Travis hurried with her into the shadows of the thick juniper hedge that bordered the property. "Now let's listen and see if we're alone. If we are, we can try to go inside," he whispered.

They started to look around the end of the hedge when Travis suddenly gestured for her to remain still.

Fox followed his gaze and saw a large, athletic-looking Anglo man in a short military-style haircut setting up trip wires around the back of the house. A closer look revealed that the front had already been booby-trapped. She'd never met McNeely, but intuition told her that he was the man laying the traps for them.

Travis edged back behind cover, and they left the hedge, returning quickly to the truck. "Under these circumstances, we can't go in there without backup. Since we don't have it, we're going to have to pass for now."

"Let's call Casey and Ashe, then stick around until they arrive, and make sure whoever's there doesn't go anywhere."

"I don't like it," Travis said after a brief pause. "If McNeely spots us and starts shooting, some of the residents who are home might be injured."

"We have to do something. We can't just allow him to move on. If you don't like my suggestion, come up with a better one."

He glared at her. Gone was the soft, yielding woman he'd held. That was the problem with Fox's passionate nature. A man would always have one hell of a time controlling her.

"I'm contacting Carl Andrews," he said at last. "He's monitoring our frequency. I'll ask him to send word to Ashe."

"Of course, if no help shows up," she said, "then we'll know for sure that Andrews is the inside man at the Marshals Service.

"That's one of the biggest reasons we should leave now."

"We can't do that and you know it. But don't worry. I've got another plan," she said.

Travis rolled his eyes. "Hang tight while I call in." Several moments later, he switched off the radio. "The storm's gaining strength," he warned. "The signal was getting a lot of interference."

"The storm will be our ally this time, covering up any

noise we make," she said. "Let's go back to the house. We can avoid the trip wires because it's still daytime and we know approximately where to look for them. We'll be careful to remain out of sight, but get close to an open window and take a look inside. That'll let us get some information while avoiding a confrontation."

"Bad idea. What if things go wrong? We have no guarantee that backup will arrive, and we might be spotted. If that happens, I wouldn't lay great odds on our chances of staying alive once they get what they need from us."

"Even if Andrews is the inside man, he's not going to be stupid enough to tip his hand. He may delay the request for backup, that's true, but he won't ignore it altogether. If you want to hedge our bets, call the tribal police and talk to Ashe directly."

He used the cell phone, but was unable to reach his brother. He then used the radio again but, this time, insisted on speaking to Gray. It didn't take long.

"Okay," he said, finished. "Let's go see what we can do."

The wind, which was rapidly increasing, grew to gale-force intensity and, five minutes later, the rain started to come down in thick sheets. Reaching the house at last, they edged in behind one of the piñon trees close to the window and could hear at least three men speaking inside. Fox concentrated, trying to understand the language they were using, but only one word struck a cord with her: "Kiselnikova."

Images of herself as a child writing the name—*her* name—on lined paper danced in her head. The last name of Sorge had been another phoney identity, that's why she hadn't recognized it before. Then, suddenly, a new image took shape. She was inside the house, running and afraid, doing her best to find a secure hiding place. The echoes of a fear she didn't understand gripped her. It was the same terror that always slammed the door on her memories. But this time she fought hard not to let go of the mental picture. Yet, even as she struggled to hold on to it, the image slipped away, dissolving into nothingness.

Frustration ripped through her, but instead of giving in to it, she shifted her attention once again to the conversation going on inside the house. Although she listened carefully and the language sounded vaguely familiar, she just couldn't make it out.

"They're speaking in Russian," Travis whispered.

"Hey, how about some English here," an American voice suddenly interrupted.

There was silence for a long moment. "We have been told that she will come here soon," an accented voice replied. "When she does, the woman goes with us, and the man dies. That's all you need to know."

"I can agree to that."

"McNeely," Travis mouthed.

"But what makes you think she still has the information you need?" McNeely added. "From what you've said, she was a kid when it all went down."

"She has the account numbers," the accented voice said. "She's the only one who could. And that money is ours."

"I don't care whose money it is—not as long as I get paid," McNeely said.

Travis peered inside the room cautiously, then quickly ducked down and pulled her away from the window. The rain was starting to let up, and the wind had stopped completely. "We're going. They've got a high-powered rifle and I'm willing to bet it was the weapon used to kill Prescott. My guess is that there's a skilled sniper in there, and that's information we need the others to know before they get here."

"Wait," she whispered. "I want to find out who told them to wait for us here."

"No." He mouthed the word, his eyes filled with intent.

Travis's tug on her arm was relentless. She had no choice except to follow him.

They'd just reached the hedge when they heard the wail of sirens. A breath later, two police cars suddenly appeared from each end of the street. Travis saw McNeely charge out the back door. Another armed man he didn't recognize followed instantly.

"The cops are too far away. I'm going after them. Stay here and help the officers."

Travis raced around to the back of the house. As a third armed man darted out the door, Travis intercepted him and immediately kicked the gun out of his hand. His enemy recouped quickly, launching a vicious counterattack.

Fox saw Travis lose hold of his own pistol in the fight. Knowing she had to help Travis, she raced toward him, but someone opened fire from inside the house.

At that instant only one thought ran through her mind. The police would shoot back, and one stray bullet could end Travis's life. As she approached the men locked in battle, she saw the long hunting knife in the hand of Travis's adversary. Her stomach sank. Travis had nothing with which to defend himself.

"Fox, stay back," Travis said, his voice low and lethal.

Travis was crouched low, his hands extended as he dodged two knife thrusts in sequence. Travis was quicker, but without a weapon, he was at a disadvantage. She had to do something right now.

Picking up a piece of firewood from a stack underneath the veranda roof, she threw it as hard as she could at the man with the knife. He saw it coming and ducked. The firewood sailed past him, missing Travis's head by mere inches.

Seeing an opening, Travis aimed a disabling kick at his adversary's knee. The man grunted and fell to the ground, and Travis was on him in a flash. Two more shots were fired from somewhere close by as Travis pinned his opponent, the knife now at the man's throat.

Two armed policemen came rushing around the corners of the house. Their guns were trained on her and Travis. "Don't move!"

"Officers, these men came after us," Fox said quickly as the policemen came up and one of them handcuffed her. Travis placed the knife out of reach of his captive, but refused to let his opponent up until they were both handcuffed.

"We'll sort it out later, ma'am," the officer said, then started reading her her rights.

Fox's throat felt so tight she could scarcely breathe. If the others came after them now, they'd be sitting ducks despite the police. And she and Travis would be easy targets in jail. "We called the police. We're not guilty of anything except defending ourselves."

"The only call SFPD received was from a Mrs. Perea, who lives across the street. Are you her?"

Fox considered lying, but then decided against it. "No." The thought suddenly occurred to her that perhaps neither Andrews nor Gray had relayed their call.

"There are two more men, armed and dangerous, around here somewhere," Travis said as he was pulled roughly to his feet. "One is an ex-Army Ranger named McNeely."

"We'll look into it," the officer snapped.

The rain and the wind chilled Fox to the bone as they, and the man Travis had captured, were led to waiting squad cars. This was turning out to be one very bad day, after all.

Chapter Fourteen

The police officers transported Fox and Travis together because she had refused to quiet down unless they did. As they rode in the back of the squad car, Travis was acutely aware of everything about her, from the warmth of her body to the way her wet clothing accentuated her soft curves. Images flashed in his mind as he visualized the way she'd looked as she'd responded to him when he'd made love to her.

Muttering a curse under his breath, Travis tried to discipline his thoughts. He couldn't seem to stop wanting her. Even now, when they were in serious trouble, he couldn't stop thinking about her in that way.

He tried to concentrate on his next move. As soon as they gave him his one telephone call, he'd contact Ashe at the station. He needed his brother's help and the U.S. Marshals Service's clout to get him out of this mess.

His gaze strayed back to Fox. It hurt him to see her in handcuffs. He wanted to take the damn things off her wrists and pull her against him.

Fox looked up at him and gave him a reassuring smile. Her courage never ceased to surprise him. Sensing his concern, she was letting him know she could handle this. But, he'd seen the way her bottom lip had quivered for a fraction of a second before she'd bitten down on it.

A sweet ache pierced him. Cursing the handcuffs that kept him from reaching for her, he started to say something when she shook her head.

"I'm okay," she mouthed, defiance shining in her gaze.

As usual, she didn't want his comfort. Her self-possession challenged him, stirring his blood.

They arrived at the station a short while later and were led inside. Casey came out of one of the offices, badge in hand, and met the arresting officer. "Release this man and woman. I'll accept full responsibility. They're in my custody now."

Fox stared hard at Travis. "You just *had* to go one-on-one with that guy, didn't you? You really do pick the most awful times to go macho on me."

"You were the one who insisted on staying there, just in case they tried to escape. Did you all of a sudden forget that part?" he managed through clenched teeth.

"You didn't just catch one of the bad guys. You got us both arrested." She looked at Casey and shook her head. "These Redhawk brothers are just trouble waiting to happen. Run away as fast as you can before it's too late for you."

Casey bit her lip to keep from laughing as she led them into an empty office. "Have a seat, guys. I'm sorry I couldn't get here sooner. It took us longer to requisition the chopper than it did to make the trip. We also had some problems flying through the storm."

Travis looked behind her. "'Us'? You mean my brother is here, too?"

"Yes. He's taking care of some red tape right now. Now tell me, what happened? We heard about your radio call, but your message was really cryptic."

"We didn't know much at that time, but we have a lot more we can tell you now," Fox said, then recounted the conversation they'd overheard back at the house.

"What I can add to that," Travis said, "is that the man I fought is a trained soldier and his fighting style was definitely Russian. He also had a tattoo on his arm. I never got a really close look at it, but I think it might have been Cyrillic in origin. I've seen similar ones during intelligence briefings."

"I'll have it photographed and sent in for analysis. What we do know so far is consistent with that. The suspect's name is Yuri Lazarev. Ashe and I are going to question him at length soon." Casey looked at Travis, then at Fox. "Anything else?"

"That's about it," Fox said. "Except for McNeely definitely being part of this. Travis recognized him."

Travis nodded, then sat back, trying to unwind. He was dead tired, but he always felt this way after action. He'd be okay in another hour or so, not counting bruises.

"How about giving me a few minutes with Lazarev?" Travis suggested. "I bet I can get some answers from him."

"Not a chance. We'll be keeping things strictly by the book. I don't want some hotshot lawyer throwing the case out."

"What about the gunshots I heard coming from inside the house?" Fox asked. "There must have been another man who didn't escape."

"He's dead. We have an ID. He's a Farmington man by the name of William McNeely."

"I had a feeling that was him. Billy's Stan McNeely's cousin and a Ranger wannabe." Travis considered everything he'd just learned. "Lazarev is or was a soldier. I'm certain of it. That gives me some common ground with him. Let me in on the questioning. I may be able to help you."

"This isn't the military, Travis. It's in the hands of the U.S. Marshal's office and local agencies now, and we'll handle it our way. Sit tight. I'll be back shortly.'' Casey stood.

TWO HOURS LATER, TRAVIS was ready to punch the wall, but neither Casey nor Ashe had come to join them yet.

Fox had been quiet—uncharacteristically so. She'd undoubtedly sensed his vile mood and was keeping her distance.

Another half hour passed before Ashe finally came in. He raised an eyebrow as he studied his brother's bruised face. "You look like hell. The other guy looks worse, though, so I guess you handled yourself okay.''

"You couldn't have taken him, little brother.''

"If it comforts you to think that, go right ahead," Ashe countered with a lazy grin.

"Don't get too cocky. There are at least two more who got away," Travis said.

"Stan McNeely was one, I gather," Ashe acknowledged. "You said he's bad news, right?''

"Very bad news." Travis noted that his brother had used the man's name. According to Navajo beliefs, the name of one's enemy was an important weapon. The Diné believed that the power inherent in the name could be used against its owner. Not a traditionalist, Travis wasn't counting on that, but he decided to use the name often, too. At this point, he'd take whatever help he could get.

"I understand it took three cops to get Lazarev out of the squad car and into the station," Casey said. "McNeely can't be any worse than that.''

"It's what's in a man's head that makes him a lethal adversary. Lazarev is big, and a skilled fighter, but when I faced him, his heart wasn't in the fight. What he really wanted to do was get away. With McNeely, it's a different story. The fight itself is what makes him come alive. He savors it. That's a far more dangerous mind-set," Travis warned.

"I ran Lazarev's tattoo through our files," Casey said. "It's the mark used by a gang of Russian criminals, most of them ex-soldiers, who've been operating in the United States off and on for many years. They're called Boyebaya Gruppa. It literally means 'combat group.' Traditionally, they've been responsible for some really nasty crimes here and in the eastern block."

"And they're the ones who murdered my natural parents?" Fox asked.

"I can't say for sure yet. What I can tell you is that being arrested carries a high price for anyone in this particular gang. If they even suspect that Lazarev cooperated with the authorities, he's a dead man. Since we've let the word out that he's being most helpful," Casey added, "Lazarev knows now, as we do, that he'll be a dead man within hours if he ever makes bail."

"So why isn't he talking yet?" Travis asked.

"He wants to try and cut a deal with us first," Casey replied. "He's asking for complete immunity and protection in exchange for his testimony. We can grant that, but only if the information is worth it. So far, all we've got is a hint that the man who killed Prescott was the one who disappeared along with McNeely. The sniper is running their operation. They all answer to him."

"He has told us one other thing," Ashe said. "Fox's family name is Kiselnikova."

"He's telling you the truth," Fox said softly. "I remember that much now. But I don't have the account numbers they're looking for. I wish I did. It would give me some leverage."

An incredible restlessness gnawed at Travis. Instinct urged him to remain a moving target. "I really don't think Fox and I should stick around here."

"We're in a police station. Where would it be safer than here?" Fox countered, then rolled her eyes, realizing what she'd just said.

"Prescott got killed outside a courthouse, surrounded by the law, remember?" Travis smiled grimly. "The presence of the police doesn't always make places as safe as we'd like them to be."

Casey nodded. "You're right, especially because the sniper is still out there. And in New Mexico, all he needs to do to get another high-powered rifle is break into a deer hunter's house. We've got a lot of them around here."

"Is there any way we can get some cash?" Travis asked.

"No problem," Casey said. "I'll be right back." She stepped out of the room and returned several minutes later with a roll of bills. "Stay in touch."

"Where's our vehicle?" Travis asked.

"It's out front," Casey said. "I won't even ask you where you got it."

Travis smiled. "It's not stolen, really. Look at it as an example of creative thinking and a friend who's in a position to cut through the paperwork."

"And a result of sore feet," Fox added.

As Travis left with Fox, a purely instinctive fear overtook him. He wasn't worried about himself—he'd faced far worse. It was Fox, and what might lie ahead for her, that made his guts turn to ice.

"I wish I knew who we're really fighting." Fox climbed into the truck, looking in every direction. "The men who came after us were only following orders. We need to capture the one in charge of the operation, the Russian with McNeely. He'll hold the key to everything, including how Prescott became part of their gang and the identity of the person inside the Marshals Service who's leaking information."

"Let Ashe and Casey tackle that part. You have to concentrate on remembering your past. After that, everything else will fall into place," Travis said.

As they headed south along the interstate, Fox studied the road signs. "We're going to the car dealership in Albuquerque?"

He nodded. "We should be there by six, at least. Most dealers are open late this time of year."

"We can't go looking like we do right now. We have to stop someplace and clean up a bit first. My clothes still have caked mud on them from the storm and that mess in Santa Fe. You look even worse. That bruise on your jaw is positively daunting. If we get near that dealership looking like this, someone's going to call the cops on us."

He'd been far more worried about McNeely lying in wait somewhere, than in presentability. "Good point," he admitted. "We'll attract security guards instead of salesmen, the way we look now."

"Lucky for you I'm here to remind you of the niceties the Rangers forgot to include in your training. Face it, Mr. Redhawk, you need me."

Travis groaned. "Fate's punishing me. That's got to be it," he muttered.

They made a quick stop at a Bernalillo shopping center, buying jeans, shirts, and fresh underwear. Sure they hadn't been followed, they continued their journey toward Albuquerque on the old highway west of the interstate.

"We'll stop at the first motel we find," he said.

Trapped in the confines of the vehicle as the miles stretched out before them, he found all his thoughts had become focused on the woman beside him. The wanting, the needing, were as natural to him now as sun was to the desert.

"What do you think about when you get moody and quiet like that?" she asked softly. "Do you think of me at all?"

Her question tugged at his restraint. Fox had never experienced physical love, he knew that. He had to be careful with her. Then he remembered how her body had opened to his caress, and how hot and wet she'd been as she'd welcomed his touch. Fire swept over him.

"Are you keeping secrets from me?" she pressed.

"I was just wondering what it would take to tame a fox," he answered at long last.

Fox smiled slowly. "With wild things, it's always best to go slowly. Test the waters, so to speak. If your approach isn't exactly right and well-timed, you're likely to get your hand torn off."

He chuckled. And that, he thought, summed up his relationship with the only woman who'd ever carved a place for herself in his heart.

AS FAR AS MOTELS WENT, it sure wasn't much, and she was glad they wouldn't be staying. Since they were only there to clean up, they decided to save money and rent only one of the closet-size rooms. Now, as she looked at the torn window screens and the flickering light fixture, she was happy that they'd stayed together. They could compensate for the lack of security this way.

As Fox pulled her new clothes out of the shopping bag, she slowly became aware of the way Travis was watching her. Emotions stirred the air and a delicious shiver raced up her spine.

Knowing how dangerous it was to allow desire to go unchecked, she tried hard to focus on what she had to do next. It didn't help. "Mind if I shower first? It was my idea, after all."

"Go right ahead. I'm used to getting down and dirty. A little caked mud and slime don't bother me nearly as much as they do you," he teased, a ghost of a smile playing on his lips.

"That explains your choice of motels," she countered playfully. "Although this place does have a certain charm...along with resident pets." She watched a cricket hop across the room, then duck behind the curtains.

"So it's not the Royal Sands. Go take your shower. We won't be here long."

Fox closed the door behind her. As she threw back the shower curtain, she saw an enormous, orange-colored centipede trying to climb up the slippery side of the tub. "Bring me your gun, Travis," she joked, opening the bathroom door again. "I refuse to bathe with creepy worms."

"You don't have to call me names," he kidded. "I have no intention of going into the shower with you." Travis saw the seven-inch centipede now scrambling toward the drain. "Oh, you didn't mean me," he said, feigning surprise.

"Disappointed? I didn't realize that worm talk would get you excited, but I suppose there's no accounting for taste."

He looked at the centipede, then back at her. "What exactly would you like me to do now? I can't just squash it, you know. They're ropy and hard to kill."

"Ah, I see. Professional courtesy."

"I could, of course, let you handle this yourself."

"I thought things like this were all part of my bodyguard's job," she answered, nonplussed. "They *are* poisonous." She glanced around and saw a plumber's helper beside the toilet. "Ah, as I said, this is one class joint." She handed it to him. "Here, pick him up with this and toss him outside."

"Forget it. That'll take too long." He grabbed a towel from the rack and tossed it over the centipede. Bundling it up, he then shook it free outside the screenless window. "Okay, miss, you're all set. Is there anything else I can do for you? Scrub your back...or thereabouts?"

"Out," she said, closing the door behind him.

As she began to undress, she could hear Travis moving about in the next room. Fox stood beneath the cold spray of the shower trying to banish the ache that suddenly filled her. Her feelings for Travis went so deep they felt like an intrinsic part of her being. Yet instinct assured her that she and Travis didn't belong together.

Hot tears fell down her cheeks as she forced herself to face the inevitable. Travis would never welcome the closeness growing between them, because accepting that kind of vulnerability went against everything he was. Acknowledging the truth at last, she felt an undeniable sense of loss.

There was only one answer now. She, too, would have to keep a tight rein on her emotions but, unlike Travis, that went against everything she was. As she considered how she was going to manage it, she had a most annoying realization. Travis had shown remarkable restraint all along. She'd been the one who'd given in to her emotions.

She took a deep breath, turned off the shower and dried off. As she saw her reflection in the mirror, she noted that her eyes were still a bit puffy from the tears she'd shed. Hoping he wouldn't notice, she dressed quickly and walked out into the bedroom.

"The bathroom's all yours."

"I won't take long," Travis said, moving away from the window where he'd been standing guard.

He turned, then stopped, studying her expression for what seemed an eternity.

Seeing the fear and sadness reflected in his eyes, her throat constricted. "What's wrong?"

He didn't answer right away and, to Fox, each of those moments stretched out and lasted a lifetime.

"I need to know if you've lost confidence in me."

Fox stared at him in surprise. "Why on earth would you think that? We're a team. I couldn't have made it this far without you."

"Then why are you holding back on me? I know you've been crying. But instead of talking to me about what's bothering you, you come out here pretending nothing is wrong."

With a sigh, she sat on the edge of the bed. She couldn't lie to him, but she knew that there were things that should not be said. She measured her words carefully. "I was crying because you make me feel crazy and none of it makes sense!"

Travis smiled, his expression gentling. "In that case, welcome to the club. If I knew how to cry, I'd join you."

She looked up suddenly and glowered at him. "You are so infuriating! You get me to admit that I'm frustrated beyond words, but then act as if my reaction is nothing but a feminine weakness you can rise above without any problem. Do you really have that much control or is it that you just don't feel anything deeply?"

His expression darkened. "I feel and I care. You know better than to ask that. I've held back with you because I don't want you to get hurt. If I didn't feel anything for you, I wouldn't worry about what could happen."

She saw the angry fire in his eyes, but she still refused to back down. "Stop being so darned careful with me. For once, just *show* me what you're feeling!"

A hunger she'd never even dreamed could be real sparked in his eyes. Travis took her hand and pulled her roughly to him. He held her tightly, forcing her to remain still as his tongue entered her mouth, seeking her fiery response.

Flames danced along her spine. He had overpowered her, but it was the strength of their feelings that made her surrender.

Travis released her a breathless moment later. "Do you understand now how dangerous desire can be without control?"

"You can meet any opponent with courage, but you're afraid of love," she replied, shaking her head slowly and turning away from him. "I don't understand that, but I know I deserve a man who is not afraid to reach out for what he wants." She took his place by the window. "Go take your shower. I'll keep watch."

His anger was a palpable force in the tiny room. As he came up behind her, she turned around, ready to face him squarely. Slowly, Travis reached out and rubbed his knuckles over her cheek in a light caress. "Sometimes you show more courage than common sense. That's one of the reasons I care about you so much. And why I *will* hold back around you. You need someone to watch over you, whether or not you realize it."

Before she could gather her wits, he walked into the next room. A moment later, she heard the shower being turned on.

No way was he getting away with a comment like that. No one had the right to tell her what was best for her. If all she'd wanted for herself was to be looked after, she would have bought a Doberman.

She strode up to the bathroom door. They'd continue their argument while he showered. With him naked and her clothed, she'd have the advantage. Ignoring the warmth that spiraled through her at the thought, she took a deep breath and prepared to go inside.

Fox reached for the door but, as she turned the handle, it clicked and stopped. He'd anticipated her and locked the door. A sound much like muffled laughter reached her a moment before his voice rose in a country-and-western song about a "misbehavin' lover."

Chapter Fifteen

A tense silence stretched out between them as they drove down the highway to the car dealership in Albuquerque's Northeast Heights. She knew he'd deliberately baited her with his comment back at the motel and there was no way she'd give him the satisfaction of an argument now.

It was after sundown by the time they arrived. Travis parked a block down from the sprawling car lot, wanting to stay as anonymous as possible. "The day shift has gone home, no doubt, and there will probably be a smaller crew there now. I don't know if that's an advantage or not."

"Let's walk around the lot and get a feel for the place," she said. "As we do that, we can keep an eye out for any employee old enough to have worked here when Prescott was around."

"There's an old janitorial truck parked around back," he said, pointing ahead. "And that janitor seems to fit the profile. Let's walk over there casually."

She sped up, eager to get started, but Travis reached for her hand, slowing her down. "Ease up a bit."

"Sorry. I'm just so tired of waiting and having to be patient."

"Don't become so focused on only one goal. Relax and keep your eyes and ears open. Otherwise you might end up missing other important things in the process," he warned.

"Is that part of Ranger training?" she asked.

"No, it's more a lesson life's taught me. I spent so many years concentrating on carving out my future that I think I missed a lot in the process."

She looked at him in surprise. "What is it that you think you missed? You've had more adventure in your life than anyone else I know, including Ashe."

He grinned. "Now *that* warms the cockles of my heart."

She chuckled, then grew serious. "Don't keep me in suspense. What is that you think you've missed?"

Travis said nothing for several long moments as they strolled across the asphalt, passing through rows of shiny new cars and trucks. "Connections. When you move continually from one thing to another, everyday things slip past you."

"Like love?" she whispered.

"That, and other things, too. Like the chance to be with old friends you share a history with."

"You and I share a history, in case you missed it," she said.

"I know. You've always worshiped the ground I walk on."

"Stuff it," she answered.

"That's the spirit. Deny everything. I'd do that, too, if I were you."

"Actually that's your problem. Half the time you even keep things from yourself."

They reached the back doors before he could reply. Travis suddenly pointed to the Shiprock Rodeo bumper sticker at the rear of the janitorial van. "I think we just got a big break," he said.

Travis greeted the elderly Navajo man who came out to retrieve supplies from the van. "Good evening, uncle," he said, using the term of respect.

"What brings you here tonight, nephew? If you're looking for a job, I've got nothing to offer you."

Travis shook his head. "What we need is information about this place," Travis said honestly. "Can you help us? We'll keep everything you say in confidence."

"What do you need to know?"

"The information we're searching for dates back quite a bit. Can you tell us how long you've worked here?" Travis asked.

"I've been cleaning this place about fifteen years. I also take care of several offices in the area. Now tell me what it is you need."

Travis decided that the best way to get the man's co-operation was to put all his cards on the table. He identified himself, and explained what he could about Fox's case.

"I remember hearing about this," he said. "My name's George Gray Eyes. My relatives keep me up with what's happening on the Rez, and I read the newspapers. I'll help you, if I can."

"Tell us about the dealership's owners and the type of people they hire."

"It's not like it was many years ago," Gray Eyes said. "When I first started here, people worked until late at night along with me. The salesmen were always excited, coming and going all the time. They called themselves 'full service,' and they'd even go and pick up owner trade-ins."

He shrugged, then continued. "These days it's a lot different. The salespeople here now are a mixture of retirees and kids with useless college degrees. Everything's more laid-back now. But, of course, after the big scandal, you'd expect things to settle down."

"What big scandal?" Fox asked.

"The former owner and the sales manager got into trouble with the police," he said. "I particularly remember that sales manager. He was one bad piece of work—a foreigner with the eyes of a coyote." He paused, gathering his thoughts before he continued. "One morning he and a few of the other top people just didn't show up for work. The company closed down a short time later. I read in the papers that the bank accounts had been cleaned out."

"How long was it before the dealership was back in business?" Fox asked.

"A new owner took over in a matter of weeks. I got my job back but the rest of the people were newly hired. I don't think they ever found the old owner or his people, though the police questioned everyone. The stories I heard claimed that they'd been running a car-theft ring right from the premises, and that's what those so-called trade-ins usually were. Some young fellows, the part-time people mostly, were doing the stealing. I remember one college kid, a really nice boy who always left a can of pop for me on his desk, was arrested. But they let him go. I don't know about the others, but I figured that particular kid was just trying to get money to pay for college."

"Do you remember his name?" Travis asked.

Gray Eyes shook his head. "When I read about the former district attorney, Prescott, I thought that it looked like the same kid, but it's been too many years and the hair didn't look right. I can't say for sure that it was him."

As they left the dealership, Fox glanced at Travis. "It really annoys me when people say that Prescott was a nice guy. He killed my parents."

"We present different faces to different people. To see the real person, you have to look past all the smoke screens."

As Fox mulled over his words, he stared at the interstate ahead, lost in his own thoughts. He took the exit through the Big I back toward Santa Fe, though he really wasn't sure where they'd go next. The only thing he knew for sure was that he wanted to stay on the move.

He glanced over at her, glad she was safe and, more importantly, here with him. He knew now that when it finally came time for him to leave and go rejoin his unit, it would feel as if he were tearing off a piece of himself and leaving it behind.

He looked at her, realizing how beautiful she'd grown these past few weeks. Her skin was tanned and her golden hair shimmered like molten gold. A different kind of desire forked through him. It was a need to unite with her, body and soul.

He gripped the steering wheel so hard his knuckles turned pearly white under the strain. It was pointless to think like this. No matter how much he cared, he just wasn't the type to get a nine-to-five and live a life punctuated by routines. To think of marrying her and then end up dragging her from base to base was just as crazy.

Aware of her lengthy silence, he turned away from his introspection. Whenever she stopped talking and started planning, there was bound to be trouble. "Don't do this," he said.

"Do what?"

"I can hear the little wheels spinning in your head. You're hatching up something. I want to know what it is."

"Force yourself not to sound so enthusiastic," she replied. "You know, for someone reputed to like adventure, you're a downright stick-in-the-mud at times."

Travis bit back a curt answer. "I'm trying to protect you even though you're constantly putting yourself in the line of fire. Considering you haven't gotten yourself killed, you should be thanking me for doing a fantastic job."

Fox made a derisive sound. "I really don't understand you, you know. You said you enjoy a challenge and not knowing what each day will bring. From that standpoint alone, you should be deeply grateful to be part of my investigation."

He groaned. "It's not *your* investigation."

"Sure, it is. I've got more at stake here than anyone else."

He would have argued with her, but he knew it would be futile. "Okay, you've had your fun. Now stop trying to evade the issue. What's on your mind?"

"I've been thinking of those account numbers that everyone seems to want, and I've got an idea." She shifted to face him more squarely.

Travis saw the flash of excitement in her eyes and the restless anticipation that made her entire body vibrate. His thoughts suddenly shifted to another time when he'd felt her trembling in his arms. Everything feminine in her had reached out to him in expectation.

He quickly looked away, cursing the passion that clawed at his gut every time he looked at her.

"I *know* I don't have those account numbers," she said. "My parents didn't, either. They were protected witnesses, and their few possessions were taken into government custody. If anything had been there, the U.S. Marshals Service would have found it. The crooks don't have the numbers, either, so that leaves only one possible answer."

"That they're still inside the house in Santa Fe, hidden someplace," he finished for her.

"That's it. We need to go back there."

"Let me call Casey and my brother. They can meet us there."

She shook her head. "You can't. Don't you see? Our most dangerous adversary is still the inside man at the U.S. Marshals Service. Casey is part of that organization and may inadvertently trust the wrong person. If that happens, we could all end up dead."

"My brother and Casey are the only allies I know we can count on. If we're going to that house again, we're going to need backup. McNeely won't be far away, believe me. He doesn't give up—ever.''

"Okay. Let's compromise. We'll meet with Casey and Ashe somewhere else and sound them out to see what progress they've made on the case. If they've found the leak, we'll play it straight. Otherwise we'll keep what I suspect about the account numbers being hidden at the house to ourselves. The Gruppa has probably searched the house many times, but let's not point out that we believe they've missed something."

"You don't get my point. I don't want to just meet with them. I want backup if we're going to the house."

"I know, but the disadvantages outweigh the advantages. Remember that if Casey does come along with us, she'll have to play it by the book. She'll need search warrants and that will mean getting more people involved. By the time all the legalities are covered, we'll have lost the small edge we have now."

"All right. That's a good point. Let's see if they've learned anything new from Lazarev and play it by ear after that."

Travis stopped at a pay phone. He made arrangements to meet his brother and Casey, filled them in on what they'd learned about the car dealership, then rejoined Fox.

As they drove toward the rendezvous, a place halfway between Santa Fe and Albuquerque, Travis could feel the hair on the back of his neck standing on end. "My brother let me know that they've made substantial progress though they still don't have the sniper who killed Prescott, but he wouldn't give me any details on the phone. That was a good precaution, but I sure wish he could have come straight out with it."

"You've always preferred the direct route," Fox said with a knowing smile. "But, in this case, I think Ashe's caution was justified."

"Ashe used to say I'd make a great cop if only I could stop trying to solve problems by ramming headlong into them. Maybe it's time I learned his way of doing things. I've got to tell you, the more I see of my brother's work, the more I'm learning to value what he does. The tribe needs its cops far more than the country needs another Ranger."

"Are you thinking of someday joining the tribal police?"

He smiled, then shrugged. "Only if I could outrank my brother. I don't think I'd want him as my boss."

As they took the exit that led to a Rio Grande pueblo, he saw his brother's tribal-police vehicle ahead in the dark by the roadside. Casey was standing beside Ashe, waiting. Travis remained next to Fox as they stopped and went out to meet them.

Ashe glanced at Fox, then gave Travis a long, thoughtful look. Although Travis instantly schooled his expression into one of polite neutrality, he had a feeling Ashe had already read his body language and knew of his deepening feelings for Fox.

"How are you holding up?" Casey asked Fox.

"I'm keeping it together, all things considered."

"I've got some new developments to tell you about," Casey said. "I had the police send me a photo of that missing car dealer. He's the Russian man we now have in custody."

"That discovery should have rattled him," Fox said. "Has he come clean?"

"Not yet. He wants a guarantee of federal protection before he tells us anything about Prescott. But that's not the way we work."

"So, basically, you're in a standoff," Fox said.

"He'll come around, especially now that we've confronted him with all those other outstanding warrants the

Albuquerque police have on him. We're in a stronger position. We just have to play it cool," Casey said. "In the meantime, I did a search through other federal data banks for the name 'Kiselnikova' and I have some preliminary information for you. Your parents were accepted into WITSEC after testifying against the Boyebaya Gruppa. At the time, the gang was, among other things, extorting protection money from legitimate businesses, trying to gain a foothold in southern Arizona. Your parents' testimony brought those activities to a halt, but in the process they became targets. The U.S. Marshals Service relocated them from Phoenix, Arizona, where they'd been living, to Santa Fe, New Mexico, and gave them new identities. At the time we didn't know the gang was also operating here."

"Why were they kept in the Southwest at all?" Fox asked.

"Your mother and father insisted. Your mother had asthma and she did better in the dry desert air than anywhere else."

"How did their enemies finally find them?" Fox queried.

"I'm still piecing that part together. The Marshals Service records have been altered, so I have to verify everything through other agencies. From what I've learned, it seems your father loved horseracing. When he entered WITSEC, he was warned not to visit any tracks—that it would be a sure way for his enemies to find him. But, at some point, he decided to indulge his habit. Your mother and father were spotted, followed home and killed."

"And I witnessed their murders?"

"Yes, we believe so," Casey replied.

Fox didn't say anything.

Feeling helpless and hating every second of it, Travis watched the interplay of raw emotions that flickered across her face. He'd gone through a lot of hardships in his own life, but at least he'd always known who he was and whom he could trust.

"And I was taken to a foster home right after that?"

Casey nodded. "You were actually taken into custody by Children's Services before the U.S. Marshals came on the scene. An attempt was made on your life. By then, our people had the paperwork we needed to take custody of you and we placed you with your foster parents. We chose the one place we figured no one would ever think of looking for you—a very remote and unpopulated area of the Rez in northeastern Arizona."

"The Johnsons must have heard about me through their government connections and decided, somewhere along the way, to adopt me," Fox reasoned. "Is that right?"

"Nick Johnson worked for the U.S. Attorney's office and that's how he knew about the case," Casey said. "Our office agreed that letting them go through with the adoption was the best thing that could happen to you."

"The rest of what we have is speculation," Ashe said. "We're figuring that years ago, when Prescott was nothing more than just another punk, he was recruited by the Gruppa and sent to New Mexico to eliminate your biological parents. He knew the area, had no foreign accent, and wouldn't be easy to trace back to them. He was probably kept in the dark about who they were, because he was expendable. Then, from the moment he did the hit for them, the Gruppa owned him."

"What about the bank accounts the crooks are looking for?" Fox asked. "Where did that money come from?"

"We think your parents skimmed off some money the group was laundering, and put it into accounts no one knew anything about," Ashe said. "From what we've pieced together, it got to be several million. That's why they've never given up searching."

"Maybe my parents were planning to eventually negotiate a trade-off with the criminals—the money for their freedom," Fox said. "They would have made sure the figure was substantial enough to give them real bargaining power. They were probably desperate to find a way to live a normal life. Living in hiding, always looking behind you in fear, is no way to live."

Travis noted that no one said anything. They respected Fox too much to try to fill her mind with empty assurances.

"Come back with us now, Fox," Casey said. "The answers you're searching for won't do you any good if you get yourself killed."

Fox shook her head and sadness tainted her words as she spoke. "There was a time when I was perfectly happy to let others make the decisions for me, and tell me what I should do. But I'm an adult now and I deserve the chance to call my own shots. I may not know much about my past, but I know myself and what I'm capable of accomplishing if I follow my instincts. I'll see this through and finish what I've started."

"All right," Casey agreed. "We'll play it your way. But watch your back, and keep your radio handy. If you get in over your head, we'll be there to back you up."

Fox glanced over at their vehicle, lost in thought. "Speaking of the radio…"

"Are you having problems with it?" Casey asked.

"I was just wondering about that beacon it's supposed to have. Can you tell me for sure how to turn it off?"

Casey went to their truck, and saw they'd disabled the radio beacon completely by disconnecting the battery contact. "You went to more trouble than you needed." She turned the setting screw on the base of the unit with the screwdriver blade of her pocketknife. "That's all you would have had to do. That breaks the connection."

Travis glanced at Fox.

"Hey, I didn't miss that look. What's going on, guys?" Casey furrowed her brow.

"We disconnected the battery after we found out we were being tracked much too easily by McNeely," Fox explained. "Andrews told us how to turn it off, we thought, but when we verified it with Gray, he said it wasn't off. He turned a different screw on the bottom. At that point we didn't know whom to trust, so we interrupted the connection to the battery manually, just to make sure."

"You turned the same screw Andrews had us turn, by the way, only you went a full one hundred and eighty degrees," Travis added.

Casey dropped back against the side of the truck, lost in thought. "Andrews could have made a mistake. I doubt he's even seen this new-model radio up close, and Gray isn't a tech expert at all. He's an administrator who hasn't been in the field for years. I don't think either man gave you the wrong directions on purpose," she said slowly.

"But you're not sure," Travis observed.

"No, I'm not."

"I have an idea," Fox said, giving Travis a hard look, warning him to be quiet. "Let's find out which marshal, Gray or Andrews, was in Phoenix when the phone call that first tracked down my whereabouts was made to the tribal police. That call, if you all remember, came from Phoenix."

"I'll check, but I'll have to go back to the office for that. There's no way I can access the information out here. But I have to say that I seriously doubt Marc Gray would turn traitor," Casey said flatly. "He's too high up in the Marshals Service, which means he's had countless heavy-duty background checks done on him. Andrews could be our man, but his record is spotless, too."

"Both need checking into, though," Ashe said.

"We'll leave that to you, then," Travis said. "It's time for all of us to get back on the road."

Casey nodded. "Normally, I'd ask you what your plans are, but you know, for once, I just don't want to know."

Her words echoed in Travis's head as he waited with Fox by their own vehicle for Casey and his brother to drive off. A chill as relentless as an icy blade pried into him. There were too many deadly secrets dogging their steps now. Trust was no longer an option. Fox had been right not to take Casey into their confidence. Casey, in her own way, was as vulnerable as they were. Her loyalties to the people she served could affect her judgment at the wrong time.

Travis glanced at Fox. There was a sadness inside her now, like a shadow over her soul. Obeying an instinct nearly as old as the land that surrounded them, he drew her into his arms.

Fox melted against him, offering no resistance and inviting his caress. His lips pressed against hers. He thrust his tongue forward, joining their bodies in the only way that was possible to them.

Though he cradled her head with his hand, the force of his kiss pushed her head back. He deepened the kiss, needing more, yet knowing it was not to be.

With a groan, he slid his hands downward, pulling her hips up and rubbing her intimately against him. She gasped and whimpered softly and, in a storm of passion, he kissed away her soft cries.

He broke the kiss slowly and reluctantly, knowing that in another second they'd both be lost.

Her breathing was ragged as she looked up at him. "I've wanted you to kiss me like this for forever. What took you so long?"

Travis grinned slowly, enjoying the taste of her that still

lingered in his mouth. He recognized the glow of passion in her eyes and knew it matched his own.

"We have to go," he said, his breathing unsteady. "It's too dangerous out here."

"You're right about that," she replied, her voice incredibly soft.

He felt her drawing away from him and back into herself. Maybe it was for the best. Everything male in him wanted her complete surrender. But that sweet victory would carry too high a price.

Even as he possessed her, he, too, would be possessed. And after that, neither of them would ever be the same again.

Chapter Sixteen

Fox kept her eyes on the road ahead. It had been so simple when she and Travis had been kids. He'd kissed her and sent a thrill all through her body. Back then it had been so magical. There had been no complications, except her dad calling out to her and interrupting the moment.

Now everything was muddled. Travis was a man determined to remain alone. He wanted her—she sensed that—but he continued to guard his heart. She'd tried to build a wall around herself, as he'd done, but it seemed to crumble whenever he touched her.

Fox ran the tip of her tongue over her lips, still tasting him there. Her heart had danced when he'd taken her into his arms. Then he'd released her and she'd died a little inside. She wrapped her arms around herself as if suddenly cold.

"You okay?" Travis asked instantly.

She knew then that he'd been watching her. She'd have to be more careful from now on. "I'm fine. We *are* going to the house now, right?"

He nodded. "I don't see a way around it, but we'll have to be careful." He paused, his expression thoughtful. "I know you believe the account numbers are hidden there, but what if they're not? Have you given that possibility some thought?"

"They're there."

"These people who are after you have searched through every possible hiding place, inside and out. You can count on it. And the police and government did the same thing years ago."

"I know. But, to me, all that says is that my parents really knew how to hide things. They were aware that, for security reasons, they might be forced to pack up and start over with a new identity at a moment's notice. That's why I'm sure those account numbers wouldn't have been far from them at any given time."

"What if they memorized them? Or maybe a later tenant found the numbers and threw them away, not knowing what they represented?" Travis countered, playing devil's advocate.

"Then we'll never end this nightmare. As long as any of these criminals are still alive, they'll continue to come after me, thinking that I know where their money is."

As they reached Santa Fe, storm clouds were beginning to gather again, and thunder rumbled in the distance. Fox shuddered.

"You're okay," he said softly.

"I know all the scientific explanations for thunder and lightning. Yet, my heart still beats frantically and I feel this incredible urge to hide."

"But you don't let your fears stop you. That says a lot about you."

Fox smiled. "I'm not brave. If I were, I'd force my memory into the forefront of my thoughts."

"Everything in life and nature moves at its own pace. It can't be forced. It's the same way with your memory, too. You can't rush a harvest."

Travis parked the truck at the very back of the narrow driveway of the Santa Fe home. With the storm, and few streetlights in the neighborhood, it was extremely dark. As they walked toward the back porch, the wind rose, lifting dust and sand into the air.

"Wind has supporting power. I think my brother would say this is a good omen."

Fox wasn't going to argue with him, but she couldn't bring herself to agree, either. The thought of facing a storm inside this house made her skin crawl.

"Maybe you should look at storms the way Navajos do. A new perspective might help you deal with your fear."

"Go on," she said.

"We believe Thunder has the power to find things," he said.

"It amazes me how much you still remember."

"Just because I chose another path for myself doesn't mean that I've forgotten what I was taught. It's a part of me—more so than I ever realized."

Fox envied him his connection to the past and how it defined him. Taking his advice, she tried to think of the storm as a good omen, but something deep inside her refused to allow her to relax. As they reached the back door, Travis tried the handle, but it was locked. A yellow crime-scene tape was stretched across its width.

"If we want in, I'm going to have to pick the lock," Travis said, bringing out a penlight and his pocketknife. "I doubt there's a security alarm here, but let me take a look."

Shielding the glow of the penlight with his body as much as possible, he searched the edges of the window but found no wires or sensors. Using a slender, almost wire-like blade, he worked on the lock until it clicked open. They were inside within a minute.

"There." He smiled, closing and locking the door behind him. "Good to know my training counts for something."

Together, using the flashlight she'd brought from the truck, they searched the empty house from top to bottom, looking inside the vents, and within each light fixture. The house was supposed to be unoccupied, so they were reluctant to turn on any lights. They were also careful to keep the stronger flashlight beam away from the windows.

Three hours later, after they'd exhausted every option, Fox dropped down heavily onto an old metal folding chair, one of the few pieces of furniture in the room. "Something inside me says that the answer is here. But we've looked everywhere. So, what have we missed?" She lifted her hair away from her neck, untangling it from the gold chain her locket hung on.

"Let me see that locket, Fox."

She slipped it off her neck and pressed the catch open for him. "It's just a picture of me and Chance. You've checked it out before."

"Take the photo out," he said, holding the flashlight for her.

She did, working carefully. The locket wasn't particularly valuable, nor was the photo inside it, but that fragile link was all she had of her past.

He looked over the photo and locket carefully once again, then handed it back to her. "There isn't anything written on the photo, nor are there any suspicious scratches or marks on the locket. And there's nothing hidden in this house—at least where we could find it. Yet, the crooks are convinced you're the key to the account numbers. What do they know that we don't?"

Fox looked out the back window pensively. "The storm seems to be passing us," she said in a faraway voice.

"But the danger isn't," he replied, coming up to stand beside her. "I have an idea," he said, after a moment.

"Hey, that's my line," she teased.

Travis gave her a halfhearted smile, then paced for several moments as if uncomfortable with what he was about to propose. Finally, he stopped and faced her. "How would you feel about going to visit one of my tribe's stargazers? They're supposed to be able to find things. I heard my brother speak of one, in particular, who's supposed to be nothing short of gifted.'' Before she could answer, Travis abruptly held up his hand and shook his head. ''Never mind, bag that idea. I'm just grasping at straws now. This is just too crazy.''

''Let's give it a try. What else have we got? From what I know about stargazers, you don't need to believe their skills will work for them to actually be able to furnish results.''

''That's true. They look into a crystal or at a star and are said to see visions.''

''I sure envy your link to the tribe,'' Fox admitted. ''I don't belong anywhere or to anything.''

''You belong to yourself, Fox, and that's where your inner strength comes from. You've accomplished an incredible number of things through determination alone because you follow your instincts wholeheartedly. You seize every opportunity the present offers, and you make the most out of life. I envy *you* for that.''

She exhaled softly. ''I seize the present because I know I may have no future. That's one possibility the little I know about my past has taught me.''

''The lessons from my past are different,'' Travis said. ''I've learned that for every bit of good life brings, there is an equal amount of sorrow. That's the price.''

''We can't avoid pain, Travis,'' Fox argued. ''By denying yourself the good that life has to offer, you're left with nothing to sustain you through the tough times.''

She could feel the darkness inside him straining toward the light. The walls he'd placed around himself were there to protect a heart that had known more than its share of pain. Underneath it all, Travis and she were more alike than he realized.

"Let's go see the stargazer," she said at last. "Even if he doesn't specifically tell us where to search, maybe he'll say something that'll jog my memory."

As they began the long drive back to the Reservation, she could sense Travis's tension growing. His hands were clenched around the steering wheel, and his back and shoulders were rigid. She knew he was torn between wanting to help her, and relying on the old ways that he'd never actually trusted.

They continued their journey south to Bernalillo, then northwest on Highway 44. Traffic became very light as midnight approached.

At last, Fox broke the hour-long silence between them. "Sometimes when it's this dark, I really wonder if the sun will ever rise again," she said.

"Hmm." He tapped his forehead as if considering the question. "It will," he said suddenly. "I can make that prediction with one hundred percent certainty."

She rolled her eyes. "That's what I get for getting too philosophical."

"Here I am predicting the future for you and, as usual, you just don't appreciate me," he teased.

"Well, if you're going to predict the future, let's go for the important questions. Will I ever meet a man who'll appreciate all my wonderful qualities?"

Travis pretended to mull it over. "No, I don't think so. I do see you meeting a wonderful guy who'll be the milk of human kindness and patient to a fault, but you'll drive him crazy."

She burst out laughing. "Gee, it sounds like you have a few things in common with this man—all except the patience-and-kindness bit, that is." She gave him a playful look. "Now tell me, in your considered opinion, how will I know this man when he does come into my life?"

"He'll be a steadfast ally, and true to the end," he said, his voice darkly heated with emotion.

Fox saw the fire in his eyes and suppressed the shiver that ran up her spine. She'd never seen desire that raw—that tempting—in any man's gaze before. Everything about him called to her. Yet instinct warned her to slow down. The answer lay not in conquering his heart, but in gentling it with love.

TRAVIS TRIED TO concentrate on the center line. It was about the only thing really distinguishable in the headlight beams except for the occasional rabbit sitting at the roadside, transfixed by the glare. He was getting sleepier by the moment, and had no one to talk to, now that Fox had dozed off. Not that they'd been doing that much talking anyway, but just thinking about her and exchanging a glance from time to time had been enough.

Knowing that Hosteen Yazzie, the stargazer, would be asleep until dawn, Travis decided to pull off the road and get a few hours of shut-eye. He wouldn't select a rest stop—those would be likely areas for McNeely and their other enemies to search. He'd just pick the next dirt side-road.

Slowing down, he found a rough track leading out into a field about five miles east of Cuba, and turned off. The road was well maintained, and he was already a hundred yards down the gravel path before Fox woke up.

"Are we there?" She sat up and looked around.

"We just passed through Cuba a while ago. I decided to pull over and get a few hours' sleep."

"I could drive for a while, if you like." Fox yawned.

Travis turned the truck around so it faced back toward the highway. This way he'd be able to see anyone who might have followed them, coming up. "You're just as tired as I am and there's no sense in driving straight through. We won't be able to see the stargazer until he gets up to offer prayers to the dawn. It's not fair to wake him up in the middle of the night since this is not an emergency. Let's just stay here, off the road, and get some rest. I'll set the alarm on my watch for three hours, so we won't over-sleep."

"You won't get a fight from me on this," Fox said wearily.

"Good, 'cause I'm too tired to argue."

Travis set his watch alarm, then leaned back against the headrest. He'd slept sitting up so many times in the military that it was second nature to him now. He drifted to sleep almost as soon as he closed his eyes.

It seemed as if only minutes had passed when a light beam suddenly flickered in his eyes. He awoke instantly and reached over to wake Fox.

"What?" she mumbled. "Let me sleep."

"Wake up, Fox, and fasten your seat belt. We have company."

Chapter Seventeen

Travis saw the source of the light immediately. It was coming from the spotlight of a vehicle that had slowed down on the highway.

"It could be a state policeman, or a forest ranger," he said. "We're on Forest Service land, or close to it. But, just in case it isn't, let's get ready to move."

Fox was instantly alert. When she saw him set the pistol down on the seat between them, her entire body tensed. "We've been spotted. Whoever that is, knows we're here."

"Yes, and they're backing up. From the outline I don't think it's a squad car. Keep your head down. They can see us inside the vehicle from where they are at and I'd like whoever it is to think we're either asleep or gone."

"Do you think it's McNeely?"

"I wouldn't be surprised. He'd probably guess we were heading back toward the Rez, and knows this is the shortest route. He'll also figure, I'm sure, that we're going to need sleep and will have to get off the road. I'm sure he checked the motels in Cuba, then kept on going, knowing that sooner or later he'd catch up to us."

"But he's got to be sleepy, too," Fox concluded.

"That's what I'm counting on." Travis started the engine, but stayed low and kept the headlights off. "They're coming this way, so get ready for a short, wild ride. And keep your head down until I say we're clear."

Fox grabbed on to the seat. "What are you going to do?"

"You'll see in a minute."

Headlights illuminated the interior of their sport-utility vehicle as the other motorist approached. Travis waited as long as he thought he could, then sat up, jamming down on the gas pedal and flipping on the headlights at the same time.

The headlights of the oncoming vehicle were centered on the small gravel road, so Travis knew he had room on either side. He guessed that McNeely, if it was him, would be on the passenger side, weapon ready.

Like in the game of chicken he'd played once or twice during his wild days as a kid on the Rez, Travis aimed his truck at the approaching headlights and flipped on his high beams. Swerving to the right at the last minute, he passed so close to the other vehicle he actually heard someone inside curse. He recognized McNeely's voice instantly and the knowledge brought a satisfied grin to his face.

Travis suddenly slammed on the brakes, and grabbed the pistol from the seat. "Cover your ears." Reaching out the window, he fired four shots, hitting both rear tires of McNeely's truck.

The sound of a weapon fired so close by was deafening, but Travis wasted no time thinking about the ringing in his ears. Almost immediately, he put the truck in gear, flicked off the headlights and headed back to the highway.

Fox grabbed the door handle and, as she looked out the side window, saw flashes of light that could only have been gunfire. "They're shooting back."

"Let them. I don't have the lights on, and they'll have to get a lucky shot at this range." They never slowed down before reaching the highway, and then bounced onto the asphalt, tires screaming. He floored the gas pedal, concentrating on keeping the truck on the road by moonlight. Ten seconds later, he turned on the headlights and realized he was going eighty down the center of the highway. He compensated immediately, slowing down and moving back into his proper lane.

"That was some rest stop," she muttered.

"At least McNeely didn't win this round."

"What makes you so sure it was him?" she asked.

"I recognized his voice when we slipped past them. He couldn't get a shot at me up close without hitting his own driver."

"Well, now that you've taken out their tires, we'll gain ground. We'll reach the Rez long before they're rolling again. No way they have two spares."

"At least I'm not drowsy anymore," he said, moving his neck from side to side and shifting his body so he could stretch his muscles. "There's nothing like a fight to get the adrenaline going."

IT WAS ALMOST TWO HOURS later, just after dawn, when they finally arrived at a hexagonal log hogan halfway up a canyon floor, miles from the closest highway. The small dwelling was surrounded by the remnants of corn stalks and harvest-ready vines of melons and cantaloupes. There were about twenty sheep in the corral adjacent to the hogan, but there were no vehicles or other trappings of civilization anywhere.

Fox shook her head. "The one thing that always gets to me is the isolation of some of these dwellings. The loneliness would drive me crazy. There are no televisions or telephones out here, and your closest neighbor is usually a jackrabbit. I don't know how anyone can stand it."

"Most people our age can't. They weren't raised this way, and they don't have the patience it takes to be happy meeting only basic needs. But it's almost like a religious commitment to the traditionalists. Here, they 'walk in beauty' as the Navajo Way requires.''

They came to a stop a hundred feet from the hogan. Fox saw the red-and-black blanket covering the entrance swaying gently in the breeze, revealing a small fire inside. They got out of the truck but did not approach, waiting for the invitation to be given.

"This hogan seems larger than the others I've seen," she whispered.

"That's because it's a 'medicine' hogan. The owner's son, who now lives in Arizona, is a *hataalii*, a medicine man. He and his father work together a lot. One of the functions of a stargazer is to act as a diagnostician. I've been told that this man we're about to see can tell when someone is going to die."

She shuddered. "Maybe we shouldn't be here, then. That's one question I really don't want answered."

"It won't come up unless you ask him, and even if you do, he probably won't tell you. To him, you're an outsider and I'm a modernist. He'll be cautious with both of us. If he consents to help us at all, it'll be strictly to guide us to the missing account numbers."

A moment later, an elderly man stepped from behind the blanket and waved for them to come inside. His weathered face was gaunt, but his eyes shone with intelligence and alertness. His skin was leathery, toughened by the sun, but beyond that, there were strong lines that defined more than his age. His face was that of a man who was sure of himself, who understood far more than what the narrow confines of his hogan would ever have allowed.

They joined him inside, where sheepskins were placed around the fire pit. Hosteen Yazzie sat on the south side of the fire with Travis, according to tradition, and gestured for Fox to sit at the north.

The old man looked down into the crackling piñon-and-cedar fire, then across the room, but didn't seem to focus on anything in particular.

Then his gaze cleared, and he looked directly at them. "You are both in a great deal of trouble." He glanced at Travis, and watched him speculatively. "It surprises me to see you here, nephew. You turned your back on the old ways since you moved from Rock Ridge to live with those schoolteachers."

Travis hesitated, then with characteristic honesty, added, "What you say is true, uncle. But I've run out of options and I need help. We're trying to find something and neither of us knows where else we can look."

With a nod, he looked at Fox, his expression gentle. "I understand your parents have been taken away from you," he said slowly. "And now, you are searching for your own identity, but that involves more than a name, so it's not something I can help you with." He stopped, then stared at the edges of the sheepskin in deep thought. "But that's not what brought you here, is it? Tell me, how I can help you?"

"I need to find a list of numbers my birth parents compiled a long time ago and then hid. My life depends on it."

"I'll see what I can do." He stood and retrieved a tightly bound pouch from one corner of the room. After placing a bit of its contents around his eyes, he sat down before them, holding a crystal in his hand, and began to chant.

Each minute that passed felt like an eternity, but Fox kept still, careful not to disturb the stargazer. As he chanted, a warm tingle ran all through her. It was as if her very essence were responding to the song.

As she glanced at Travis, she saw his eyes widen as he stared at the stargazer. She knew he could feel the man's power, too.

At last, Hosteen Yazzie looked up at Travis, then at her.

The old man knew something. His gaze pierced through her.

"You have the answer with you. It has always been so," he said.

"I don't understand," she said.

"The information you're after has never been beyond your reach. It's part of your heart."

"You mean my memories? But I can't unlock those. I've tried."

"Then look outside yourself. Everything is within your grasp."

Travis expelled his breath in a hiss. "Uncle, please speak plainly. We can't understand, and there's too much at stake for us to try and decipher these riddles."

"You come to me so that the spirits will guide you, yet you don't *listen* to the answers. I have spoken as clearly as I can." He shook his head slowly. "Like many outsiders, you come to me wanting a road map to the lost item. Now I'm telling you plainly. You already have what you need."

"*Where?*" Travis pressed.

"That is up to her to tell you," he said, gesturing to Fox. Yazzie then shifted his gaze to her. "You will find the list when your heart is ready to accept the burden it'll place on you. When that time comes, you'll understand that what is yours always comes to you and everything I've told you will make perfect sense."

"Why can't you tell us what you know more clearly, uncle?" Fox asked softly.

"Because there are lessons you each must learn first. But believe me when I tell you that you *will* find what you're searching for. It waits for you to find it. It's in no danger."

"You wouldn't play these games if you really did know something," Travis said, anger tainting his words.

The stargazer's expression was full of compassion—not surprise or annoyance. "You are the one who has the most to learn and those lessons will be hard for you to bear. You think you're protecting her, but she'll be the one who will show you what true courage is about. You trust your training and physical strength, but you have yet to learn that real strength comes from harmony and walking in beauty.''

Hosteen Yazzie paused, staring into the glowing embers of the fire, then continued. "Try to recall what it was like for you when you were a child living at Rock Ridge. You welcomed our traditions then. You were said to be like Wind and you liked the comparison because it defined you. Now you think that's where all your restlessness comes from. But you're wrong. You have to understand your heritage and learn to value it before your heart will ever find peace. Harmony comes only to those who strive for it.''

Travis rose. "Thank you for your help, uncle." He unfastened the *jish,* the medicine pouch, that he'd carried at his belt. "I've brought no gift as payment, but maybe you'll accept this.''

The old man took it from him. "You part with something you don't understand,'' he said. "Power comes in many guises, and some kinds should never be shared." He handed the pouch back to him. "Keep it with you. I ask for no payment.''

Travis led Fox back outside. "I should have known this was a waste of time,'' he said, as they reached the truck.

Fox shook her head. "You're wrong. This may sound crazy, but I honestly think he knew precisely where that list is. We'll just have to puzzle his clues out.''

"We needed answers, not guessing games. I'm sorry I suggested coming here.''

"Don't you see what's happening to you?'' There was no anger in her voice as she spoke. "You're just upset because, for the first time in your life, you tried to depend on the old ways and you think they've let you down. But you were using the old ways as a tool, and tradition and culture are much more than that. I'm not Navajo, but I do know that the Navajo ways are not like a light switch you can flick on and off at will.''

"Something either works, or it doesn't.''

"Yes, but to use something of this nature you have to understand its limitations as well as its advantages. That takes dedication and study.'' Fox paused, and in a soft, sad voice, added, "Like with anything worthwhile, it exacts a price. It requires giving it your heart.''

Travis gave her a long, pensive look. "All or nothing,'' he whispered, his gaze drifting over her in a silent caress. "My life seems to demand that at every turn these days.''

"Sooner or later we all have to decide how much we're willing to risk to get what we want.''

Wordlessly, he started the engine.

As they headed north, she wondered what thoughts lay behind his hooded eyes.

TRAVIS DROVE DOWN THE empty highway, not really knowing where they'd end up. The old man had thrown him a curveball. Like Fox, he'd had the clear impression that the stargazer had known something he hadn't wanted to share with them.

As he looked off into the distance, Travis saw a familiar sight, the stark formation of Rock Ridge. He and his brother had lived in a small house there. Their parents had been poor, but his brother and he had always had clean clothes on their backs and food in their stomachs. Love had abounded in their family, despite the hardships.

As he looked at the desert that stretched out before them, he felt a kinship with the land. In all the years he'd stayed away, he'd never felt the sense of belonging, or rightness, that he felt now, traveling across the Rez with Fox beside him.

He turned his head and glanced at her. Though she'd

never admit it, he knew she was bone weary. With only a few hours' sleep last night, interrupted by their encounter with McNeely, they'd both expended their energy reserves. They needed to hole up and get some rest. Daylight had come only a few hours ago, and already it felt like dusk.

As she closed her eyes, he tried to brush aside the rush of tenderness that filled him. He'd grown used to having her depend on him, but he relied on her, as well. Protecting her had given him purpose and, through it, he'd found a side of himself he'd never known existed. And maybe it hadn't—not until she'd come back into his life.

As she shifted, trying to get comfortable, the top button of her shirt came open. He saw the creamy white breast that lay just below the folds. Fox looked so soft and vulnerable right now, his head sizzled with wild, erotic thoughts.

Travis almost groaned when she shifted again and reached out, resting her hand on his leg. It was as if his entire body had suddenly caught fire.

He didn't realize until she drew her hand back that he hadn't been breathing. He sucked in a long, ragged breath.

"Where are we going?" she asked, opening her eyes.

"Someplace where we can safely get some rest. I'm not sure exactly where."

Fox leaned back into the seat and stared ahead, her eyes nearly shut. "Tell me honestly, when this is over and you go back to your unit," she whispered sleepily, "will you think of me from time to time?"

Her question left him stunned. How could she not know the way he felt? He looked at her, wondering if she was teasing, but then realized she was not. He'd guarded his feelings far better than he'd ever realized.

"You are always part of my thoughts," he answered.

"And, someday, do you think you'll come home to stay?"

"I don't know," he replied. A month ago he would have said no, but many things had changed since that time.

Travis kept his eyes on the road as her breathing deepened and she drifted off to sleep. The old man had been right. He needed to find himself, not as a fighter and a soldier, but as a man. He'd been fighting all his life. Now he was fighting his feelings for Fox. He cared deeply for her, but life had taught him that love was unreliable and it was hard to trust in that emotion now. Whenever he'd loved, and trusted in love, life had found a way to bring him to his knees.

Yet, even as the thought formed, he knew that it was already too late for misgivings. There was no turning back. Somewhere along the way he'd crossed the line and given her his heart. Her gentleness and her fighting spirit had combined forces and penetrated every emotional barrier he'd ever placed around himself.

Travis gazed at Ship Rock, now only a few miles to his left, as he drove toward the town of the same name. Some said that the rock formation was a guardian, a warrior frozen in stone, and an advocate of any man who went to war. Silently, he asked for help now. Though he was a warrior, far gentler emotions had won him over.

He was in love with Fox. He knew that with every fiber of his being. But the thought of settling down was totally foreign to everything he'd ever valued. He thrived as a Ranger, facing danger wherever he went.

Of course, life with Fox would be anything but tame. Excitement rippled through him as he remembered all the times their wills had clashed. Life was never simple, and when a man added a woman like Fox to the equation, there was no telling what would happen.

He smiled slowly. And that was one of the many reasons he'd fallen in love with her.

Chapter Eighteen

Later that day, they set up camp several miles southeast of the town of Shiprock, beyond the Hogback oil field.

Fox looked around her, studying the area Travis had selected. The Hogback—a tall, tilted ridge of sandstone that ran in a northeast-southwest direction for many miles—was at their backs. To the west, the mesas and canyons of the Colorado Plateau rose slowly toward the purple mountains that formed the Carrizo and Chuska ranges. Beautiful Mountain, highest of all the peaks, shimmered like a mirage nearly nine thousand feet above sea level.

Except for the tall poles of the power line to the south, the country seemed so uninhabited and open that she wasn't in the least bit worried about anything or anyone sneaking up on them.

Her gaze drifted over to Travis, who was trying to set up a canvas awning beside their vehicle that would give them some shade. It was part of the camping gear his friend had provided in his Weekend Getaway Special. She watched Travis use his knife to sharpen a wooden stake that would hold the awning secure by its guy ropes.

"Can I help?"

He shook his head. "I've got it." With a flick of his wrist, he tossed the knife down into the ground, the point embedded in the soft earth.

He was all male power and vitality, but she still liked being able to worry about him. She was sure he thought of himself as indestructible, but the inescapable fact was, they'd needed each other to stay alive.

"I want to learn how to fight," she said at last.

"Excuse me?" He was setting out their sleeping bags on a ground cloth when he stopped abruptly. "I must have heard you wrong."

"No, you heard me correctly. Remember when you were going hand to hand with that man back in Santa Fe? I tried to help you by throwing a piece of firewood at his head. He ducked and I missed but, fortunately, you were still able to take advantage of the distraction. But think about it. We would have been in a real pickle if there hadn't been a stack of firewood there. And, what if I'd hit you, instead? That's why I've decided to learn to fight. That way, I can take care of myself—and you—if I have to."

He burst out laughing. "You know, just when I think you're actually capable of being reasonable, you say something crazy like that."

"I *am* being reasonable. It's perfectly logical that I want to learn to defend myself and you, if needed."

"I don't need a woman to take care of me."

"Of course you do. If I hadn't diverted that guy's attention for you, he might have cut you badly with that knife."

"You didn't have to worry. I know how to disarm an opponent. I was looking for an opening when you threw that wood."

"But what if, next time, there's more than one guy? What will you do, then?" She glanced at the handgun he'd placed next to his bedroll. "I won't use that thing. I could point it at someone, but I doubt I'd ever really be able to shoot. So, chances are they'd take it from me. I'm aware of my limitations, you see, so I know I have to tackle this from a different angle. That's why you have to teach me to fight.''

He rolled his eyes. ''I can't do that in one afternoon, or even one evening. And if you try to take any of these guys on, they'll hurt you—badly. They're professionals with years of training. You haven't got a chance.''

''All I want to learn is how to get loose if someone grabs me, and how not to be a victim. Come on. You owe me that much, don't you think?''

''I *owe* you?''

''Well, you owe *us*. We have to stand together.''

''I've protected you this far. What makes you think I can't keep doing that?''

''You can't guarantee the future. How can you be one hundred percent certain that you won't need my help at any given time?'' Fox smiled slowly. ''A long time ago, Dad told me that one of the basic tenets of the Navajo Way is the belief that whatever happened once, may happen again. Do you remember learning that?'' She didn't wait for a reply, knowing full well that he did. ''Don't you want me to be able to get away if there's a problem and you've got your hands full?''

He considered it, then shook his head. ''No. I'm not teaching you any fighting moves. My gut instinct tells me you'll only get yourself into more trouble.''

''Okay. Then I guess I'll have to teach myself to use the pistol,'' she said, moving toward it, hoping her bluff would work. ''I'm *almost* certain I can remember everything Ashe taught me about handguns once. It was a long time ago but, heck, it can't be that hard.''

''*Don't touch it,*'' he growled. ''You'll shoot yourself, and maybe me, too.''

She smiled slowly. ''So you'll teach me how to fight, then?''

He groaned, suspecting he'd been had. "You're not going to give me any peace until I do, are you?"

"Nope."

He stepped toward her and stopped, inches away. "What if I get too rough? Can you handle it?"

She knew he was trying to intimidate her by looming over her like that, but it wouldn't work. "Of course. Now let's get down to business. Teach me anything at all you think will be helpful. I mean, I doubt I can land a good, solid punch against anyone—unless, of course, they were very cooperative and stayed perfectly still."

"Unlikely." Travis gave her a long, hard look. "The problem with fighting is that even if you win, you've got to be prepared to take a few hard knocks."

"It's better to go down fighting than to just be a victim. You, of all people, should understand that," she said.

She saw surprise, then realization flash across his features. Everything she knew about Travis told her that her words had gotten through to him and that he finally understood.

"The first thing you have to recognize and remember," he began, "is that there are a few key places in the human body that are very vulnerable. Those are areas you need to concentrate on striking, never holding back. With a man, one of the most vulnerable, accessible places is the groin. Second to that, there are the backs of the knees, the neck—specifically the windpipe—the eyes, and the bridge of the nose."

"So I should aim for those?"

He glowered at her. "Let me finish."

She made a rolling motion with her hand. "Cut to the chase. I'm a quick study."

Travis shook his head, then moved away. She thought he was going to walk right past her, but he suddenly stopped and pulled her roughly toward him. Her back was pinned to his chest. His arms were locked around her rib cage and over her arms. She could scarcely move.

"Hey, that's not fair. I can't free my arms now. There's no way I can fight back in this position."

"Not true. You still have some options. Let's start with the first thing you can try. In slow motion, okay?"

Fox nodded, suddenly not trusting her voice. Her pulse was racing. His body felt hard and incredibly masculine as it pressed intimately into hers. Even as the thought was forming in her mind, she felt his unmistakable response to the contact between them. He wanted her as badly as she did him, but his voice never betrayed him.

"First, bring your foot down hard on your opponent's instep. Use your heel. That's a painful move that will cause him to loosen his hold slightly. Then immediately elbow him as hard as you can in the stomach. When he bends over in response, bring your fist up and back and hit him right in the nose. Got all that?"

"Sure. Let's try it." She followed his instructions to the letter, pulling her punches. "Are you sure this works?"

"It'll work, particularly because they won't be expecting that from you. You might also remember that the inside of anyone's thigh is also very sensitive. Even if you're pinned, if you can reach back with your hand and pinch hard, he'll let go."

"That sounds so simple. Will it work even against someone with your training?"

"Yes, particularly if they try to pin you like I just did."

"Let's give it a try," Fox said. She pressed her back against his chest once more and waited for him to renew his hold.

"No more," he said, not reaching for her. "We've both had enough for now."

She could feel his manhood pulsing against her buttocks. A shiver of excitement darted through her. "Control and discipline," she murmured. "Do I threaten those in you, Travis?"

Her words were a clear challenge and she knew he'd never back down now.

"One more time, and that's it."

As his arms tightened around her, she reached back, found the inside of his thigh, and squeezed. "There?"

His voice was low. "Yeah, but move your hand away now, or you'll find more than you bargained for."

She obeyed him reluctantly, but remained where she was. His breath, so hot against her neck, made her tremble. A sweet fire raged through her, but she refused to give in to it. She would not surrender to a man who wasn't willing to do the same for her.

Still, that melting heat persisted, growing stronger and more urgent with each passing second. Knowing she had to counter those feelings quickly, she decided to do the one thing he wasn't expecting. Remembering what he'd said, she stepped away, then did a sweeping kick, aiming for the backs of his knees.

Travis's legs buckled and he went sprawling onto the ground.

She gasped, suddenly contrite. "You're not really hurt, are you?"

He didn't answer her. Instead, he closed his eyes and stayed very still.

She instantly dropped to her knees next to him. "Travis, say something! I didn't mean to hurt you!"

In one fluid move, he pulled her against him, rolled over, and pinned her beneath him. His dark eyes smoldered as he grinned slowly. "*Never* trust your opponent in a fight. Cheating is often the fastest way to win."

Her senses stung with awareness. Travis's heartbeat shattered against her own. In his eyes, she saw pure male triumph. He shifted over her and spread her thighs, settling between them.

Ripples of excitement flowed through her as she felt their lower bodies touching intimately. As he rubbed himself against her, a little cry escaped her lips. It was the sound of a woman who needed a man, and everything male in Travis recognized it.

He kissed her, sending his tongue deep into her mouth. His lips slanted back and forth, sucking and mating, alternating between exquisite tenderness and the hardness his passion demanded. At long last, his breath ragged, he drew back.

There was a wildness in Travis's eyes as he looked down at her. She understood then that his control had been stretched to the limit. The passion that drove him now was too powerful for even him to master.

"You do things to me no one has ever done before," he whispered darkly, nuzzling her neck. "And you feel so right beneath me." He pushed himself into the cradle of her thighs, wanting her to feel him and needing her softness.

Poised over her and balanced on one arm, he unbuttoned her shirt, then loosened her bra. "So lovely," he said, baring her breasts.

The bones of his face seemed to sharpen as he gazed down at her. Then, moving slowly as if to savor each precious second, he lowered his head and drew her nipple into his mouth.

Pleasure shot through her and the new fire that blazed inside her made it impossible for her to draw a full breath. She could feel his body harden even more, although until that moment, she hadn't thought it possible.

Long, heated moments passed before he kissed her again. Wild lights danced in her head as she sucked at his tongue and he gave it to her, letting her love him.

When he drew back this time, his eyes were smoldering and his body was shaking with a passion he could barely keep leashed.

"I want to feel you naked against me. I don't want any barriers between us." His voice was a fevered whisper as he shifted off her and began undressing her. "I want to make you mine here, in this place where Wind and Earth meet as one."

Fox didn't resist him. She'd given Travis, the boy, her heart one moonlit night years ago. But now, it was the man she loved.

"Is it only my body that you want?" she whispered. She knew in her heart it was not, but she needed to hear him say it.

His features were intense, his eyes glittering as they held hers. "You're a part of me, Fox, but you've known that all along. I need to be inside you, to share your fire, to take everything you've got to give me and give you all I have in return."

They were the words she'd longed to hear. She reached for his hand and brought it to her breast, then guided it over her heart. "Then take what's already yours."

He sucked in a ragged breath. "I'll never give you reason to regret this day, Fox. I'll love you the way a woman like you was meant to be loved."

He released her hand and stripped off his shirt and jeans, letting her watch him. As he stood before her, naked, his manhood swollen and pulsing, she opened her arms to him.

Travis stretched out beside her and loved her with his mouth and his hands. He brought her to a fever pitch, readying her for the final joining.

"Take me now. No more games," she begged, an unbearable pressure building within her.

"It should be slow," he said, his voice an unsteady murmur in the shade of their small shelter. "But the gods help me, I just don't know if I can do that now."

He moved over her, determined to let her feel the very tip of him only and get used to his body that way. But at that moment, she thrust upward. Hearing her cry out, he froze. "Hurt?" he managed, struggling for control, though he was at the ragged edge.

"No...yes, but just for a minute," she managed, feeling her body melt around his. She began moving again, wriggling her hips to take him deeper inside her.

"So good!" He groaned her name and held her hips steady, stopping for a moment, trying to slow things down for her sake.

Travis wanted to be tender, but her inexperienced movements were too much. He thrust inside her, riding her hard, taking her over the edge time and time again, then finally joining her and spilling his seed into her.

Afterward, as the sun went down, Fox lay in his arms. A peace unlike anything she'd ever known before settled gently over her. She'd never dreamed it could be like this; that love would make her feel so complete. It was like a fairy tale—magical and wonderful—but, oh, so true.

He cradled her tenderly, tucking her head beneath his chin. "Tell me you don't regret what happened," he murmured, tilting her chin upward. "I need to hear you say it, but only if it's the truth."

As she gazed into his eyes, she understood. She could destroy him with just a few words. His heart, laced through his plea, was reaching out to her. The toughened soldier, the loner, had taken the biggest risk of all when he'd surrendered to love.

"I will never regret today, not for as long as I live."

Travis held her tightly. "Sleep now. I'll watch over you."

She closed her eyes, exhausted, but fulfilled in a way

she'd never known before. Today Travis had trusted her
enough to allow her to see him at his most vulnerable.
Without words, he'd asked for her gentleness, knowing
she'd be capable of nothing less. No promises of "forever"
had been made between them, but that didn't matter now.
The future was not theirs to claim. The shadow of their
inevitable parting lurked just beyond the bend. But those
tears would wait. For now, secure in the afterglow of their
love, they would share each other's warmth.

Chapter Nineteen

Morning came like a thief and, as the sun's rays bathed the tops of the distant mountains, Fox knew their night of magic had passed. Sadness encompassed her as they ate the rest of yesterday's food, then broke camp. All the obstacles that had stood between them before were still there. Nothing had changed—yet everything had.

"I think we should head off the Reservation and lie low for a while," Travis said as Fox climbed into the vehicle. "We certainly don't have many options left right now and it's better not to act without a clear plan."

"There is one place we haven't searched for that list of numbers," she said. "And it's possible that it's been there all along, hidden in something from my past."

"Where's that?"

"The school. I know that Mom kept some of my baby stuff as mementos in her office. It's possible she inadvertently stored away more than she'd intended. Nobody was looking for numbers when Ashe and Casey checked out the place weeks ago."

"We can't go to the Johnsons' school," he said flatly. "The people who are after you may have gotten the same idea, and it's too easy a place to stake out."

"Then we'll have to arrange to meet Casey and Ashe there. They can be our backup, and also speed up our search because they can rule out places they've already looked. It'll give us a chance to get an update from them, too, and see if they've turned up anything new. We have to let them know about McNeely catching up to us, anyway."

"Just because Casey and Ashe will be there doesn't mean we won't be in the line of fire," he warned. "Keep that in mind."

Ninety minutes later, after breakfast in the parking lot of a fast-food place, and a quick call from a pay phone, they arrived at the school. Casey and Ashe were waiting by the doors. They'd brought a set of keys.

Ashe led the way inside. "Let's divide this place up."

"We can search Mom's and Dad's classrooms," Fox said, "their offices, and whatever places we can think of that only they had complete access to. And keep in mind that one of the best ways to hide numbers is to put them with other numbers. We're going to have to check any list that looks even the slightest bit suspicious or out of place."

Two HOURS PASSED. Fox glanced at Travis as he checked Nick's file cabinet. He obviously didn't like doing this. To go through the possessions of the dead was offensive to him as a Navajo. But these days, he made no effort to disguise it. He had accepted the part of himself that was, and always would be, Navajo.

After an exhaustive search, Casey sank down in one of the empty chairs. "We've looked everywhere. It's time to call it quits here."

Fox sat at a secretary's desk a short distance from Casey, determined to hide her disappointment. "What about your prisoner? Did you ever get anything out of him?"

"Not yet, but we will."

An eerie silence fell over them as they accepted that they'd reached the end of the line, and still had no answers.

"The people after me are convinced I have those account

numbers or, at the very least, know where they are,'' Fox said at last, thinking out loud. ''They must have either some solid evidence or a very good reason to believe that. They wouldn't be doing all this solely on a hunch.''

She saw the others nod in agreement, and continued. ''For a long time I kept thinking that Chance, the bear, was the link, but that was off base. There's nothing in Chance. We checked him out.''

Casey nodded. ''I could have told you that. After the murder, the police took it in, looking for trace evidence. When they discovered that your parents were living under an assumed name, they searched through everything, including the bear's stuffing.''

''Then what are we missing? As far as I can tell, I only have one other thing from my past life, and it's this locket.'' Fox reached up and curled her hand around it. ''But I've already searched it, and there's nothing in there.''

''I took a look at it, too. There's no inscription on either the metal or the photo,'' Travis added.

''Refresh my memory. Tell me about the photo,'' Casey said.

''It's just me as a kid holding Chance,'' Fox answered.

''Can I see it?'' Ashe asked.

Fox undid the clasp, then flipped open the lid. ''It's just as I said—'' Fox stopped speaking abruptly as she looked down at the photo.

''What's wrong?'' Travis asked.

''The photo... It looks different.''

Travis came up and took a look. ''It's the same photo of you and Chance. How's it different?''

''There's something about the eyes....''

''Let me see.'' Ashe took the locket from Fox's hands. As he started to pull out the photo, a black dot slid downward toward the bottom of the locket. "Something's weird here. It looks like part of Chance's eye is coming off."

He placed it under a desk lamp, taking a closer look. "This isn't part of the photo. It's something that's been carefully placed over the photo."

"A microdot of some kind?" Fox asked.

"Maybe, but I can't be sure until we check it out."

"Let's go down to the science lab," Fox said. "There are microscopes there. I may not be able to verify what it contains if it is a microdot, but what I can do is make sure that it's not just a piece of the image cracking off because of age."

At the lab a few minutes later, Fox used tweezers to place the dot between a cover slip and slide, then put it on the stage of the microscope. "I can see numbers. This is no dirt spot. I have a feeling we've just found what we've been looking for."

"I'm going back to the police station and have the local experts tell us exactly what's on this," Casey said, carefully taking the photo, then placing it and the slide with the microdot in an evidence pouch. She sealed that inside another pouch, then labeled it.

"Wait, slow down," Fox said. "This may be our only chance to catch the inside man at the Marshals Service. But to do that we're going to have to set things up carefully. We'll need to work with another agency that the inside man at the Marshals Service won't be able to infiltrate."

"We can go to the FBI office in Albuquerque," Casey suggested reluctantly. "But, first, I need to know exactly what you have in mind."

"It's a great plan," Fox said, ignoring Travis's groan. "All we'll really need is luck and little ingenuity."

KEEPING THEIR OPERATION a secret from everyone in the Marshals Service, they took a commuter flight from Farmington to Albuquerque and went directly to the Bureau offices there. Four hours later, they had what they needed.

Casey stood with Travis, Ashe, and Fox in the outer lobby of the facility, just east of downtown. "The Bureau will keep the real microdot and the account numbers they extracted from it. What I've got here," she said, holding up an envelope, "are two new microdots with phoney information in them. We're ready to roll. But from this point on, things are going to get nasty."

"I've been preparing for this moment ever since the day Prescott came into my life," Fox said. "I'm ready."

Casey gave her a nod, then looked at Travis and Ashe. "I'm going to independently give one of these microdots to Carl Andrews and the other to Marc Gray. I'll tell each of them that the other man is our suspect, and I'll insist they keep the information completely confidential until we figure out what the numbers represent. The moment either of them tries to access the phoney accounts, we'll know who the inside man is, since each microdot has a different set of account numbers leading to a separate account."

"It'll be a great sting operation," Ashe said. "If they don't access the accounts right away, they'll risk losing all that money. Good thinking, Fox, and a great job, Casey."

"It's a matter of having the right plan and the right contacts," Casey said. "But now we'll be under fire from all sides. I've gone out on a limb by getting authorization directly from Washington and getting the Bureau involved."

"And we still have McNeely and his companion to contend with," Travis added. "But that's where I come in. I know how McNeely thinks, so I can use that to reel him in."

"You're our point man, then," Ashe said. "Go on. What's your plan?"

"McNeely found, and then lost us the other night outside Cuba, but that's a situation he intends to rectify. What he'll do is backtrack to where we've hidden out before. There's only one place left standing on the Rez we all have ties to—the lodge by Rock Ridge. I'd be willing to bet he's got that place staked out, hoping we'll show up there sooner or later.''

"But we can't count on that, because the bad guys are really short on manpower, now that two of them are out of the picture,'' Casey said. "It could take forever. And if we happen to corral the inside man at the Marshals Service first, it's likely McNeely will cut and run. We need to stack the deck more in our favor. We have to find a way to lead him exactly where we want him to go.''

Travis nodded thoughtfully. "Leading him to the lodge purposely is going to be tricky. It'll have to be done subtly, or he won't fall for it. The only way I can think of doing this is to somehow let him know we're on our way up there. He'll either try to follow or ambush us. But if your people give us backup, we'll be able to turn the tables on him before he even knows what hit him. I know that area like the palm of my hand.''

"How can you make sure word gets to McNeely with any degree of certainty?'' Casey asked.

Travis considered for a long moment. "McNeely has a cousin who works at the Last Stop Café, which is on our way. They've always been tight, and I bet she knows exactly what McNeely has been up to. We can stop by long enough to pick up some food and, while we're there, drop a hint or two about our destination. McNeely's cousin is sure to recognize us and pass on what she overhears to him.''

"Sounds like a good plan,'' Casey said. "Now we have to come up with a timetable. We'll all have to work in unison and on a variety of fronts. I'm also going to need to make sure we have trustworthy backup,'' Casey added. "You and Ashe know the area around Rock Ridge better than anyone else. I want you two to work out the details of the trap we set for McNeely.''

"The first thing is to lead him away from the lodge itself into the surrounding terrain, which will give you the advantage,'' Ashe said, then began discussing possible strategies with his brother. At long last, they settled on a plan. "Get a flight back, pick up your vehicle at the Farmington airport,'' Ashe told Fox and Travis, "then head back to the Reservation. It'll take Casey and me at least two hours to get things rolling.''

As they left the building, Fox's thoughts were racing. She knew that the next part of the battle belonged mostly to Travis. He needed to settle the score with McNeely. He wouldn't rest until that was over.

They drove to the airport in the rental car and then, sometime later, the small commuter plane took off toward the northwest. Looking out the aircraft window at the ground dropping away, Fox remained locked in the privacy of her own thoughts.

They'd both changed so much. Through Travis, she'd discovered that the home she'd longed for was in reality something other than a particular place. Home was a place the heart could find rest.

Her feelings for Travis had awakened an entirely new world to her—one filled with gentleness and kindness, even in the midst of violence. But love had to be welcomed and accepted by two people, or it would never find the fertile ground it needed to grow. And, above all, love had to be believed in before it could overcome whatever stood in its way.

Chapter Twenty

After landing in Farmington, Travis and Fox picked up their vehicle and began the drive back to the Rez. She sat quietly beside him, but he was certain her silence was temporary, much like the calm before a storm. Soon, she'd come up with another plan, and do her best to force him to follow it, assuring him it was better than his. She was a constant challenge, and not an easy woman to live with. Yet the thought of a lifetime with her, trying to tame her while she tried to tame him, made a stream of raw and reckless excitement course through him.

It was precisely because he did care about her and because he loved her that he knew he had to end it. What could he possibly give her? After his time in the Rangers was over, he wouldn't reenlist, he knew that much now. But that meant finding a new career and building a new life. She deserved a man who was settled, who had a nine-to-five job and would come home every night.

He stole a long, furtive look at her, feeling the weight of sorrow. He wanted to believe that no one would ever incite her passion as he had, or her anger or her loyalty. But he understood the realities of life. If he left her, eventually she would find someone else.

The thought of Fox with another man filled him with a sudden, intense jealousy that burned through his mind like acid. Travis stared at the road, forcing himself to focus on the job he had yet to do here.

"Do you really think McNeely will come after us at the lodge?" Fox asked, interrupting his silence.

"I don't doubt it for a moment."

"If he does, he's going to want to kill me, and you, too," she said, looking directly at him. "I'm right, aren't I? And it won't be just because of the account numbers. This has more to do with pride. McNeely feels that he's got to be the only one left standing."

"That's true. But I'm a better fighter, and I'll have better backup too. He won't win." Travis's grip on the steering wheel tightened as he saw the worry on her features. "Don't let this upset you, Fox." He gave her a cocky grin. "Come on, you *know* I can tear him apart and, just for you, I'll even put him back together in a new and interesting way."

She laughed. "Lack of confidence was never a problem for you. But I'm worried that you may not be thinking clearly. You hate McNeely's guts."

"I resent him for the hell he's put you through. You've got that right."

"And if you get a chance to square off with him, you intend to take it, don't you?"

"In a flash, but it won't happen. I'll never get that lucky," he added, scowling.

Fox sighed. "Listen to me. Even if you do get the chance, I don't want you to fight him."

"Why? You think he can take me?"

"I don't know who can take whom, and I don't care. That's not my point." She paused, then began again. "I don't blame you for feeling the way you do. I know this has got something to do with those boy-type hormones."

"What's this, a complaint? Here I thought you were quite happy with the way my 'boy-type' hormones work. I

could have sworn you gave them rave reviews last night."
He held her gaze and smiled.

She blushed and looked away.

He didn't have the upper hand often, but this round was
all his. "Look, Fox," he said, his voice gentle. "I won't
initiate a confrontation. But I won't walk away from it,
either. I could give you all kinds of assurances, but you
deserve better than that from me." Travis wanted to hold
her, to do something to soften his words, but this wasn't
the time. "The one thing you can count on is that I will
never make you any promises I can't keep."

He saw it on her face the second he uttered the words.
She was remembering last night, and the words he'd never
said. There had been no commitment between them. He'd
shown her his love in every physical way he could, but
he'd never offered her any tomorrows. Now, as he looked
at her, he wanted to do just that. He wanted to ask her to
go with him and stay by his side, no matter what his future
held. But putting his needs before hers wasn't his definition
of love.

"It'll be over soon, Fox. Just hang on tight," he said,
his eyes again on the road ahead.

"And after that it'll be back to the Rangers for you,"
she said with a thin smile. "It's your passion."

He shook his head. "It was at one time, but I don't
belong there anymore. The problem is that once I leave the
Rangers, there isn't much I'm qualified to do. I need a new
challenge, something that'll keep me going and moving.
I'm not at all sure where I'll end up."

He wasn't ready to discuss it with anyone, but he'd had
one idea he intended to pursue. Maybe he could become a
cop for the Bureau of Indian Affairs. It would be a risky
job, but then again, it would suit him. That was why he
knew Fox and he would have to make a clean break long
before then. But the inevitability of their final parting

knifed at his gut. If he could find the courage, he'd end it before he returned to his unit.

The cell phone rang and, as Travis got the go-ahead to put the operation in motion, a new tension filled him. "It's time to head over to the Last Stop," he said. "Casey and Ashe have turned over the phoney microdots to Andrews and Gray, as planned. Now it's up to us to do our part."

"After all these weeks trying to dodge these people, it's finally my turn to go after them. I've been looking forward to this moment for a long time." Fox paused, then added, "Let's give them something to remember, Travis."

"Count on it."

THEY ARRIVED AT THE Last Stop Café, a popular eatery about halfway between Farmington and Shiprock, a short time later. The hot, fresh food renewed Travis's energy though he ate light, knowing what lay ahead. As he looked at Fox's plate, he saw she'd scarcely touched the green chile omelet.

Travis knew that she was frightened—though mostly for him—and he was determined to try to make it easier on her. He decided on the only strategy he knew for sure would work.

"Don't start getting jumpy on me now, Fox—not after all we've been through," he challenged, and had to suppress a smile when he saw the angry spark in her eyes.

"I'm not 'jumpy,' as you so eloquently put it," she replied in her best "haughty" voice. "I'm cautiously anticipating what's ahead for us. There's a huge difference. Showing caution is a sign of intelligence." She paused. "Are you getting this, or am I going too fast for you?"

He chuckled. "Welcome back," he muttered.

"I'm eating light, by the way, for the same reason you are. I know I'll need to be quick on my feet. I remember our lessons in fighting."

Now he was worried. "Have a heart. Tell me you're not considering the possibility of trying to fight McNeely or his pal."

"Only if I have to." She smiled, then added, "But don't worry. If I'm too rough with them, you can hold me back."

Travis cursed himself for ever having taught her any self-defense moves. "There's McNeely's cousin, Lori, manning the cash register. Let's go."

As they stopped to settle their bill, Travis could see from the woman's eyes that she'd recognized them, though he'd avoided making eye contact. As Lori rang up the tab, he turned to Fox. "It's a good place for us," he said softly. "One bad experience there shouldn't keep us from going back. Ever since high school, it has been our family's special place. I think we should use it now. With those log walls, the building is like a bunker."

"I agree with you," Fox said. "And, it's so quiet up there, it's easy to hear anyone come up."

As they headed out, Travis glanced back and saw McNeely's cousin already on the phone.

"You really think it'll work? Will she figure it out?"

"It doesn't matter. McNeely will, from what she tells him."

"Your training and his are identical," she said slowly. "That really scares me. In a fight, you're evenly matched."

"I need you to believe in me, Fox, okay?"

"Of course, I believe in you. And I'll be there, ready to help."

He groaned. "Thanks for the reassurance."

"Don't mention it."

Despite the lightness of her tone, Travis could see the lines of worry still etched on her features. He found himself wishing he could pour out his love for her now while he still had the chance, but he remained silent. Despite what he'd said, he suspected that neither McNeely nor he would walk away from the fight. No matter who won, they'd each inflict damage on the other. But Fox was wrong about one thing: They weren't evenly matched. Travis knew that to fail would mean leaving Fox to McNeely's mercy; that knowledge would give him all the edge he needed.

As he hardened his thinking, Travis forced his feelings for Fox to fade into the background. He was still the only major obstacle that stood between her and her enemies, and he wouldn't let her down.

"It's time for me to call my brother and let him know when we expect to arrive. Then I want to do a little reconnoitering and make sure we've picked up McNeely." He turned off onto a dirt track that led to the cabin, took out the cell phone and called his brother. After he was finished, he parked the vehicle in an area beneath some pines. "I'm going to check and see if I can spot McNeely anywhere."

Travis and Fox walked to a place below the crest of a hill from where they could see the entire valley stretching out below them. A vehicle several miles behind was approaching slowly, its dust trail barely visible.

"You think that's McNeely?" Fox asked.

He nodded. "It's either him or his partner," Travis said, hurrying back with her to their vehicle. "Things are going according to schedule."

By the time they reached the lodge, Travis's muscles were taut. He could sense the danger pressing in on them. "I can feel McNeely itching to make his move."

"Let's lead him over to Casey and Ashe's position, then."

"We need to make it look as if we're going for a hike. Otherwise he'll suspect something's up," he said.

Travis found a knapsack in the cedar chest and placed a blanket inside to bulk it up. Fox rolled up another blanket, tied it with a rope, and strapped it to her back. They worked wordlessly, the tension between them an almost-palpable presence.

"Fox, stay close by me," Travis said, his voice hard and deadly. He checked the clip on his pistol, made sure he had spare ammo in his pocket, then placed the gun into his belt.

He had to think like a soldier now. Their survival was at stake. Any mistake could be fatal.

"Wait. I want to add icing to the cake," Fox said, producing a pencil and sticky notepad from her purse. Quickly she wrote a message.

> Ashe, in case you come up tonight instead of tomorrow, we've gone for a short hike, looking for piñon nuts. Hope you've brought plenty of food. We should be back before dark.
>
> Fox

Travis grabbed a tack from an old note somebody had stuck on a log ages ago. As they stepped outside, he attached the note prominently on the door, then led the way across the small clearing in front of the cabin.

Chapter Twenty-One

Making sure they left tracks McNeely could easily follow, they entered a narrow, winding canyon lined with piñons and brush, proceeding at a brisk clip. A clear stream flowed beside them, sparkling in the sun as it bubbled swiftly across the rocks.

Travis led the way toward the scooped out amphitheater-like cave that formed the dead end of the canyon. It had been a favorite picnic spot of theirs once.

"I remember this place," she said. "I'll keep up, but don't forget it's been a long time since I've done any rock climbing."

"There's a foot-wide hidden trail to our left that was placed there by my ancestors," he said, gesturing ahead. "Ashe and I never told anyone about it. That will take us above the cave, and eventually lead us to the top."

Though Travis had climbed the hidden trail many times before, it still took a few minutes for him to locate it among the rocks and brush that had grown there since his last visit.

Parts of the ancient trail consisted of steps cut out of the rock face, and the rocky terrain and stunted piñons clinging to the steep sides helped their passage. They picked their way carefully across the hard sandstone. Their footsteps, and even their breathing became amplified by the concave surface of the cliff. Travis knew from experience that anyone farther down the trail would hear them easily, but there was nothing that could be done about it now. With luck, Casey and Ashe would move in before McNeely came after them.

Halfway up the secret trail, Travis stopped and looked below. Two figures in tan and light green clothing were coming up the creek bed, and both had shoulder-held weapons.

"McNeely is the one in the rear, partially hidden," Travis indicated in a whisper. He knew that for the moment they wouldn't be heard because their pursuers were beside the running stream. "He's always playing it smart, taking any available cover and letting someone else take point."

"Is it training or intelligence?" Fox asked.

He knew she was hoping to find at least one Achilles' heel in her enemy, but he couldn't lie to her. "McNeely's no rocket scientist, but he's good at what he does. He's cunning and that's what makes him dangerous."

As they continued their climb up the cliff, Travis stayed close to Fox. The hairs on the back of his neck were standing on end. The shooting would start soon. He tried to keep her in the shadows while making himself a slightly clearer target. Though it was possible the Russian ex-soldier would try to take Fox alive, he had a feeling McNeely's plans were different: that he wanted Travis now. In his eyes, killing Fox would weaken Travis and it was an edge Travis was certain McNeely would use.

"Quit trying to screen me with your body," Fox snapped. "You're making yourself an obvious target."

Before he could reply, a bullet impacted into the rock just above her, and the echo of a rifle shot rang across the canyon.

"They're trying to keep us from getting to the top," he said. "Don't try it. Just get behind cover." He gave her a nudge in the right direction.

"Where are Casey and Ashe?" she asked, fear in her voice.

"They'll be here for us," he assured, though he had wondered the same thing. "Keep moving." Maybe his brother had encountered problems of his own. The thought worried him, but he couldn't dwell on it now.

Another round hit perilously close to Fox. As flying bits of rock stung them both, she yelped, and ducked her head. For one heart-stopping second, he thought she'd been hit. He reached her position, putting his body between the sniper and her. "Can you move?"

"I could until you shoved me against this rock," she said. "Under different circumstances this might be fun, but right now, I'd like to be able to get out of here."

Grinding his teeth, he pulled her with him into the shadows beneath a rock overhang.

He started to say something to her when the sudden roar of a helicopter drowned out all other sounds. The agile scout craft swooped over the ridge to their left, dropping down and hovering above the creek. Gunfire from the police chopper raised puffs of dirt around the two men below, and they dropped their rifles, raising their hands. As the aircraft closed in, the rotors churned up a cloud of dust. One of the men suddenly took off, sprinting uphill, and Travis lost sight of him.

"It's McNeely. He's coming up. He knows that the only chance he's got to finish the fight is to close in on us. The chopper won't fire on him if he's near us. We have to get farther off the trail. Hopefully, he'll think we ran on up to the top of the cliff when the helicopter arrived."

The helicopter's engines slowed then, and died out quickly, leaving only the distant whoosh of blades. Travis knew the helicopter had landed, dropping off reinforcements to take the prisoner and pursue McNeely. Now, with backup on the ground as well, the odds seemed more in their favor.

Travis pulled Fox into a large crevice in the rock face as the sound of footsteps from below grew louder. Travis listened to McNeely's labored breathing. He was almost upon them.

As McNeely reached their position, Travis suddenly stepped out and delivered a hard, fast punch to his stomach, dropping McNeely like a bag of grain onto the trail.

Travis heard Fox come out of hiding as he pressed his pistol into McNeely's back. McNeely, on hands and knees and groaning in pain, still gripped his own weapon in one hand.

"Don't even think about it, McNeely," Travis growled.

"You couldn't have done this without bringing in reinforcements, Redhawk."

Travis never took his eyes off McNeely's pistol. "Ease your hand off that weapon."

Fox moved farther out onto the trail, grabbed the pistol, then tossed it down the cliff. "Let's get that out of the way before somebody gets hurt."

Travis glanced at her for only a second, but in that instant McNeely rolled and kicked out, knocking Travis against the cliffside. The narrow ledge didn't give either of them much room to maneuver.

Travis was struggling to regain his balance when McNeely pulled out a small backup pistol from his shirt pocket and grabbed Fox's arm, swinging her toward Travis so she was between the two armed men. McNeely held her tightly just below her breasts, effectively pinning both her arms. His grip nearly choked the air out of her lungs. She had no room at all to try any of the moves Travis had taught her.

"I may not win this battle, Redhawk," McNeely said, laughing grimly, "but you're going to lose, too." He aimed his weapon at Fox's head. "I'll kill her unless you do exactly as I say."

"Don't listen to him. He'll kill us both anyway," Fox said raggedly.

Travis aimed his pistol at the top of McNeely's head. "If you shoot her, there won't be a place safe enough for you to hide. Even if you manage to get off this cliff, I'll find you."

"I'm trembling."

"You should be. Suicide missions were never your thing."

McNeely pointed with his chin toward the helicopter that was hovering a hundred feet away. "Better wave them off, Travis. I always get an itchy trigger finger when I'm nervous."

Travis gestured for the helicopter to back off, and it dropped down out of their view. They could hear it below, possibly landing. "Okay. Here's my deal, McNeely. Let her go now. You can have me." He placed his pistol on the ground in front of him.

"Kick it over the side."

"Don't you dare do that!" Fox cried. "He'll kill you!"

Travis slid the weapon down the slope, still watching for an opening.

McNeely eased his hold on her slightly then. Taking full advantage of the little mobility she suddenly had, Fox reached back and pinched McNeely as hard as she could in the thigh.

McNeely howled in pain and, as he doubled over, Fox slipped out of his grip. In a lightning-fast move, Travis delivered a sharp blow to McNeely's windpipe. McNeely crumpled to the ground, gasping for air. As he struggled to stand again, he slid on the loosened gravel and started to slip over the edge. But before he could lose his footing completely, he grabbed hold of a root that jutted out from the stone face. That one-handed grip was all that kept him from falling to his death.

Travis lunged forward and gripped his arm, steadying McNeely's hold. "Stay still, or I can't help you."

"Why are you?" McNeely managed, his voice not more than a croak.

"Because I'm not you. Give me your other hand," Travis said. When McNeely hesitated, Travis added, "Work with me and I'll pull you up."

Fox moved forward in a crouch. "Let me help, Travis."

"No! Stay back," he warned, but before he could finish, McNeely reached out and grabbed Fox's wrist with his free hand. She struggled, but he held on, pulling her down to her knees and dangerously close to the edge. Travis locked his arm around Fox's waist and held on to her.

"I'll cut your arm off if I have to," Travis said, his voice deadly. "Let her go."

"Not until you pull me up. She's my insurance."

"Let her go now," Travis ordered. He stared hard at McNeely. "I can't pull you up with just one hand, and I won't let go of Fox. It's your call. Or I can just stay put and let the marshals shoot you. If you're lucky, you'll be dead before you hit the ground."

The helicopter came up directly behind them. "Look down, McNeely. Can you see the red laser sight on your rib cage? All I have to do is nod to the sniper. He'll take you out, and we'll be rid of you forever. Decide now, before they do."

McNeely released Fox, and Travis pushed her quickly out of McNeely's reach.

Using both his hands, he pulled McNeely up slowly. The moment he was back on the ledge, McNeely threw a punch at Travis. Using his attacker's momentum against him, Travis stepped aside, then hurled McNeely against the cliff, pinning him there face first.

"I can't breathe," McNeely gasped.

"Good. Choke," Travis snapped.

Ashe arrived at their position just then, having come up from where the helicopter had landed below. He placed one careful hand on his brother's shoulder. "It's over now. I've got him."

Travis didn't move.

"Stand down, soldier," Ashe said. "You did your job, now it's my turn."

Travis eased his hold, and his brother handcuffed the prisoner.

Travis watched in stony silence as Ashe prodded McNeely down the trail. Voices from below told them more help was coming.

"It'll be okay. Your brother knows what he's doing," Fox said.

"I wanted to kill him for putting you in danger," Travis said.

"But you didn't. I don't think I've ever been more proud to be—"

Travis looked down at Fox, then gathered her gently into his arms. "Finish what you were saying."

She shook her head, leaning against him.

"Tell me," he murmured in her ear.

"To have been yours," she finished hesitantly.

"What we have shared is something that no one will ever be able to take away from us, Little Fox." He brushed a kiss on her forehead, then took her mouth in a long, deep kiss.

Travis finally drew back and gazed down at her, wondering how he'd ever live without her. He couldn't imagine never hearing the music of her voice again, or feeling the tenderness of her touch. He needed her softness, her gentleness. His world had so little of either. Fox had been his light, and without her, only an endless night stretched out before him.

BY THE TIME THEY arrived at the police station, Fox's spirit felt heavy. She wanted to talk to Travis, to ask him when he planned to leave, and about his return. She couldn't imagine him not wanting to come back now—not after all they'd shared. How could he walk away from something that was powerful enough to light up the night sky? But, for once, her courage utterly failed her. She remained quiet, hoping that her heart would speak to his in that silent language only he could hear.

They went inside the building a moment later. Casey met them as they were escorted into the squad room.

"I want you two to stick around while I question McNeely's ally, Viktor Kiktev," Casey told them. "We believe he's the sniper who killed Prescott."

Fox shuddered. "I have no desire to be within a million miles of either McNeely or his pal."

"They can't hurt you now," Casey said. "And I do need you here, in case we have to verify something."

Fox nodded once. "All right. If it'll help to put an end to this."

Fox sat in one corner of the large room while Casey, Ashe, and U.S. Marshal Gray took turns questioning the prisoner as he was being fingerprinted and booked. Deputy Marshal Andrews stood to one side, watching the proceedings but saying very little. In the midst of the questioning, an officer came into the squad room, took Casey aside, and handed her a computer printout.

Casey studied it for a moment, then set it down on the table. "I've just received some new evidence," she said to their prisoner. "If you choose to identify the others you worked with, we may be able to make things easier on you. Cooperating right now is your only real option. If you wait much longer, you risk not having anything to bargain with at all.''

Casey pushed the printouts toward Kiktev. "We now have the list of account numbers you've been searching for all these years. They were hidden in Fox's locket, though nobody knew that until yesterday. But curiously enough, those accounts are empty. It seems that millions of dollars were withdrawn and deposited in new accounts all over the world earlier today.''

Kiktev's eyes narrowed and his expression became deadly as he studied what Casey had placed before him. Suddenly he looked up and his gaze locked with Carl's. "Did you think you could have it all?"

"Wait a minute," Carl Andrews said with a laugh. "You're not actually going to believe anything this man—'' He took one casual step toward Fox.

Travis moved between them, and faced Andrews with clenched fists. "Not one more step.''

Ashe came up to stand beside his brother, his hand on the butt of his holstered pistol. Casey moved in on Andrews, quickly disarming him.

"Hey, you've got the wrong man," Andrews protested. "You'd take the word of a criminal over mine? I'm a Deputy U.S. Marshal. I've been set up.''

"Yes, but it was your own greed that sprung the trap,'' Casey said. "You played dumb when we brought you the microdot and pretended not to know what was on it, but you got on the phone as soon as we left. The money you think you transferred came from phoney accounts we'd set up. The real microdot went elsewhere.'' Casey looked at Kiktev. "And now we even have a corroborating witness for the prosecution.''

Gray studied Casey speculatively. "So I have the real microdot?''

Casey shook her head. "Yours was phoney, too, sir. We

knew that the inside man had to be one of you, but we weren't sure who it was. So we came up with a plan. Each microdot had different account numbers. The banks we'd listed all cooperated, and as soon as someone tried to move the money, we were contacted."

Gray's eyes flashed with anger. "How could you set this up without authorization from the Marshals Service?"

"I did have the Service's cooperation. I just circumvented the chain of command and went directly to Washington with my request. You see, there was a problem with the radio beacon and, for a long time, that pointed to you," Casey explained.

"I'm not a tech expert," Gray said.

"We know that now, sir," Casey added.

Gray's face began to turn red, and Fox knew Casey would have a lot of explaining to do later.

Casey handcuffed Andrews, then turned him over to an officer. As he was taken away, still protesting his innocence, Casey turned to Kiktev. "We have Yuri Lazarev in custody. He's claiming he works for you, as did Prescott. Apparently we've caught everyone in the gang who was working in this area, or so he says."

Kiktev said nothing.

Casey continued pressuring him. "We know that you are the regional leader of this operation. You'd better cut a deal now, before your lackeys bury you."

Kiktev transfixed Fox with an icy glare. "It was your parents who began your nightmare when they stole my money. This was nothing personal."

"You've tried to kill me, and you've murdered people I loved. It *is* personal. I hope you see my parents' faces before you for the rest of your life and remember that it was their daughter who brought you down."

While the law-enforcement team focused on the Russian

prisoner again, Travis and Fox quietly walked out of the squad room together.

"It's really over now," Travis said. "You've got your life back."

"And now I can finally go after anything I want, right?" She looked at him and smiled.

Travis stared hard at her, his heart beating double-time. "You don't know what you're asking for—"

"Life doesn't come with guarantees. You just have to take things one day at a time. All I'm asking is to love the man I've chosen and to be loved by him in return."

Before he could reply, several officers rushed past them, reporting for the new shift.

She looked around the lobby and grimaced. "Let's go someplace else. I've had it with police departments."

As they stepped out into the desert night, the full moon above them, a night bird screeched overhead. "The police are needed here," Travis reminded her gently. "They're not your enemies, Fox. The harmony that has been restored to you came through them."

Fox gave him a surprised look. She hadn't expected him to be defensive about her statement. "I'm grateful for what the police have done but, now, I need to look after my own life."

"Tell me, how would you feel about being married to a cop?"

"I'm not in love with a cop," she answered, puzzled.

"But you are in love," Travis murmured, taking her into his arms. "Do you love me, Fox?" he asked, tilting her chin upwards.

"You know I do," she said in a breathless whisper.

"I'm coming back to the Rez, Fox. At first I thought I'd join the Bureau of Indian Affairs, but that could take me away from the *Dinétah,* and I belong here. So I'm going to apply to the tribal PD."

"A cop," she whispered, her heart hammering. She held her breath, knowing what he'd say next and longing to hear the words.

"As a cop I won't be able to give you a high degree of security. But I can give you a lifetime of love and my loyalty forever. Will you be my wife?"

A hot wind swept over the desert floor. "Earth and Wind... Together we're bound to stir up a lot of dust storms," she said with a smile. "Are you sure you're up to it?"

"I wouldn't have it any other way." He lowered his mouth to hers, showing her with one kiss far more than words could ever have expressed.

Fox surrendered with a soft sigh. It was their time at last. Their destinies, written in the stars, had been fulfilled. "Forever" began one moment at a time, and a lifetime of love waited to be explored.

Epilogue

Six weeks later

Travis and Ashe parked their pickups a few miles from the hogan where their wedding ceremonies would be taking place shortly. The grooms weren't supposed to arrive until the wedding began, so they'd decided to wait until all the guests had passed them by, before traveling the final distance. Balloons and ribbons tied to sagebrush and tumbleweeds marked the gravel road. One large cardboard sign with the word "WEDDINGS" printed in large block letters, and a directional arrow, stood by the highway.

Travis paced back and forth by the road, as restless as a caged tiger. He'd been away for six weeks, and it had seemed more like six months. He'd had to return to his Ranger unit immediately after the criminals had been arrested. His leave was all used up by then, so he hadn't been able to come back to the Rez until now, to testify in court. His brother, Casey, and Fox had worked tirelessly to take advantage of the time and make the double wedding possible, since this would be his only time off until his discharge, months from now.

"I'm glad Casey and Fox decided to make it a double wedding," Ashe said. "But I'm not sure about this blend of traditional and Anglo ceremonies that they worked out," he added with a wry smile.

Travis said nothing as he walked back and forth.

Ashe glowered at him. "Will you stop pacing? It's a wedding, not an execution."

"I'm worried, brother. Something's not right with Fox. I can sense it."

"It's the wedding. She had to plan a lot of the details by herself, since Casey had a lot to do before the trials. Fox is just tense. Give her a break."

"It's more than that. She's different," Travis insisted.

"Different how?"

"I don't know—just different. I haven't even had a chance to be alone with her since I got back yesterday. Today, in particular, has been impossible. I couldn't even get hold of her on the telephone. I should have insisted we schedule the wedding for morning, before the first trial starts. Maybe it would have cut down on all the fuss."

"It's our custom to have wedding ceremonies at sundown to give people time to arrive," Ashe reminded. "Distances are vast on the Rez. There's a rightness about that time of day, too. After the guests leave, it's said that the mantle of night covers the groom and bride and blesses them with harmony." He paused. "But the truth is, Fox didn't want to see you today any more than Casey wanted to see me. The grooms aren't supposed to see the brides before the wedding. That's part of our customs, and also a big part of the Anglo way, too. We've got to respect that." He rubbed the back of his neck with one hand. "Things sure get more complicated when you blend two cultures."

"The ceremony is certainly going to be one of a kind," Travis said, exhaling softly. "A ceremony in a hogan with a preacher in attendance."

"I'll say." Ashe looked off into the distance. The sun

was sinking behind the mountains. "It's time to go, things should be beginning about now."

When they arrived at the newly-built hogan Ashe and his fellow officers had constructed for the occasion, the women were waiting. Casey looked beautiful in a white lace blouse and a white long skirt, blending the Navajo and Anglo style. Ashe's face lit up as he saw her.

Travis searched the crowd for his bride, then saw Fox come out of the hogan. She was dressed in a flowing, white satin, floor-length dress. Just looking at her tore his breath away. With her long blond hair caressing her shoulders, she looked like a goddess come to life.

He gazed admiringly at his bride-to-be. There was a glow about Fox that seemed to go beyond the radiance of a bride. The power of her femininity tugged at him. Yet, another instinct rose inside him as well—the need to protect this woman he loved so dearly. His reaction puzzled him. She was in no danger here, and he didn't think of himself as an overly protective man. But there was something different about her, something he was picking up on at a level that went beyond logic.

There was no time for him to think about it. A line of people formed by the women, and he and Ashe were led into the hogan. The brothers walked clockwise around the fire, then sat on the west side, facing east. The shawls draped on the walls and on the door told everyone the ceremony was about to begin.

Casey entered next, with the traditional basket of cornmeal in hand, and sat to Ashe's right.

Then Fox entered, and holding another small basket, repeated the process. As she walked toward Travis, he couldn't take his eyes off her. His heart was pounding when she poured water into the gourd and washed his hands, signifying a cleansing of the past.

As he, in turn, gently washed her hands, their eyes met.

The look she gave him reflected the love she felt for him...and something more. His bride, his woman, was keeping a secret from him. His muscles were tense as they concluded the Navajo ceremony, eating the cornmeal placed before them.

Travis then walked outside with Fox, followed by his brother and Casey. The guests were pressing in all about them. One more step to go before he'd be able to steal a chance to talk to her. He waited as the Anglo preacher began his part of today's ceremony. First, Casey and Ashe exchanged traditional wedding vows, and then the rings. Tears shimmered in Casey's eyes. When his brother, at long last, gently took his bride into his arms, a sigh rippled through the crowd.

Then it was his turn, and all eyes were on him and Fox. He'd memorized the vows Fox and he had written. They were a part of him now.

"You are mine from this day forward," he said, his gaze on her alone. "I'll be beside you in sickness and in health. One heart, one mind, one spirit. Now and forever." His hand shook slightly as he slipped the ring on her finger.

His heart stood still as she repeated the words to him. His new wedding band shone brightly in the muted firelight.

"I now pronounce you husband and wife," the preacher said.

Travis gathered her into his arms. Her lips were sweet and, for those precious moments, he nearly forgot his other concerns.

Hearing the chuckles in the crowd, he reluctantly eased his hold. "Soon," he whispered, and was rewarded when he felt her tremble in his arms.

As the guests began moving to the buffet tables that had been set up, Fox drew him into the shadows.

"You're very tense. I can feel it," she whispered, her

hand on his forearm. "Is it that you didn't expect this large ~~a wedd~~ding?"

"The wedding—you—are beautiful," Travis said, his voice reverberating with emotion. "I'm glad all our friends are here to celebrate with us." He smiled slowly as he looked around. "But small and simple would have been okay, too."

Her eyes sparkled. "Well, simple's out of the question, but I think I can handle the 'small' part of your wish."

He looked at her, puzzled. "Have you and Casey cooked up something else?"

She smiled. "No, actually, this is something you and I cooked up." Fox took his hand and placed it on her belly. "We're going to have a baby, Travis," she said, her eyes never wavering from his.

It all made sense now—the secrecy, the glow about her. "I'm going to be a daddy?" he managed, his voice an awed whisper.

She nodded. "So what do you think?"

"That it just doesn't get any better than this." He kissed his bride, the future mother of his child, showing her what he couldn't put into words. Today was the first day of a beautiful future.

HARLEQUIN®

INTRIGUE®

BROTHERS OF ROCK RIDGE

by award-winning author Aimée Thurlo

The dark, sexy and mysterious Redhawk brothers become a family once again to track down their foster parents' killer and their missing foster sister. But Ashe and Travis have no idea what dark danger—and steamy passion—awaits in their hometown of Rock Ridge....

REDHAWK'S HEART
#506, March '99

REDHAWK'S RETURN
#510, April '99

THE BROTHERS OF ROCK RIDGE—
As different as night from day...
but bound by a vow to protect
those they love.

*Available at your favorite
retail outlet.*

HARLEQUIN®
Makes any time special ™

MURDER AT THE MOVIES

CHARLENE WEIR
GEORGE BAXT
MAXINE O'CALLAGHAN

MURDER TAKE TWO
by Charlene Weir

Hollywood comes to Hampstead, Kansas, with the filming of a new picture starring sexy actress Laura Edwards. But murder steals the scene when a stunt double is impaled on a pitchfork.

THE HUMPHREY BOGART MURDER CASE
by George Baxt

Hollywood in its heyday is brought to life in this witty caper featuring a surprise sleuth—Humphrey Bogart. While filming *The Maltese Falcon*, he searches for a real-life treasure, dodging a killer on a murder trail through Hollywood.

SOMEWHERE SOUTH OF MELROSE
by Maxine O'Callaghan

P.I. Delilah West is hired to search for an old high school classmate. The path takes her through the underbelly of broken dreams and into the caprices of fate, where secrets are born and sometimes kept....

Available March 1999 at your favorite retail outlet.

HARLEQUIN®

I N T R I G U E®

COMING NEXT MONTH

#513 THE STRANGER SHE KNEW by Gayle Wilson
Men of Mystery

Ex-CIA agent Jordan Cross was given a new face and a new life.
What he didn't know was that his new identity belonged to a man
with dangerous enemies—and now he's put an innocent woman and
her children in jeopardy.

#514 THE BODYGUARD by Sheryl Lynn
Elk River, Colorado

J. T. McKennon was everything a man was supposed to be. Loyal,
strong, responsible and determined—not to mention the way he could
kiss. And as a bodyguard he was the ultimate protector. But as far as
Francine Forrest was concerned, he was the one brick wall she could
not move. Without him she'd never find her kidnapped sister. But
could she avoid falling in love with him in the process?

#515 A WOMAN OF MYSTERY by Charlotte Douglas
A Memory Away...

More than muscles and a handsome face, Jordan Trouble was a
professional protector. And while the cop in him wanted to know
what caused a beautiful woman's amnesia, the man in him wanted to
know how she did what no other had—made him feel alive again.

#516 TO LANEY, WITH LOVE by Joyce Sullivan

A note from her supposedly dead husband sends Laney Dobson's
world into a tailspin. But the clues she and Ben Forbes follow lead
to the revelation of a lifetime of deceit—and unexpected passion in
Ben's arms.

Look us up on-line at: http://www.romance.net